KISS ME, KILL ME

Terri-Ann,
I hope you enjoy it.

X.

KISS ME, KILL ME

Louise Mullins

An Aria Book

This edition first published in the United Kingdom in 2021 by Aria,
an imprint of Head of Zeus Ltd

A CIP catalogue record for this book is available from the
British Library.

eISBN 9781838938079

PB ISBN 9781800245990

Typeset by Siliconchips Services Ltd UK

Cover design © Lisa Brewster

Aria
c/o Head of Zeus
First Floor East
5–8 Hardwick Street
London EC1R 4RG

www.ariafiction.com

Printed and bound by CPI Group (UK) Ltd, Croydon, CR0 4YY

MELANIE

Before

A bee flew past me, heading for one of the ceramic planters filled with violet- and tangerine-coloured flowers, parked either side of the open French doors. Mum was buzzing round Maddison as usual, offering to top up her plastic beaker with more squash while I wrung my hands, my stomach growling.

Maddison sat beside me on the lawn to show me her light pink nails. 'My mummy painted them,' she said proudly.

'They're pretty.'

She smiled in response.

Mum gazed at Maddison adoringly as she topped off her glass with the sparkling juice that made her wobble. I wished she'd look at me that way.

The doorbell chimed.

Mum turned and gave me a warning look. 'Take care of Maddison for me, Mel. Especially near that pool. I'll be right back.' And off she trotted on her heels, clackety-clacking across the concrete and into the house.

I saw Mum through the glass as she pelted across the lounge, her stick-thin figure disappearing as she exited the room and entered the hall to answer the door.

'I'm bored,' said Maddison, frowning.

'What do you want to do?'

She wore a look of deep thought then squealed, 'Let's play I-Spy,' grinning, eyes bright.

'Okay. You go first.'

Maddison patted my hand and said, 'I spy with my little eye, something beginning with…'

I zoned out Maddison's voice when I heard Mum yelling. 'You can sit and bloody swivel if you think I'm going to hand any money over to you!'

Dad's upset someone again.

I heard a man's voice then, loud and insistent. 'Listen, love, if he doesn't sort it out then I'm going to take him to court which will cost you far more than a couple of hundred pounds.'

'It's not our problem if someone you paid to fit a window to your property screws it up.'

I turned towards Maddison. 'Sorry, what letter did you say?' But she wasn't there.

She was gazing down at her reflection on the surface of the water from the edge of the pool.

'Maddison?' I stood and moved closer to her. 'Mum's put me in charge. She told me not to let you go near the pool.'

She took a step forward as if daring me to stop her.

I stared at her wide eyes, clear skin, perfectly plaited pigtails and shiny new shoes. The ones Mum couldn't afford to buy me. And I had the urge to shove her in.

BETHAN

Now

Ipractise my shock-horror face in the mirror for the seventh time. 'My husband, he's... dead,' I say, the pitch of my voice heightening with each syllable.

The staircase creaks.

I squeeze out a few tears and prepare for my pièce de résistance: quivering mouth, trembling hands and uncontrollable sobbing that's not so hysterical it will draw the attention of the police.

A floorboard groans.

I think I have perfected it but when I glance up at my reflection my impression of the grieving widow still looks fake. Perhaps it will appear more authentic once I have been bereaved.

Humphrey's footsteps, painfully slow and telling of his age, reach the landing. I close my eyes and imagine running from the room and shoving him in the chest, his hand sliding off the balustrade as he falls backwards and hits his head on the edge of the oakwood skirting board while he reaches out for me, his mouth shaped in an O, his eyes wide with disbelief.

'Bethan, darling, there you are,' he says, breathless from the exertion of climbing the thirty-odd-step staircase.

I pout and turn my cheek for him to kiss. I don't want his slobbery lips on mine.

He smells of Tom Ford's soap and Creed's aftershave: basil, leather, neroli and bergamot.

His thick grey hair bounces on his head as he straightens to survey me. 'Are you heading into town?'

'You know I am,' I sigh, unscrewing my cherry-red lipstick. I apply a thick amount before smacking my lips together to ensure it is evenly spread.

He shoots me a disapproving look. 'Will you be needing any money? It's just that—'

'Well, of course I will. You don't expect me to buy dinner with thin air, do you?'

He glances down at his slippers then catches my eyes in the mirror as I snap the lid onto my lipstick and drop it into my patent leather Gucci bag.

I run my fingers through the soft waves of my blonde hair and smile, catching a flash of heat spreading across Humphrey's cheeks as I stand.

He reaches out to me and grips the sleeve of my chenille jumper with two worn fingers as I turn to grab my coat from the back of the ornamental chair.

'I love you,' he says wheezily, his hand shaking as he places several fifty-pound notes, retrieved from the cigar box on top of his bedside cabinet, into my hand and squeezes my palm around them.

I slip the money into my purse, clasp it shut and drop it into the bag. 'You too.'

I glide my arms through the sleeves of my coat and zip it up.

'Drive carefully,' he says, wearing a serious expression.

I roll my eyes and pout, and he slips one hand around my waist to draw me close so that I can feel his heart beating against my jaw. Then he tilts my chin up with his other hand, so that I cannot avoid his gaze, and says, 'Look after yourself, darling. I don't want anything to happen to you.'

I push his hand away from my face and watch his features sink.

You should be more concerned about yourself.

I enter the supermarket car park, the brakes screeching when I'm forced to stop suddenly for a man in a car the size of a roller-skate to exit the disabled space I couldn't see was taken behind the rear bumper of an SUV. He smiles and holds up his hand in thanks and I reply with a flip of my middle finger. He looks away and I reverse the Range Rover into the space he's just vacated until the parking sensors bleep alarmingly.

I jump out, lock the car and head to the trolleys, limping.

I enter Waitrose through the automatic doors and glance at today's newspaper headlines:

COLLISION ON M4 KILLS TWO, CARDIFF DRUG DEALER JAILED, MISSING MAN BELIEVED TO HAVE COMMITTED SUICIDE.

I avoid the cheese and chocolate aisles, though the trolley appears to move towards the alcohol without my input. I grab two bottles of premium whiskey – Johnny Walker and Bushmills – a bottle of cognac – Rémy Martin – and Belvedere vodka. I nudge two bags of ready chopped mixed vegetables into the trolley and spend the remainder of my trip grabbing items and throwing them in until I have a pile of food that looks like a child was asked to choose what to eat for their dinner. I'm not even sure how much of it can be cooked together.

I pick up a bag of potatoes and a small glass bottle of rapeseed oil and head towards the small collection of magazines stacked beside this month's top shelf literary fiction. I leaf through *Woman & Home*, *Vogue*, *Horse & Hound*, *Vanity Fair*, and eventually slap a *Country Living* on top of the pile of items I've gathered. When I catch sight of the immaculate couple fronting their beautiful home on the cover of *Home & Garden*, I'm instantly reminded of the photoshoot Humphrey and I took part in when the same magazine publicised our Garden Of The Year Award for our wildflowers.

My hair was dyed black and straightened. The candyfloss-pink dress I wore looked stark against my fake tan. The sunglasses covered my eyes. I told the photographer I was photosensitive as I'd just had laser eye surgery. He said my pose added mystery to the shot and congratulated me on my model figure.

At the till I watch the woman in front of me take far too long to fill her bags, try paying with the wrong card and discuss with the cashier the extent of her husband's recovery from a 'particularly nasty bout of the flu', as if there are levels of the virus.

I huff and roll my eyes enough times that she eventually apologises for taking so fucking long.

The cashier looks like something has crawled up her arse and died.

'Would you like help with your packing,' she says nasally, halfway through the process.

'No, thanks. I'm fine.'

I pay with Humphrey's debit card, smile when I'm bidden a good day, dump the bags in the trolley and wheel it out of the shop. When I reach the car, I toss them into the boot, slam it shut and shove the trolley into the rear of another that's been left in the car park causing both to skid along the uneven concrete, out the other side of the trolley park and into the door of a shiny GLA, leaving a nick in the paintwork.

I hurry back to my parking space to find a man inspecting the top of the dashboard through the windscreen with a smug expression on his face.

'You know you're parked in a disabled bay,' he says.

'You know you can mind your own fucking business.'

The woman on his arm raises her eyebrows and I limp the final few feet towards the driver's door, puff and moan as I hoist myself into my seat, and slam the door on their muttered conversation about feigning sickness and immobility to cheat the benefit system.

The tyres squeal under the pressure of my foot as I accelerate out of the parking space so fast it causes a puddle of water to spray onto the front of the man's geography-teacher-style corduroys.

I glance into my rear-view mirror and smile at the wide-mouthed woman with pinched cheeks and watch her strike the man's arm with a little more force than could be ethically considered playful when it's obvious his gawping gaze was fixed solely on my cleavage.

When I reach Cardiff Road, the traffic has built up and when I glance at the time on the dashboard, I note that it's almost lunch. Ignoring the low fuel light blinking an amber warning, I cut off the B-road onto a country road and navigate myself towards home. Reaching a small roundabout on top of a hill with a sign directing me to the golf club, I continue until I hit a familiar route as the diesel gauge drops to red.

I have about ten miles left.

I flip down the visor and blink away the sunlight spilling through the pastel-blue sky, hitting the wing mirror and bouncing onto my face. I squint as I reach a narrow bend before descending to a hump in the road that dips suddenly and jerks the suspension so violently, I must clench my stomach to stop myself from vomiting.

The two bottles of champagne I drank last night weren't such a good idea. But skipping breakfast was.

My head begins to throb now that the paracetamol I necked this morning has worn off. I narrow my eyes further against the glaring sun, the pressure building behind them as I reach the three-storey, ten-bedroom property surrounded by golden fields and rendered private by a row of thick blossom-filled trees.

I follow the beige grit path past the horses chewing on wheat in the pasture to my right and hold my breath to the scent of manure that seeps through the car via the air conditioning as I cross the cow field to my left. I park directly in front of the house with the dry sandstone fountain so close behind me that when I exit the car, I must hold the boot lid partway open to avoid denting it on the structure while removing the shopping bags.

I tread through a puddle. The water spurts upward and across the back of my white trousers and soaks through my canvas boots. 'For fuck's sake.'

I head into the house, carrying the bags and I'm hit first by the smell of poached eggs and the sound of 'Mariage d'amour' by Paul de Senneville (Marriage of love) then Humphrey's disapproving gaze. 'I didn't think we needed that much in the way of groceries. It's only a dinner party.'

'That's the problem. You don't think.'

'I didn't mean to offend you, darling. It's just that we must be careful now that I'm no longer working. You should try to be less frivolous, mmm?'

'You invited them over.'

'Yes, but I expect them to be fed wholesome, homemade food, not expensive, ready-prepared meals.'

I push past him and barge through the kitchen door. Muriel is there with her apron on and wearing gloves to disguise the fact she doesn't wear a ring.

'What are you doing here?' I turn from Muriel to Humphrey, who smiles and tries to placate me with a warm hand on my lower back, steering me down the hall and into the morning room where there's less chance of his ex-housekeeper hearing my raised voice.

'You've brought her back. Why?'

'I'm not feeling as agile as I once was, and you don't seem to have the time to keep the rooms tidy anymore so—'

'You don't think I clean the house as well as her.'

'I didn't say that.' He smiles and reaches out to touch me, but I step away from him and slam the backs of my heels into the conker-brown skirting boards.

I fight the urge to stab the letter opener I spot parked on the French mahogany desk behind him through his pompous throat.

'I know you've had your differences, but I'd like you to try and get along with her.'

A flash of red-washed lingerie zips across the insides of my eyelids while I clench my hands into fists. 'She ruined my white underwear, or have you forgotten?'

'I know you think she did it on purpose, but I assure you she isn't malicious.'

'What is she doing in my kitchen?'

'Muriel is just helping out until you...'

Start behaving like a married woman.

'She's a pretentious bitch.'

'She's a friend.'

'I'm your wife.' I blink hard and bite my lip until I taste the metallic tang of blood.

'Yes, you are. So perhaps...'

It's time you started acting like one.

I cross my arms and tap my foot. 'Spit it out, Humphrey.'

He takes a second longer than I have the patience for, and I spin round to stomp down the hall.

'I understand how difficult it is for you to adjust. You've been privileged. And that's partly my fault. I should have supported you to find something more productive to do in your spare time, away from the house. And now that I've retired, I'm going to be around more often. We can spend more time together. Though we may get in each other's way if you don't find something to occupy yourself with when I'm not around.'

The last of his words die as I re-enter the kitchen to find Muriel holding a packet of ham up to the light to inspect the label. 'Overpriced,' she says.

'For you, perhaps,' I say, hauling the bags up from the floor to deposit on the dining table.

Jealous cow.

I begin to stow away the food haphazardly, aware that I'm being watched. Wild rice, tagliatelle pasta, parmesan cheese and raw Manuka honey are stored on top of jars of pesto and sundried tomato sauces, and packets of lentils and couscous.

Muriel sighs and glances over my shoulder. I follow her gaze to where Humphrey stands with a reproachful look on his face. His eyes are pink and tired-looking. There are deep grooves beneath the sacks of sagging skin beneath them. Under his wide protruding nose, flecked with dry patches and age spots, his mouth twitches.

'Muriel,' he says, 'you should go. You've been a tremendous help, but my wife informs me that your services are no longer required.'

She presses her lips together and stalks forward, holding her hand out at mid-height. Humphrey takes her hand and shakes it firmly, and she curtseys.

'I'll deposit the last of your wages into your bank account this evening.'

She darts her eyes to me then back to him. 'If you're sure?'

He nods, once. 'Thank you for everything you have done for me and my wife.'

She turns to me, takes my hand in hers and digs her thumbnail into the space between my thumb and forefinger until my palm goes slack, her features unchanged.

I smile and pull back my hand. It tingles.

Humphrey grasps me tight and holds me against his rounded stomach so that I can feel his heartbeat against my neck. I squirm. 'Bethan will take responsibility for the manor from now on. Won't you, darling?'

'Of course.' The numbness in my palm slowly begins to dissipate and a flush of heat spreads across my cheeks, along with the jarring pain that begins to bloom in my hand.

I wait until she's gone before I glance down at the half-moon indent where Muriel's nail had dug into my flesh so hard that she'd managed to pierce the skin.

'Our guests will be here at seven. I expect you know what you're cooking?'

'Yes.' I can't disguise the resentful lilt in my voice.

'No red meat. I need to lower my cholesterol,' he says, rubbing my shoulder and stroking my neck.

I think of all the fat congealing inside his heart, causing it to bloat and clogging up his arteries. His hand grasping at his chest while he strains to breathe. His eyes wide and his face the colour of a plum. 'I wouldn't worry about a bit of fat.'

'Heart attacks are the number one cause of death for men in this country.'

I move forward, the backs of his fingers brushing lightly against my spine as his hand falls to his side. I close my eyes and imagine he's someone else: handsome and muscled. When I open them, they land on the gun cabinet.

There are worse things to die of.

DI LOCKE

Then

The signalman was shaking when I arrived. I retrieved the tartan blanket from the boot of my car which I kept in case of situations such as this and threw it over him.

'I'm not cold,' he insisted, teeth chattering.

'You're in shock. Detective Inspector Locke,' I said, flashing my ID card at him and the uniformed officer stood beside him.

'I shouldn't have opened it.'

'I know it must have been an awful sight, but I'm pleased you did.'

He frowns.

'If you hadn't, we might never have found them.'

'Them?' he said, eyes wide.

'I meant in plural terms, because we don't know yet whether the individual is male or female.'

His shoulders dropped and he nodded.

'What do I call you?'

He'd already repeated the information twice. Once during

13

his conversation to the call handler when he'd dialled 101, and again to the police constable who was watching him like a hawk.

He gave me his name, date of birth and address. Then I asked how he'd come across the suitcase.

The PC listened and watched to ensure his version of the event matched the one he'd given previously.

'Staffing cuts mean I'm sometimes tasked with checking the lines. People throw rubbish off the overpass. Sometimes stuff lands on the rails. Not only if the object is large could it cause an accident, but fly-tipping attracts vermin. Rats can chew the cables, causing signal failures, and aluminium foil and cans on the tracks can cause short-circuiting. Both can lead to derailment.'

I glanced down at the gardening gloves covering his trembling hands. 'They send you out in the dark?'

'The first train's at 7 a.m. I've got a Maglite and I've got LED motion sensor lights set up down there.'

'So you were removing rubbish from the tracks.'

'I dumped a bicycle wheel, some wood and a couple of bags of soiled nappies I'd found into a rusted shopping trolley and dragged it up onto the verge. That's when I smelt what I thought was a dead animal. The suitcase was buried beneath the undergrowth. It looked like it had been there a while. It was light and rattled, and as I pulled it out through the nettles, I saw that it was stained. But I couldn't tell if it was blood or Ronseal. I know you're not supposed to open bags you find. Especially near transport links. But when I inspected the ground there was a tenner sticking out of the mud. I thought maybe... I don't know.'

He thought the suitcase was filled with money. Was hoping he could keep it.

'I unzipped the suitcase and about a hundred dried maggots fell onto my foot. There was a bone protruding through them. I called the police, then my supervisor.'

Car headlights drew my attention to the vehicle that was cruising down Lodge Road.

I motioned to the PC. 'My colleague is going to need to take a formal statement from you in a moment. And a mouth swab to collect your DNA so we can eliminate it from any we might find on the suitcase. He'll drive you down to Newport Central to do that and bring you back here afterwards.'

'Where are you parked?' said the PC.

The man pointed to the opposite side of the road, past my own car. I nodded to the PC and excused myself to meet the lead technician.

The van pulled over and the crime scene investigators exited it, donned in white coveralls. The driver had yet to zip his suit up to the bridge of his nose to mask the lower section of his face, drop his hood down to his forehead, apply the visor attached, slide on a pair of gloves and slip the shoe coverlets over his feet. He opened the back doors of the white van and retrieved some cables, a camera and a silver case that contained the equipment that would be used to collect items that surrounded the suitcase which were deemed significant in identifying who it belonged to or who dumped it.

I'd called Jones on my way out the door of the house that I, my husband Johnno, and stepson Jaxon were renting in Pontypool. He was here now, hair uncombed and a red mark beside his left eye which told me he slept on his side and had been out of bed for less than fifteen minutes. It shouldn't have taken him longer than me to get here. I'd had to travel eight miles to Carleon.

He parked his car behind the van and walked towards me.

'I need you to oversee the evidence collection.'

He glanced over my shoulder and down at the floodlit rubble where the female PC was guarding the crime scene. 'I'll start the scene log.'

I heard him introduce himself as Detective Constable Jones to the witness, and the PC stood beside him as I strode to the CSIs.

'Who's the lead technician?'

The driver raised his hand in the air.

I got his name and gave him mine.

'What have we got?' he said.

'Skeletal remains inside a suitcase. We're assuming they're human.'

MELANIE

Then

I swung my legs over the pool and dipped my toes into the chlorinated water that glinted in the sunlight and rippled with the gentle breeze. It was cool on my small, bronzed legs.

I heard my mother gasp then cry, 'Mel!' before I felt her grab me from behind and pull me away from the edge. 'What the bloody hell do you think you're doing? Have you got a death wish or something?'

She didn't tell me what I'd done was wrong or explain why.

She walked across the patio, snatched a sweet pastry from the plastic dish on top of the table and shoved it into her mouth. Then she took a tall glass filled with sparkling liquid, her grip tightening around the stem while she chewed then swallowed the small sugar-glazed puff of grease and raised the glass to her lips.

I licked mine in memory of the sweet bubbles that, when

I'd stolen a sip while she dozed earlier, had made my mouth tingle and my tummy warm.

She spoke sloppily and complained that her tongue was furry then turned her back to me.

I gazed up at the dazzling orb in the sky that made my skin sore and dangled my hot feet back over the ledge and into the water to feel its gentle caress lapping at my ankles.

Seconds later she dragged me by the wrist forcing me upright, swung her arm back as far as it would go, and slapped me hard across the face. I fell backward, using my elbows to absorb the shock, but they grazed across the rough concrete as I landed.

Tears pooled in my eyes as I inspected the gashes, but I was too stunned to cry.

I stood, wiped the blood from my elbows with my damp palms and looked at my mother. At her smudged green eyeshadow, the pale lines across her bare shoulders where yesterday's dress had hung from her rake-thin body, and at her heaving breasts that swung pendulum-like behind a tight, strapless bikini top that was covered in bright, multicoloured birds. Her face contorted into a mixture of what appeared to be irritation and regret.

I glared at her and stomped my feet until they hurt, arms folded tight against my tummy, hair clung to my forehead with perspiration. 'I hate you!'

'What's wrong with her?' My father appeared in the doorway, clutching the phone to his chest, the cable taut.

His shirt was dark around his armpits and his hair dripped sweat from his nose and left wet trails down his face that reminded me of the slime left on the path after heavy rain had invited the slugs out of their hideaways.

'Who are you talking to?' said my mother, eyes narrowed.

'A client.'

'Charge him double, then maybe I could afford an electric fan and *she* could play indoors.' Her finger pointed behind her, at me.

'Shut your damn mouth, woman, or I'll—' He turned back into the house at the distant voice of a shrunken male and raised the phone to his ear. 'Yes, I'm still here. Sorry? Oh, I was just talking to my wife.'

He slammed the French doors shut behind him and trod across the living room, his feet sinking into the carpet before he perched on the sofa, tapping his foot against the floor as he spoke.

I couldn't hear him, but I could see his forearm muscles constrict and loosen while his foot began to hit the floor faster as though in tune with the conversation.

My mother sidled up to me and huffed. 'Come on, brat. I'll take you to the park.' She flicked her sunglasses that were perched on her mane of copper hair and they fell over her eyes.

She poured herself another glass of 'grape juice' and I watched her take a long series of gulps until it was empty, while I fastened the clasps on my white T-bar sandals.

She wiped her mouth with the back of her hand and belched, placing the glass back onto the table with a clink. She bent to inspect the shard of crystal she'd chipped off the stem, straightened, and shrugged. 'Come on. I haven't got all day.'

I walked slowly towards her and followed her into the stuffy house where my father was hissing something unintelligible down the phone. His Adam's apple jerked up and down as he slammed his hand onto his thigh with a resounding smack then gesticulated wildly for us to leave.

My mother's chin jutted out as she gritted her teeth in the same way I did when forcing myself not to say something, snatched my hand and tugged me through the living room, down the hall and out of the front door.

The road was quiet. The houses on it were attached to one another and made from the same red brick with pointed roofs, and small front gardens.

There was a lady knelt in the grass, snipping at the peach-coloured roses that grew next to the wall separating our garden from hers while we trod down the path. Her husband appeared to be humming a tune while he mowed the lawn. The lady smiled at me as my mother closed the gate. But as we passed her house, the woman shook her head at my mother and tapped her husband on the shoulder. He pressed a button on the mower and the loud whirring stopped, though the smell of petrol still lingered in the air. 'That's his wife,' she said.

'Living off her conman husband's immoral earnings,' he tutted.

She nodded at him, holding eye contact with my mother.

'The rain came right through Mrs Galloway's kitchen window. They didn't bother to seal the gap between the frame and the wall after installing them.'

My mother stopped mid-step, twisting so fast that she bent my hand back. I jerked away from her and a sharp pain shot from my wrist and up to my elbow. 'My husband's a double-glazing salesman. Not a bloody window fitter. And it's not him or the company he works for that you should be insulting but the idiot Mrs Galloway paid to screw her windows in after he'd nailed her!'

The woman's face turned scarlet and she clamped her hand over her face. Her eyes darted to her husband who was smirking while he rubbed her neck and lowered his voice to a soothing tone so quiet, I couldn't hear his words.

Across the street Mrs Galloway stood erect at her half-open living room window, her chiffon curtains rustling in the breeze.

My mother's rah-rah skirt swayed as she walked, her heels clacking along the pavement at a pace that made me breathless.

My thoughts were on what I would do when we got to the playground. Would I zoom down the slide or swing through the air first?

When we reached the field dotted with daisies there was a line of kids queuing at a yellow and white van. A man handed a boy an ice lolly decorated in sugar strands which he unwrapped and began to lick, his face beaming.

'Can I have an ice cream?'

My mother stopped and lowered her glasses to the tip of her nose to glance down at me.

'Samantha!'

She tilted her head at the sound of her name, released my still-aching hand and shooed me away.

I watched her move towards a man wearing blue jeans and a white T-shirt. He was leaning forward with his arms resting against the top of a bench on the other side of the metal fence separating the playground from the football field. A lit cigarette in his hand emitted smoke that curled upward to the linen-white, fluffball clouds. She halted mid-stride, swung round to press fifty pence into my hand, motioned to the climbing apparatus and said, 'Take it over there to eat. I'll be back in half an hour.'

I went to follow her, but she frowned and continued towards the man whose moustache was neater than my father's. My mother's eyes lingered on the tattoo of a swallow that covered part of his left shoulder. She traced it with her fingertip then hissed at me to 'Go and play.'

'I'd like to play with you,' he said, winding his fingers through her hair and nibbling her neck with his eyes on me. My mother whooped and tried to detach herself from him, but he cracked his hand against her bottom, and she laughed.

I turned away and moved cautiously to meet the line of kids that had grown rapidly, queuing in front of the serving hatch of the ice cream van.

When I looked back the man had his arm over my mother's shoulder, her hand was in the back pocket of his jeans, and he was pointing to a white car parked next to a wall as they walked in its direction.

I hesitantly joined the line, kicking dirt up into the air as I shuffled forward. I stood sandwiched between a scruffy-looking woman, her twin daughters sleeping facing one another with a raincoat over the Silver Cross pram to protect them from the sun, and an oversized boy who scowled at me every time I caught his eye. I tapped my foot in the same way my father did when he was frustrated.

The man behind the counter had a curly beard and a belly as fat as Santa's. 'What are you having?' he asked, leaning over the counter to hear my reply against the backdrop of squealing kids, barking dogs, squawking seagulls and chattering adults.

'What can I get for this?' I handed him the money.

He flicked the silver coin and it spun on his palm until he slammed his hand over it then slid it into his pocket. When he caught me staring at his wizardry with awe he grinned and said, 'Party trick.'

He turned his back to me, then a minute later produced the biggest ice cream I'd ever seen. He winked at me as I took it from him, open-mouthed.

I bit the top off the chocolate flake and sucked the strawberry sauce that had run down my hand from between my sticky fingers.

I scanned the area opposite for my mother, but she, the man and the white car were gone.

My thumb pierced through the waffle cone and crunched under its force. I felt something soft and cold under my nail. Then the ice cream slopped onto the ground and squelched beneath my shoe.

BETHAN

Now

The fire alarm screeches, and my heart begins to pound. I rush into the kitchen, snatch a tea towel from the sparkling granite countertop and open the range oven to a blast of black heat and a stink so strong my eyes water. I cough and splutter while Humphrey waves his Versace suit jacket beneath it, presses the reset button, his face blotchy and creased with displeasure, then slams the kitchen door on me.

I sift blindly through drawers until I find a familiar bunch of keys and feel my way through the smog to the back door to open it, watching the smoke being dispelled by the growing wind and towards the patio where two of Humphrey's old work colleagues are puffing on cigars bought duty-free during a recent business trip to France.

Gerald and Derek's wives, Roberta and Kimberley, are stood beneath the canopy of the gazebo, sipping Hendrick's and singing along to electro, Eighties soundtracks emanating from the Wurlitzer Jukebox. I can see them talking, laughing, and moving to the music through the steamed-up kitchen window.

I stare at the burned steak and charred chips, and feel my limbs tense. I swipe the ruined food into the pedal bin and dump the anodised oven trays into the sink to deal with later.

At least I can't fuck up the salad.

I rip open the bags of ready mixed pea shoots and watercress and shake them into a large ceramic bowl. I grab a serrated knife from the magnet above the steel kettle and slice the cucumber leftover from the punch, adding finely chopped spring onions, sweet peppers, goat's cheese and olives. I inspect the fridge and realise I forgot to buy dressing. I grab the jar of sea salt and crush the chunky crystals together with some black pepper using the pestle and mortar until both are ground into a fine ash-coloured powder. I sprinkle the lot over the salad leaves and pour a light drizzling of olive oil and balsamic vinegar into the bowl before sifting it with a ladle. Then I peel back the cling film, sniff and add a splash of cider vinegar into a bowl of coleslaw, stirring it to get rid of the offish scent of three-day-old carrot and grated white cabbage. I carry it all through the house into the dining hall on a steel tray. No one says anything, but I feel their eyes on me as I move around the table aligning everything, perfecting the placement of the napkins, and ensuring the proper cutlery is in the correct position.

I dash back into the kitchen, cut the bread Muriel baked this morning into chunks using the vegetable knife, spread garlic butter across the soft centre of each slice, and lick the remainder off the blade before shoving it onto a tray and into the oven. I watch it like a hawk and bring it out crispy and golden brown, seven minutes later.

I dart a look at the pile of dirty crockery in the sink and open the glass-fronted cabinet to grab one of the six blue and white china plates that hang from the panelled wall inside. I spin the plate on the counter while placing each individual cut of garlic bread onto it until it becomes a pyramid of gluten. Next, I remove from the fridge the cooked chicken that's been sitting in its own juices inside a Tupperware box since lunchtime and carve it into thin strips using the same serrated knife I realise is meant only for bread, not cutting salad or meat.

Oh, the pomposity of it all.

I inhale the seasoning coating its skin and lick my lips, my mouth watering.

Roberta enters the kitchen. 'That smells delicious. Would you like a hand?'

'No, thank you.'

She watches me stumble into the dining hall, the plates heavy, the stiff material of my shoes starting to bite the tips of my toes. I drop the plates down onto the table too hard. The one holding the bread cracks in half. I don't bother to replace it, or start again.

'Is that a Spode?' says Rupert, one of Humphrey's associates, as I run back to the kitchen, open a bottle of Chablis and pour it into a champagne flute. I gulp it down so fast it spills from the corners of my mouth and down my chin.

Thank fuck it's white.

Humphrey finds me glugging the tepid liquid from the bottle while dabbing at what's dripped down my throat with the tea towel. The lip of the bottle pops as I withdraw it from my mouth and I splutter as I swallow while he tries and fails to retrieve it from my hand. 'Calm down. We've got all evening.'

I purse my lips and narrow my eyes at him, tightening my grip on the bottle. I slug back as much as I can in one go then plonk it down onto the counter and move fast to the open door of the fridge, noting the glacial rivulets at the back of the Bertazzoni have defrosted.

'I wish you wouldn't interfere,' I say, turning the dial back up a notch before I remove the fresh cream pastries from the top shelf of the side-by-side fridge-freezer, feeling Humphrey's breath on the back of my head as he returns the bottle to the middle shelf of the fridge, where it stands among Dom Pérignon, Bollinger and a Domaine de la Romanée-Conti.

Humphrey gasps when he spots the latter. 'Red doesn't belong in the fridge!'

I huff. 'It'll be room temperature half an hour after I've taken it out.'

'It'll taste dry.'

My hand tenses around the wrapped pastries. 'It does anyway.'

'Do you know how much it cost?'

'The thirstier they are, the more they'll wash down. The drunker they get, the more they'll forget the taste.'

'Almost two thousand pounds a bottle.'

I squeeze the thin cardboard packaging that crinkles in my palm. 'Grab another from the basement.'

He inhales sharply, nostrils flaring. He closes his eyes, then opens them on the carved white meat. 'Chicken's far healthier than steak anyway. So just serve that, then you only need to put white wine on the table.'

His condescending tone causes my thumb to pierce the cellophane wrapping protecting the triple chocolate éclairs. I lick it from behind my thumbnail and he tuts, turns away.

'Are you sure I can't do anything?' says Roberta from the stool she's perched on at the breakfast bar where I'd forgotten she was. She's quietly sipping the punch I made using half a leftover watermelon, some mint leaves I pilfered from the overgrown herb garden out back, the last of the seedless grapes and two kiwis. 'I feel like a spare part,' she says, her mouth looking oddly swollen, unable to hold a smile.

I'm wondering which salon she uses to have her lips plumped up when she fingers her upper lip to examine it then glances down into her glass. Her eyes widen in horror and she stands abruptly. The glass falls from her trembling hand. It crashes to the floor, leaving shattered pieces glittering the slate tiles.

Humphrey spins round and grabs her by the arms to steady her. 'She's allergic. Didn't you check?'

The way he holds her, the concern he shows, tells me he's wrapped his hands around her flesh before.

Gerald appears in the doorway smelling of maple whiskey and wood. He moves towards us, stops in front of Roberta, doesn't acknowledge the fact Humphrey has just released his wife from an overly affectionate grip, and takes Roberta's spindly hands in his. She opens and closes her mouth several times before she speaks, but her words come out fuzzy, her tongue too swollen to talk properly.

'Allergic to what?'

'Kiwi fruit,' says Gerald.

I walk over to the sink, stepping over the shards of crystal, and fill a sherry glass with ice-cold water, which slops from the rim and splashes across the floor as I make my way to her. Roberta takes it from me, her hand shaking. She nods, saying, 'thank you.' But through her swollen mouth it sounds more like 'fuck you.'

I slip and trip across the floor, sloshing through the water and giggling at my own incompetency. I tug off a yard-long stretch of kitchen roll from the holder, bunch it up and throw it onto the floor to soak up the water. Then I use the dustpan and brush that's leaning against the wall beside the cabinet to sweep the broken glass up into several folds of today's edition of *The Times* before depositing it in the bin. I check the floor for any glass I might have missed then wipe the tiles dry and toss the wet kitchen towel into the pedal bin.

I lean on the breakfast counter to remove the stilettos from my aching feet, wobbling on one painfully high-arched heel, using Humphrey's arthritic arm to stop myself from toppling over.

'Come here, Roberta,' says Gerald, glancing from her to Humphrey, arm raised with his elbow pointed north. She stands and links her arm through his. 'Thank you for a splendid evening.'

'You haven't eaten yet.'

He gives Roberta a sympathetic smile. 'I'll take her home. She should rest.'

'You can't leave here hungry.'

'She'll be alright. Though she might not be able to talk for a few hours.' He aims a wink at Humphrey, who reciprocates with a one-sided smile.

Roberta nods in apparent agreement of her husband's

sexist comment that she'd be better seen and not heard, and he hoists her off the bar stool. I step aside to allow them past and watch from behind while he escorts her from the kitchen, down the marble floored hall and into the dining hall where the sound of clinking glasses and raucous laughter grates against the backdrop of Enya – Rupert's choice, no doubt. Gerald says goodbye to the other guests and apologises on Roberta's behalf. She holds her palm over the lower quarter of her face to avoid having to display her misshapen mouth and I follow a few paces behind to stand in the doorway and see them out, like the respectable wife Humphrey wants me to be.

I watch him walk them to the glossy black Mercedes and wave them off.

'It's not her fault,' Gerald's words float through the air. Humphrey turns to look at me before whispering something inaudible in his ear.

I fight the urge to yell at him in front of witnesses.

Humphrey turns back and rubs his eyes and the tip of his nose, a look of exasperation on his face as he re-enters the house.

I glare at the two of him and they shake their head. I blame my double vision on the wine, but it's probably the bottle I drank before it.

The rest of the evening passes quickly or maybe I'm just too pissed to notice the time. Unfortunately, I remember the tedium of every conversation that occurred between Roberta the Trout Pout leaving and the others starting to talk more shit than usual, so I know I didn't black out. I listen to everyone recommending accountants, architects, interior designers and holiday apartments.

Eventually I become so bored I join in.

'I don't have a passport.'

Derek frowns and Kim cannot hide her surprise, though she looks permanently startled since her recent bout of Botox.

'You've never been abroad?'

'No.'

Humphrey, one eye drooping, the other roaming, cuts in. 'I took her to Scotland for our honeymoon.'

'In Rupert's Cesena,' they sigh in unison.

I struggle to deconstruct their shared joke.

'You must visit Rome,' says Kim, leaning over the table and almost losing her balance. She plunges her finger into the centre of an éclair to retrieve the stale cream and circles the tip of her finger with her tongue before pushing it just past the knuckle into her mouth and sucking on it, her eyes focused on mine, unblinking.

I manage to hold a straight face while she repeats the strangely erotic movements a second and third time. Then perhaps tiring from my lack of response she leaves the table, swaying her hips, dancing out of sync to the piano concerto now playing at a volume I consider background noise, while humming a tune of her own.

The food is eaten, the port is opened and the men retreat to the study to play cards, while I find myself alone in a secluded spot of the Victorian garden.

Kim waltzes towards me from the ivy-covered porch, her heels clopping along the wooden bridge to cross the pond. Her eyes are set on mine, if a little unfocused. And her feet keep moving left while her torso leans right.

She lands heavily on the dry-stone wall that lines the

path where moss and weeds have already begun to sprout between the cracks since Frederick the gardener last tended to the land. I squint at the lichen, which has climbed the cyclamen and strangled it, before redirecting my gaze to the blurred contours of Kim's face when she exhales something that's caught up in the night-time breeze.

'Pardon?'

I must lean into her to hear her speak, so quiet is her voice. 'The men are keeping themselves amused.' Her eyelids flicker as she lowers her head to rest it on my shoulder.

She pins a few stray hairs back into the clip supporting her long mane of auburn hair and I strain not to shove her off me as her chin digs into my collar bone. 'It seems that way.'

'I know what people said about you before you married Humphrey.' She starts picking at the hem of her dress. 'I didn't listen. The age difference between me and Derek is half yours.' She pauses, pulls a thread of cotton from the stitching. 'I didn't mean... what I'm trying to say is you're good for him. He seems alive.' She tugs hard on the thread until it snaps then unravels it from the coil around her finger and drops it onto the ground.

Not for long.

'He loves you.'

I look back at the house, the shadows behind the glass, where a stream of dim lamplight piercing through an inch-wide gap in the stiff velvet curtains of the study tells me the men's game is getting serious. 'I know.'

She snuffles, sits upright, brushing her cheek against my collarbone as she stands and straightens her spine, causing her to appear taller than her five foot six inches.

'I'm hammered,' she slurs.

I dip my fingers into my bra and pull out the small baggie of cocaine I was saving for later. 'Want a line?'

She stares at it for a few seconds then stumbles back, holding onto the railing for support. 'How much have you got left?'

'About a gram.'

She nods and looks at the ground then turns and follows the path back to the house, wiping her runny nose with the heel of her hand.

In the bathroom, the door locked behind us, I try to pull the elaborately moulded mirror off the wall but it's too heavy, so I remove the loose tile from behind the sink, run the sleeve of my gown beneath the tap and use it to wipe the dust off the tile before placing it onto the back of the toilet lid. I empty the two-inch-wide see-through snap-bag onto the tile and chop the white powder into a fine line that runs from one end to the other with my credit card. I notice some of the powder has wedged itself into a small groove in one corner of the tile, so I lick the tip of my forefinger and dab it away, rubbing it along the gums above my top front teeth, the tingle reassuring me of the alert sense of wellbeing I am about to feel.

I hand Kim the rolled up fifty-pound note and watch her snort it, sniff, then pull a menthol cigarette from the pocket of her Armani trousers and light it before I can switch on the fan to dispel the smoke.

I hoover up the last of the coke and sneeze as it hits the blood vessels in my nasal cavity, my sight sharpening as it reaches my brain.

I catch the blood that drips from Kim's left nostril with

a bit of toilet roll. She moves my hand away from her nose, holds it in mid-air and stares at me, her expression unreadable.

'What do you want?'

She lowers her chin, looks up at me doe-eyed and presses herself against me.

I kiss her delicately, surprised when she reciprocates as I wasn't sure she was this way inclined. Her mouth is soft, her tongue tastes sweet.

There is a *rat-a-tat-tat* on the other side of the door.

'Are you in there, Kim?' says Derek.

I keep my voice low, but my breath gives away my rising adrenaline. 'Go.'

She moves away from me, backs into the door, turns and inhales the last of the blood to preserve the indignity of being caught out. Of failing to maintain the feminine ideal.

I catch the faintest eye-roll in the mirror as Kim exits the bathroom ahead of me, a slight blush creeping up her cheeks.

She doesn't wear guilt well.

Derek gives her a concerned look that turns to one of perplexity when he sees me.

I wind past them and down the hall. As I reach the bottom step of the staircase the loud shrill of the smoke alarm cuts through the silence, turning the accusing atmosphere surrounding me into one of panic.

When they've vacated the house, I stand at the window looking over the veranda and down on the commotion, at the worried and harried people Humphrey has known for decades.

It wasn't my cooking this time but Kim's cigarette that set the first-floor smoke alarm off. Despite the fact I turned the fan on, and she dropped it in the toilet before she opened the door to Derek, who saw and recognised the tiny clump of white powder stuck to the dried blood up her nose. The cigarette remained inside the bowl instead of sinking into the water. Humphrey took too long to key in the code and reset the alarm, so the company who maintain the system alerted the fire brigade.

I watch Rupert's driver reverse around the fire engine, and Derek opening the door for Kim to sit inside the Volvo. I wait for them all to pass the courtyard before I release my hold on the curtain. It drops down over the luminescent moon.

I'm seated in front of the mirror brushing my hair when Humphrey falls into the room and clamps his hand over mine. For a seventy-year-old man he's surprisingly strong. The pressure of his palm weakens my hold on the solid silver brush, and it clangs onto the polished wood of the chalk-white oak dresser, leaving a dent.

He dismisses my clumsiness for once and nuzzles my earlobe like a salivating dog, and I close my eyes to evoke the image of my dream man: younger and slimmer.

I let Humphrey trail his damp mouth from my neck to my throat, but when he hooks his fingers into my bra strap and runs the backs of them downward to stroke my breast, I push the chair back causing him to leap backwards.

'I'm going to freshen up.'

I sit on the edge of the freestanding claw-footed bathtub inside our ensuite, unscrew the bottle of Rohypnol that's saved me from feigning orgasm twenty-four times, pop one of the four capsules into my mouth and swill it down with a handful of cold tap water.

If I must climb on top of him, I don't want to remember it in the morning.

I slip out of my silk robe and push my lacy babydoll down to expose more of the crease between my breasts, add a touch more sparkling rouge lipstick, smack my lips together and shimmy into the bedroom to find Humphrey lying comatose in the centre of the bed, arms spread wide, shirt buttons undone, trousers halfway down his thighs, his breath stained with the smell of black truffles.

'Thank fuck for that.'

Despite the mini bar in the lounge and the basement full of decade-long aged wines and wood-distilled spirits, he's not a big drinker.

The drugs I slipped into his last glass of cognac seem to have already begun to take effect.

I try to rouse him. First by shouting his name into his ear, then by shaking him. He stirs when my actions become more forceful, then turns onto his side and begins to snore. I try to raise his sleep-weighted hand and when that doesn't wake him, I shove him hard in the back, but he won't budge.

I fall back onto the feather soft pillows stacked against the headboard of our king-size bed. Squeezed between the fat oaf beside me and the Baroque-style bedside unit, I cross my arms and wait for the tranquilisers to kick in.

DI LOCKE

Then

According to the preliminary report provided by the forensic anthropologist the incomplete skeleton had been inside the suitcase for at least two years. Despite the skull being missing, Dr Ward was able to tell from the wide subpubic angle and broad sciatic notch of the pelvis that the person was a female. Structural analysis suggested she was Caucasian. Pockmarks were present on the symphysis pubis bone where ligaments had torn during childbirth. And the rate of fusion on the caps of the bone shafts suggested bone growth had almost completed, placing her at around twenty to thirty-five years old. But without teeth it was difficult to determine a more precise age.

It wasn't just Jane Doe's head that was missing, but her hands too. To prevent identification. Placing her cause of death firmly in the murdered category.

I called Dr Ward to let her know I'd read the email she sent me the morning after Jane Doe had been discovered. Because there were two things that she couldn't assess without consulting a Home Office pathologist her report was merely preliminary. Dr Holland had just left her office.

'Any idea how she died?'

'She has a couple of fractured ribs, and a healed wrist joint. But there's also peri-mortem trauma to her right ankle and shin suggesting she was struck at least twice with a blunt object. Due to the placement of her injuries it's likely she was kicked. But that certainly wouldn't have killed her. My guess is her head was not only removed to decrease our chance of identifying her but to make it difficult to uncover her cause of death.'

'It's possible she suffered a fatal head injury?'

'We won't know unless we find her skull. And if or when we do, we'll know it's hers because she was dismembered with a sharp implement that has a distinct cut.'

I felt my jaw tense and my stomach churn.

'Dr Holland and I agree that the blade was convex with an evenly pointed angle, larger than a knife, and had a nick in the metal approximately half an inch in diameter near the point.'

I gritted my teeth as bile crept up my throat. 'A sword?'

What kind of monster murdered someone, chopped them up, squeezed their body parts into a suitcase and then dumped them like a bag of rubbish?

MELANIE

Then

I stomped from the ice cream van into the playground and headed to the swings. At the sight of my fury, the girl sat on the one I had my eyes on jumped off. I grabbed it before it swung back and hit her in the face, catching a familiar shape bounding towards the entrance from the line of trees she cut through from her house.

I watched Maddison slam the gate behind her and pound towards me. She jumped onto the swing beside me and reached her hand out to mine. I took it and we swung like two links in a chain.

'If you close your eyes and lean your head back it feels like you're flying,' she said.

I swung on it for ages with my eyes shut, feeling the roaring wind comb my hair back and forth as I pushed out with my feet and soared upward, kicked at the clouds then retracted them in a whoosh of air.

Time didn't exist when we were together.

'I've got to go,' said Maddison, a while later.

I opened my eyes as she retracted her hand from mine and shot across the playground.

I didn't feel the pain when I jumped off the swing and landed on my knees. I just picked out the grit that was embedded into the soft fat protecting my kneecaps and rubbed the bloodied dirt off them. Then I trod over to the roundabout and pushed it hard until all the kids hopped off it holding their stomachs, leaving me alone with the boy I'd noticed had been standing beneath the slide watching the other kids squealing as they sped down it but making no move to traipse up the steps to glide down it himself.

He smiled and looked down at the soft furry toy in his hand. I followed his gaze. 'He's a Care Bear.'

'Does he look after you or do you take care of him?'

He seemed to be contemplating my question for a long time before he replied. 'He makes me feel calm when I'm angry.' He held it out to me. 'Do you want to hold him?'

I took it from him. 'Do you get angry often?'

He looked back at a denim-clad man who had both hands raised, face red, words unintelligible from the distance between us. The woman, who I guessed was the boy's mother, was backed into the chain-link fence while the man seemed to be closing in on her. When I blinked, I saw my own parents arguing.

'Depends if I'm spending the weekend with my dad or not,' he said.

I hugged the bear, felt nothing but its soft fur tickling my chin, then held it at arm's length and pushed it back into the boy's hand. He looked disappointed so I reached out and took his other hand and led him towards the slide. I felt his hand tighten as we grew closer, his arm tense. 'It's not as high as it looks.'

He dropped his gaze.

I gave his palm a squeeze. 'Why don't we go down together?'

I let go of his hand when we reached the queue of kids waiting to climb the five-foot-high incline. He watched the others ascend and when it was his turn, I pushed him to go on ahead, met him at the top and sat on the cold hard steel so he had no option but to park himself between my thighs. He moved to put his arms out to the bars, and I caught them at my sides and shuffled forward until the only way off the apparatus was down. We slid slowly to the bottom together, and when the boy turned to me his face was beaming. 'You can do anything if you work for it,' I said, echoing my grandmother's words.

He nodded and we walked back to the end of the queue to repeat our movements. Only this time he went down alone.

When I got to the bottom the girl who'd jumped off the swing to let me have a go on it earlier re-appeared. She barged past me as I made my way back to the queue that had diminished to just the three of us.

He was nearing the top when I felt the first drop of rain. I looked up at the gathering clouds and as my eyes returned to the boy, I saw the girl nudge him. He grabbed for the handrail to prevent his fall.

When I saw her again, the girl was lying on the ground screaming and crying with blood pouring from her nose, a split lip, and was missing a bottom tooth. The boy was stood over her. As he glanced up at me the rain began to spit. He shook his head and I mouthed 'payback.'

A woman appeared at the girl's side the instant she heard wailing. She picked her up and carried her to a bench. A woman with a pram retrieved baby wipes from the tray beneath it and handed the pack to the girl's mother to clean up the blood that had soaked through the girl's dress and stained her blonde hair crimson in parts.

The boy's mother climbed the fence and ran towards him. Kids and adults gathered around the bench muttering comforting words. A boy held the girl's tooth out for her, but her mother said, 'I don't have any milk to put it in.'

The woman with the pram said, 'My daughter drinks cow's milk.' She peered into the changing bag hung from the handlebar, pulled out a bottle, unscrewed the teat, and said, 'Drop it into there.'

She took it but her hand was shaking so much she spilled half the contents onto the concrete before screwing the teat back on and re-applying the lid.

I skidded down the wet slide and searched for the boy who'd been stood beside me at the top of the slide but caught sight of my mother instead as she exited the white car. She walked round to the other side and leaned through the driver's window to where I saw the man with the moustache. He reached out and brought her face toward his with a hand gripping her jaw and kissed her. I turned away to avoid eye contact and saw the boy on the other side of the gate with his back to me. I was willing him to turn around so I could wave goodbye when a girl behind me said, 'There she is.'

My mother waved her fingers at the man. He smiled

back then sped off, leaving a trail of dust behind him. She spun in the direction of the park and aimed for the gate I was heading for when a boy stepped in front of it to block my exit and pointed at me, his finger inches from my face. 'That's her.'

I looked back at the bench where the girl's mother cradled her whimpering daughter against her chest. The woman's face was scrunched up with disgust and her eyes were filled with accusation. Another boy stepped in front of me and I pushed past them both, pulled back the heavy gate with a squeak, and skipped towards my mother.

'What happened?' she said, noting the group of people who were staring after me.

I fluttered my eyelashes. 'A girl fell off the slide.'

'I hope *you* were being careful.'

'I can look after myself.'

She nodded and patted my back. 'We'd better get home.' She spun her watch strap round and read the time on the Quartz's face. 'It's almost five o'clock. Your father will be wondering where we are.'

My father was watching the TV when we returned, his eyes on the ball the Cardiff City players were kicking around the pitch. When it hit the net, he jumped off the chair and shouted, 'Goal!' He kicked the coffee table over in his excitement and the pint of beer that was on it flew across the room and hit the TV stand.

He punched the air, his eyes flitting from my mother to me and then he ruffled my hair. 'Did you have a good day, princess?'

I nodded and copied my mother's smile.

'Good.' He turned his attention back to the TV. 'What did you do?'

My mother widened her eyes at me in silent warning.

'We went to the park and Mummy bought me an ice cream.'

My mother's shoulders dropped and her face relaxed.

'That's great,' he said, fetching the empty glass from the sodden floor and refilling it with another can of beer before slouching back in his seat.

He turned towards my mother without averting his gaze from the screen and placed a hand on her shoulder. 'Clear that up, will you, love?' he said, motioning to where the beer had soaked into the carpet.

'Sure.' She sighed and left the room.

I lingered in the doorway and watched her enter the kitchen. She returned to the living room with a cloth and some Jif, knelt on the floor and began to scrub the carpet. When she stood, her forehead was dripping with sweat and her smile had faded.

I sat on the sofa and twirled my hair between my fingers until I'd created a spiral, watching my father watching TV and my mother tidy the room around him. 'Can I play in the garden?'

She frowned. 'You've been in the sun all day.'

I shrugged.

She stared down at me kicking the heels of my bare feet against the sofa and sighed. 'Fine. Go on.'

I headed straight for the mulberry bush at the bottom of the garden where a gap in the hedge gave me access to our neighbour's patio. It was behind their shed and to the left that the apple tree stood, out of their line of sight.

I stepped over creeping thistle, buttercups and dandelions, their heads rust-coloured from the heat. Nettles stung my shins and the tiny white petals of ground elder tickled my ankles. I tugged on the lowest branch of the tree. The apple I retrieved had maggot-holes in it. The red skin on the next was wrinkled. I reached up and shook the branch that was second up from the ground. Two large unripe apples landed on the brambles with a thud. I walked round the tree and did the same again, collecting four this time. I knelt and gathered them all to my stomach then raised the hem of my cotton dress to act as a makeshift basket to carry them inside the house.

My mother was dusting the floral ornaments she collected on top of the fireplace when I re-entered the house. I left the apples on the kitchen counter beside my mother and at the sight of my flushed cheeks and grubby feet she recoiled. 'Look at the state of you.'

I glanced at my scratched legs.

'How did you get dried leaves in your hair?'

I shrugged though I thought it was obvious.

'You need a good scrub.'

I was in the bath when the doorbell chimed its shrill cry. Barbie had been drowning Ken and when the door opened, she removed her feet from his neck, and he bobbed up to the surface of the water.

'She's been stealing again,' our neighbour said from the doorway.

'You're mistaken.'

'She's trodden all over my primroses. The footprints lead into your garden through the hedge.'

'They're only weeds.'

'I suppose that makes it alright, does it?'

'What's all the commotion?' my father roared from the living room.

'The nosy hag from next door is accusing our Mel of nicking her rotten apples.'

'Tell her to go and get f—'

'What my husband is trying to say is that he thinks you need a good hard f—'

My father pelted to the door and slammed it in her astonished face before my mother could finish.

My mother was baking apple pie when I entered the kitchen sometime later. She sensed me immediately and didn't bother to turn around. 'Don't think you're getting any pudding, young lady. I didn't bring you up to nick old Mrs what's-her-face's sour fruit.'

'Where did you think she got that from?' said my father, blowing smoke from his cigarette out of the partway open window while waving to dispel it quicker.

My mother stared at me for a long time then said, 'She doesn't get her thieving from me.'

'Just your manipulative streak then.'

I was sent to my room hungry, forced to endure the smell of sweet pastry wafting upstairs, imagining the taste of cinnamon-sugar-coated apple pie lagged in custard. My stomach grumbled.

'Would you like to go to the park again tomorrow?' Mum said, later that night while tucking me into bed.

'Will you buy me another ice cream?'

She folded the sheet down and smoothed it under my arms. 'Sure.'

'Okay then.'

She nodded, straightening, then backed out of the room and closed the door.

I heard my father's footsteps on the staircase five minutes later. I lifted the sheet and buried my head under it and tried to keep my breath even while I listened to him pee then pull the flush. I heard the splash of water hit the sink.

The loose floorboard creaked as he trod across the landing. His feet shadowed the gap of light beneath the door. The handle turned and my father entered my bedroom. He crept up to the bed and I felt my heart hammering against my chest as his weight landed on the edge of the mattress beside me. He leaned over me and kissed my forehead and my entire body began to shake.

'Daddy's special princess,' he whispered into my ear. His hot breath stank of ale.

BETHAN

Now

I listen to the tweeting birds through the broken seal of the double-glazed bedroom window, open one eye and see the light streaking between the blackout curtains. My tongue sounds like Velcro as I tear it off the roof of my mouth and when I swallow, I taste ashtray and vomit.

I roll over, stomach churning, to reach for the glass of water I usually leave on my bedside. I swipe the unit, feel the solid ivory lamp, then brush against something plastic I can't distinguish that crashes onto the floor, forcing me upright with a yelp.

My head is pounding and whirring like a cement mixer, my heart is thudding and I feel queasy. I struggle to adjust my hungover eyes to the sharp room while I pat the bed to find the empty space where Humphrey should be lying beside me, cold.

What a shame *he* isn't.

The bedroom door wheezes open. 'Good morning, darling.'

I glare at Humphrey and pitch a pillow at his head, but it misses and almost knocks the tray – containing a freshly baked waffle covered in thick yoghurt and mixed berries, and a glass of freshly squeezed orange juice – out of Humphrey's hands and onto the floor.

He moves carefully towards me, lays the tray on the bedside unit and collects my La Prairie crème from the Persian rug. The lid is cracked, and a hundred pounds worth of anti-wrinkle cream has spilled down the side of the pot. I snatch it from him and feel something caked into my fringe as I shake my head and growl. When I toss the duvet off my jittery legs, hoist myself off the bed and wobble to the mirror to investigate, I pull my hand away and leg it into the ensuite before I throw up for what could be the second or even third time according to my puke-matted hair.

'You didn't drink *that* much last night,' says Humphrey, from the doorway.

He enters the bathroom and stands over the toilet bowl I have my head over and places both hands on my shoulders before giving them both a squeeze. 'You must have eaten something that didn't agree with you.'

It could be the rehashed coleslaw.

Or the tranquilisers.

I'm sick until my ribs ache and my throat is sore.

Though he turns away as I spit bile into the toilet then flush, Humphrey hands me a rose-scented makeup wipe from my cosmetics bag and retrieves a towel from the airing cupboard and hangs it over the heated rail to keep warm. 'You might feel like eating once you've had a wash.'

I nod, incapable of much else.

I lock the door on him then step behind the curtain and stand beneath the shower, feeling the heat rise from my shivering feet to my dizzy head and inhale the steam, allowing my pores to open and my skin to clear, as the water rains down on me in a cleansing torrent.

Once I'm satisfied that I no longer smell like an alcoholic hobo I pat myself down, blow-dry my hair, brush my teeth and slap on enough makeup to alter my identity: primer, foundation, contour pen, highlighting pearls, eyeshadow, eyeliner, mascara, lip plumper, lip stain, lip gloss and finally setting spray. Then I open the door to a blast of cold air, reacclimatising my limbs to the natural heat of the sturdy old building. Or rather it's lack thereof.

I dress, choose a pair of Louboutin's that match the zebra print Dolce & Gabbana bodycon that clings to my curves, nibble on the browned edges of the waffle and take a swig of the bitter orange juice before spitting it back into the glass. Then I take the tray downstairs, dump it onto the kitchen counter, and retrieve the keys to the E-Class from the safe.

As I grab my Burberry from the coat hook Humphrey spins me round to face him and pecks me on the cheek. 'Where are you going? Do you need money?'

'Shopping, and yes. I've got the credit card, but it's maxed out. If you could—'

'I'll put five hundred on it as soon as I find my glasses.'

I spot them in the lounge through the half-open doorway, stretched over the armrest of the sofa.

'Here.' I hand them to him along with his phone.

'Where would I be without you?' he says, thumbing the screen to log onto the online banking app.

In a coffin a lot later than planned, I expect.

I study his thumb-strokes but after the 8 he turns so I can't see him hit the final four digits.

He smiles and I let him draw me into a hug and inhale the white musk and jasmine perfume I've dabbed behind my earlobes. He sighs, satisfied when I don't stiffen or pull away. 'Drive carefully.'

I smile back and step on my toe with the heel of my shoe to stop myself from laughing at the irony of his ignorant comment.

I did a Google search using a burner phone I bought from a pop-up shop in Newport town centre six months ago. I dressed down, wore reactor-light glasses which I smashed up and doused in bleach before dumping in the river later, a wig and hat which I burned in a field several miles from home while Humphrey played golf afterwards, altered my facial expressions and mannerisms to match those of an actress I'd seen on EastEnders the night before, and inherited a northern accent. I ensured there were no CCTV cameras outside the shop by checking their locations on the council's website, paid with cash and gave the man who served me some spiel about wasting paper to ensure he didn't print off a receipt.

When researching how to get away with murder I discovered offenders get caught because they make mistakes or leave trace evidence at the crime scene.

Humphrey may be twice my age, but he's fit and healthy. He's never worked with toxic chemicals, doesn't suffer from any known psychological or physical illness, has no history of criminal behaviour, is far too intelligent to get into a fight with someone and has the money to afford to pay a professional for services involving DIY. Which rules out industrial disease, Sudden Adult Death, suicide, murder and carbon monoxide poisoning.

After Alzheimer's, cardiovascular disease, pneumonia, cancer, suicide and homicide, the sixth leading cause of death in men is accidents. Typically manufacturing, poisoning, or road traffic accidents.

I did some random searches using the burner phone – best places to visit in south Wales; places to stay off-grid in south Wales; longest road in south Wales; least used road in south Wales; highest road in south Wales; and road in south Wales with largest mortality rate – leading up to the question I needed answering: how likely is it that a person could survive driving off a bridge and onto a motorway?

The statistics were pleasantly bleak.

It turns out that the A470 route through the valleys is the most dangerous road in south Wales. And is notorious for what police term run-offs (vehicles drifting out of lanes and into oncoming vehicles or crash barriers).

Searching for the commonest causes of RTAs threw up the following results: being distracted; dangerous driving/ recklessness; adverse weather conditions; potholes; tyre blowouts; and breakdowns. The conclusion being the majority of RTAs are due to human error.

While a post-mortem examination will reveal the injuries a victim obtains, investigations into RTAs by the Home Office are conducted by coroners via an inquest, the aim of which is to assess a range of contributory factors including negligence and illness, considering vehicular maintenance and insured risk against what is often the primary cause of an individual's fatality – mechanical failure or automotive malfunction – to determine the cause of the accident. When a serviceable fault is found the individual's death will be reported as thus: accidental, an incident no one could have predicted would have occurred.

The number one avoidable cause of mechanical failure is braking, followed second by electrical systems. It seems logical that if you add a dash of drunkenness, a sprinkling of fog and a spritz of dark sky, a man unused to the effect of alcohol on his bladder and who is prone to speeding while distracted by the loud music emanating from the speakers of his car is unlikely to notice the warning light on the dashboard alerting him to a problem with his premium drive.

Next, I Googled how to cause a car crash. It's surprisingly easy to cause a blowout with a set of low tread tyres and misaligned wheel camber. Add some faulty brake lines to ensure either the cables or master cylinder is leaking fluid. Decrease the vehicle's stopping power with some corroded or distorted brake discs and worn pads. Perhaps include a rusted, debris-laden calliper piston that intermittently sticks. Supplement this with a loose axel joint or loss of steering fluid to compromise performance of the suspension and tracking. The addition of a headlight bulb that needs replacing or a set of worn windscreen wipers during heavy rain will also affect the driver's visibility. But I needed to stage an accident on a one-year-old car, so I settled for a fault with the Anti-Lock Braking System.

The ABS sensors attached to the wheels can be damaged by impact, electrical overload or extreme temperature changes. But without involving someone else to detect and interpret the hidden fault codes then erase them from the Engine Control Unit my only option was to play amateur auto-electrician.

A YouTube video showed me where the unit was situated and how to remove the fuse that modulates the braking pressure within the Traction Control System, preventing the tyres from skidding or hydroplaning, and replace it with a blown fuse that would cause the brake pedal to become unresponsive and seize during an emergency stop.

I could have rammed a car into Humphrey's or forced his vehicle into someone else's but the element of risk I'm undertaking increases in the unfortunate event of a witness describing the blonde woman who fled the scene. I'm not going to be in the car with Humphrey when it careens off the road, rolls over and lands upside down, there aren't any ANPR-camera-free-zones nearby, and the nearest roadside clifftop or flyover is too far away from the house. So spiking his drink, waiting for him to lose consciousness, getting him into the car, driving him to the highest point of the valleys, dragging him onto the driver's seat, wedging his foot onto the accelerator and releasing the handbrake isn't feasible here.

As he has no heirs and no descendants Humphrey's money would be kept by the government if an inquest concluded he died as a result of murder and I was suspected to be at fault. But the rule of forfeiture only applies to his estate, not the other properties he owns or the savings and investments in his Eastern bank accounts. So I figured a failproof two-pronged approach would protect me from legal ramifications by suggesting I sign a prenuptial agreement.

In my preparation I've provided Humphrey with a false sense of security. Playing the ditzy trophy wife to my generous, gullible husband has been marked off my internal rota as complete.

Now it's time to implement phase two.

We're staying in the holiday cottage he owns just a few miles south of Mount Snowdon next week. The three-year-old Mercedes-Benz Sprinter is only three and a half tonnes, so I don't need a Category C licence to drive it. Which is just as well because although I have a driving licence, I've never taken a test.

The van is heavy, north east Wales is expecting a midweek storm according to the MET office, making the weather perfect for an accident, and practising on a similar engine one final time I'm positive I can tamper with the Sprinter in the dark, wearing gloves, in under a minute.

I need the brakes to lock and the fifty thousand pounds' worth of steel body and titanium alloys to tip. Adding some lethal objects to the cargo should increase the level of injuries Humphrey sustains and decrease the possibility he will survive. Although Daimler's German engineering is top notch and their commercial vehicles are built to withstand the toughest of terrains and the worst collisions, so I've got to stack the rear shelf of the cabin with bags of unmixed cement to ensure it at least tips, and preferably rolls over.

Six months in the gym three mornings a week and I'm capable of hauling a sack truck containing four stacked 50kg bags from the house and wheeling them into the garage. Sixteen should do it.

Humphrey stands in the doorway waving as I speed off.

I glance into the rear-view mirror, watching the manor shrink in the distance.

It won't be long before it's mine.

DI LOCKE

Then

To identify a killer, you have to start with the body. Jane Doe's hard tissue DNA didn't match the profiles of any recorded missing persons in the UK. So we had to use other means to identify her.

While DC Winters compared Jane Doe's demographics – sex, estimated age, ethnicity, and the evidence of childbirth and injuries common in victims of domestic abuse – against the medical records of missing persons in south Wales, DC Chapman compared known ex-convicts and registered sex offenders living in hostels or released from prison within a ten-mile radius of the crime scene, around the time the maggots found inside the suitcase were believed to have been alive.

None of the CCTV cameras in the area were close enough to the overpass to pick up anything significant, they were wiped every three months as they belonged to a private company across the street, and they only gave a view of customers entering and exiting the factory car park.

Jones was sitting in front of his laptop, staring at the screen, and making notes of every vehicle spotted on ANPR cameras that were near to the crime scene back in 2015, to check for repeat journeys. But as he had no idea what he was looking for – although we suspected a van was used to dump the body the suitcase could just as easily have been transferred in a car boot – he could only narrow the potential car down to 317; 209 of them belonged to locals, with a good knowledge of the area, and 198 of those could be eliminated based on mobile phone data, in-car Satellite Navigation signals, and alibis. Leaving 119 potential suspects. And that was only if the person who dumped the suitcase was the same person who'd murdered the woman inside it, and the individual hadn't travelled to Carleon from elsewhere to dispose of her.

Sixty-six of them volunteered to give us saliva samples to compare to the skin cell traces of the unknown male DNA we found on the suitcase. Forty-four of them were already on the system, so we didn't need their permission to compare their profiles to the four and a half million samples we have filed on the NDNAD database. Seven of them refused to give a sample, claiming it was a violation of their human rights. They changed their minds when we arrested them for obstructing a police officer which led to the extraction and retention of their DNA, allowing us to eliminate them from the investigation. One of the two we hadn't been able to contact was a drifter. We managed to track him down to a squat in Cardiff. His DNA matched the profile taken from a burglary six months before, that left an elderly man battered and bruised, which resulted in his conviction. The final one led us to the Newport Butcher.

MELANIE

Then

Ilay on the floor with my ear pressed to the thin carpet. A glass broke. My mother screamed something inaudible. Then my father's deep voice bellowed, 'Lying, cheating slag!'

Something got knocked over. My mother cried. My father lowered his voice.

I crept back into bed and shook beneath the sheet, chanting quietly. 'Please don't hurt Mummy... please don't hurt Mummy.'

I fell asleep with my hands clenched into fists and my teeth bared.

I woke hours later to the sound of birdsong and the smell of pancakes, my fingers cramped and my jaw aching. I almost deceived myself into thinking that I'd dreamt what had happened the night before. Until my father slammed the front door, his car engine roared into life, the wheels span and the exhaust backfired. He left in a cloud of black smoke without looking back.

I pressed my hands against the cold glass and turned away from the window. I dressed, then padded downstairs.

My mother was stood at the sink with her back to me when I reached the kitchen. When she heard me enter her hands stalled on the dishcloth.

I sat on the chair closest to the door and furthest from her, where only I could see Maddison peering into the house at me from behind the hedge. I shook my head, mouthed 'I can't play today' and she retreated.

The silence was physical. And when she eventually spoke it sounded like her mouth was full. 'Why did you tell your father?'

'Tell him what?'

'About Jason.'

'Who's Jason?'

She threw the soapy plate into the sink and it broke into pieces. 'The man you told your father I left you alone in the park to drive off with.'

'Oh.'

'Oh? Is that all you have to say?' I didn't recognise the woman who turned to face me. Her eyelids were puffy and black, one side of her face was swollen, and her upper lip was split.

'You didn't tell me not to tell him.'

'Well, now he's gone. Taken his things and left us. And he won't be coming back,' she lisped.

Although her eyes were mere slits, I felt her hatred burning through them.

'Frosties or Coco Pops?' she said. The wound to her mouth reopened and blood dripped down her chin and onto the lino.

I pointed at the Frosties.

She poured the sugared flakes into a bowl and added a splash of milk, then slid it across the table and threw a spoon next to it which clanged before landing on the floor.

When I'd retrieved it from under the table my mother had dashed from the room.

As I sat and ate, her footsteps shuffled around upstairs.

When she returned to the kitchen, she'd dolled herself up, but nothing could disguise the thumbprints around her throat or the look of terror on her face, double the size it should be, as the post fell through the letterbox and landed on the mat.

She flinched when I scraped the chair back to stand, wiping off my milk moustache with the back of my hand. Tears formed in her eyes and her mouth wobbled.

I left the table and plopped my empty bowl and spoon onto the counter.

She hobbled down the hallway and winced as she opened the front door and stood, head down, one shoulder drooping while tears trickled down her powdered face and dripped off her jaw, darkening the neckline of her brass buttoned top.

'Can I have a double scoop this time?'

'A double scoop?'

'Ice cream.'

'Ice cream?' She shook her head. 'We're not going to the park.'

'But you said yesterday w—'

'You're going to your grandmother's.'

'Where will you be?'

'Here,' she said, spreading her arms wide and twirling on unsteady feet.

I got the hint. She did look scary.

I left the house with my mother stood behind the door to hide her bruised face. I crossed the road past Mrs Galloway's and took the shortcut I recalled my mother using on one of our rare visits to her childhood home together.

When I reached the familiar lane that led to the muddied path of Liswerry Pond I was hit with the sweet scent of cannabis. I turned my head to the group of older boys milling around on bikes, one of whom I recognised from school though I couldn't recall his name.

His weekend attire was as scruffy as his school uniform. He watched me walk along the water's edge. Two ducks, one making an odd puffing sound from its beak, the other flapping its wings swam towards me. A twig snapped and I heard someone cough, my spine tingling as the boys grew closer. I watched a swan waddle to its mate, hiss as one of the boys tossed his cigarette on the wet soil beside it, lurch to avoid a boot to its side, then plunge into the dark water and skim across it to the island where a capsized rowing boat had been left to rot.

'Where are your parents?' he said, surveying the area.

I stared up at his large frame eclipsing the sun.

One of his mates stepped forward when I didn't answer. 'I asked you a question,' he said, pushing his face into mine.

'My father walked out on us this morning and my mum's at home.'

'So, you're on your own?' He smirked and poked my shoulder.

I jerked sideways, almost losing my footing.

I stared at a spot on his face.

'What are you looking at?' He reached for the rash of whiteheads that covered his forehead, nose, and chin.

I pointed at the patch of red circling a large spot on his left cheek. 'That.'

He lunged for me but was drawn violently backwards. My eyes went from the boy to the old man with rotten teeth who held a bag of worms in his other hand. 'You want to end up in that pike-infested water?' he snarled, twisting the back of the boy's T-shirt between his grubby fingers so that it tightened around his torso, exposing his plump midsection.

The boy shook his head, eyes wide.

'Or maybe I should feed you some of these.' He shook the bag and the worms clambered over one another, fighting to escape through the opening.

'No!' He tried to wriggle free and the old man smiled.

One of the boys reached out to grab the bag from the old man but he was elbowed away. 'Did your mother never tell you not to pick on girls?'

The boy continued struggling while the old man wound the fistful of cotton in his hand until the neckline was taut across the boy's throat and he began to choke. As he started to gasp the man released him, and the boy fell onto his knees, inhaling air loudly through his mouth. When he stood, his grey jogging trousers were grass-stained at the knees and his face was red.

The old man looked each of the boys in the eyes. 'If I see any of you round here again, picking on a kid who's smaller than you, I'll let him off his lead.' He motioned to a pit bull who sat unmoving on the reeds of the bank where a fishing rod bounced. He walked slowly backwards, reached behind him, and in one smooth move, withdrew the line, wound in the fish, removed the hook from its mouth, stamped on its body and clobbered it over the head with a mallet.

He held the fish out to emphasise his point and the boy and his mates were gone in a flash, kicking up dirt as they fled. The old man winked at me and patted the wild rye that bordered the pond. 'Do you want a go?'

'I'm going to my gran's.'

'Maybe next time,' he said, stabbing a worm onto the hook and casting the line out as fluidly as he'd brought it in moments ago.

'What will you do with that?' I pointed at the fish.

'Take it home and cook it for my cat.'

'Don't you eat them yourself?'

He screwed up his face. 'Carp, no.'

A moorhen divebombed the surface of the pond and sprayed water into the air. It fell in a perfect arc.

'This pond appeared by accident, you know.'

I blinked and turned my attention back to the old man. 'Really?'

'Quarrymen from Aberthaw hit an underground stream near the railway line, over there, while excavating,' he said, pointing to the tracks. 'The water burst through the limestone to create this pond.'

The sunlight reflected on his digital Casio watch-face. 'I've got to go.'

He wrapped the fish in a carrier bag and dumped it in a holdall filled with tackle that was parked on the grass beside his rod and a small fold-out chair. 'Don't forget what I said. Ask your mum if you can join me for a bit of fishing sometime. Maybe after school? I'm here every day until six. That's when my wife expects me home.'

'Okay. Thanks.'

'Good manners,' he said. 'You were obviously brought up well. Unlike those yobs back there.' He titled his head towards the trees where between the branches, in the distance, I could see the boys stumbling up the hill in the heat.

I had to cross the field the boys had taken to get to my gran's. When I reached the withered common crouch, I turned right and passed the school, the newsagent's, and the pub. I crossed the roundabout and turned left to follow the houses to the stream, careful not to slip off the embankment.

My gran was hanging the washing on the line to dry, stopping to mumble something, her leg twitching as if she was preparing to kick an invisible ball, when she heard the creaking gate. She looked down the steps to where I stood assessing her mood by the clothes she wore and the time it took her to fold the tablecloth over the thin piece of rope and click three pegs onto it from the ones she had attached to her apron. There weren't any in her hair today.

She waved me forward and squinted at me as she turned my head from side to side, her fingers digging into my jaw. She narrowed her eyes when they fell on mine. 'You've got the devil in you, girl.'

'Can I have a drink?'

She appraised me, relenting when she gazed up at the fiercely bright sun and sneezed.

I sat cross-legged on the prickly dry lawn that itched my legs while I waited for the beaker of orange squash. She appeared carrying a plate of cheese spread sandwiches, and a bowl of pink wafers. 'The tap water's been poisoned again.'

'How do you know?'

'There are bubbles in it.'

'I can drink it without.'

'Go on then. You can get it yourself. You know where everything is, don't you?'

'Yeah.' I jumped up and headed inside the house. The hallway was cool and dim. I had to step over piles of dirty laundry, stacks of books with their covers ripped off, and food wrappers, to enter the kitchen.

I climbed onto the greasy counter and opened the cupboard door to peer inside. It was where she usually kept the bottle of Kia Ora. The door sprung off its hinges and fell onto a stack of leaflets my mother would have pushed back out through the letterbox. I grabbed the bottle, opened the lid and took several large gulps of the strongly concentrated sugary drink. It stung the back of my throat. I spluttered and spat and after replacing the lid went to put it back into the cupboard, stalling when I found Gran's medicine – the pills she was supposed to be taking twice a day.

I emptied the last two 5mg tablets of Haloperidol from a blister pack and did the same for the unopened packet of Olanzapine. The last lot she'd collected from the chemist were still in the paper bag at the back of the cupboard, jammed between an old cereal box and some outdated tins of chicken in white wine sauce.

The capsules were easy to crush with a teaspoon on a plate but not so easy to disguise. Unable to find a clean glass I emptied most of the juice from the plastic bottle into the sink, then brushed the powder into it and shook it hard until my arm hurt.

When I returned to the garden Gran was explaining to her neighbour with exaggerated hand gestures how the CIA had her under surveillance.

'They fly over the house in a silent helicopter. They've got brick-penetrating radar that tracks my whereabouts. The lasers send computer signals back to HQ to tell them I'm home.' She put her hand to her face and snickered. 'I trick them by leaving the lights on during the day, so they waste fuel looking for me.' Her face grew solemn. 'But then they influence my dreams or start stealing my thoughts and implanting them back in wrong when I'm asleep, so I have to stay up all night.'

I held the bottle out to her. 'Drink this.'

'I'm not thirsty,' she said.

'It's very hot,' said the woman, who was snipping away at an overgrown shrub.

'Yeah, Gran. You don't want to get dehydrated.' I pointed at the blue sky.

'You're right,' she squealed. 'I need to stay fit to fend them off.' She clapped her hands and ran towards me, grabbed the bottle from my hand, flung the lid onto the grass and glugged it down. Then she spun and hopped into the house.

Her neighbour's gaze followed.

'Mum's picking me up later.'

She nodded and smiled.

BETHAN

Now

I stand inside the porch and stare at Humphrey holding the edge of the car door, waiting for me to leave the house and follow him to the E-Class.

'We're not going in that.'

'The Sprinter's due its first MOT.'

I scan the grounds. 'Where is it?'

'I had the garage collect it this morning.'

'We're driving a vehicle with low suspension through steep, winding, single lane roads across a mountain range?'

'It's Snowdonia, not Everest. And we're not off-roading it.' He senses my fury and lowers his voice. 'Come on, darling. I want to leave before rush-hour.'

I slam the door behind me, raise my nose to the air and totter along in my heels. The moment I sit he leans into the car and lays a hand on my thigh.

I shove him off me. 'You're a fucking liability.'

He straightens, sighs and closes the door. He walks around the car and hesitates before hopping onto the driver's seat, clipping on his seatbelt and turning the key. The engine starts with a roar, though his foot is barely touching the pedal.

This vehicle is too bottom heavy to tip over, but it might roll down a ravine and into dense woodland. If he's not wearing a seatbelt, shatters the windscreen with his head or his ribs get crushed into the steering wheel and pierce a lung, he'll die.

I'm no longer bothered how he's killed so long as I return home from the holiday cottage alone.

I Google how to deactivate an airbag on an E220 and await my Galaxy S10's instructions.

I stare, silently, through the windscreen at the glacial mountains, most of which are clouded at their tips by thick mist. The ones that aren't look as though they're dripping icing from their peaks.

Aside from the sound of the tyres on the asphalt, only the tooting and chugging of a steam train in the distance can be heard. A plume of smoke draws my attention from the tall, blue-grey summits that separate the land from the sky, to the railway. A piece of track poking out of the moorland where nature and industrialisation collide, distracts me long enough that I involuntarily unstiffen my crossed legs and unfurl my hands from the cashmere scarf around my neck that I feel like ripping off to choke Humphrey with.

The sun drops too quickly, leaving streaks of violet and a haze of russet to paint the horizon. We zip past the entrance of a waterfall, leading to a freshwater lake, replete with an arched transporter bridge and a set of viaducts. We drive in awe alongside slate villages, between tangled treetops, and past the craggy hillside of a derelict stone-age settlement that is somehow still standing. Humphrey turns off the A-road in Talsarnau, Gwynedd at a coach-house, slows the car to a crawl up a scraggy hillside lane and eventually stops the car outside a barn conversion set several miles off-road, thirty minutes later.

Under an indigo sky dappled with twinkling stars, it looks like a witch's hut – something from a grim fairy-tale.

My arse has gone numb, my lower spine aches and I'm salivating at the thought of a crisp white wine to slurp while dipping the toasted olive bread into the melted extra-mature Cambrian cheddar we bought in a farm shop during our one and only stop to refuel the tank.

'Welcome to Bwthyn Glowyr Lan y Dŵr. Waterfront miner's cottage to you, my Welsh Rose.'

I suck in both cheeks and nibble the spongy tissue there until I almost chew through my own face.

There's a large ominous structure shadowing a massive hole carved into the earth beneath us. The ripples on the water sparkle from the thin half-circle moon, disguised by heavy black clouds that light their northern edges. 'I wasn't expecting it to be so—'

'Quiet?'

'Dead.'

As he treads towards the wooden door of the foreboding unlit entrance, his phone pings. Mine vibrates as I exit the car to walk off the pins and needles in my legs, and while I pull it out of the glovebox to read the latest quote of positivity from one of the motivational speakers I follow on Instagram, Humphrey presses his phone to his ear.

At least the place has Wi-Fi.

'Yes? Ah, great.' He frowns, then directs his gaze to me. 'Just a parking light, marvellous. The key's with Muriel. Park it in the three-way when you're done, won't you? Oh? Right. Thank you.'

I guess the van has been delivered home. And by the look in his eyes he's just been told the rear shelf was full of ready-to-mix cement. It's a good job I hid the blown fuse between the tongue and lace of my white Rock-stud trainers, packed snugly inside my suitcase, or he might guess who replaced the one inside the Sprinter with a dud.

I wait beside the car boot for Humphrey to collect our cases. The stony path looks too treacherous for my heeled Valentino's, so I'm not going to risk damaging the wheels of my baby-pink, snake-print Globetrotter by dragging it across the uneven tumble-stone walkway.

I'm expecting him to ask me what I was planning to build with all those bags of cement I'd stacked inside the Sprinter, but I suppose he's so used to my peculiar interests and artistic indulgences he doesn't bother.

Inside, the Llanberis cottage set deep in the heart of the Caernarfon valley is as yuppyish as I imagined it would be. The charred wood effect beams that shrink and darken the living room meet at a gold chandelier. The floors throughout are polished oak, and the kitchen is a smart rustic version of a pre-war pantry and diner. My eyes skate over a marble shelved larder, a reclaimed wooden table with copper pans hung above it, and land on an open copy of The Times dated June 21st 2018.

'When were you last here?'

He leaves both suitcases in front of the door that leads to the utility room. 'Last summer, before we met.' His voice sounds strained from the exertion of hauling the heavy items the thirty yards from the car.

'Who manages the place?'

'A friend.'

I walk over to the window. There's a stone-built wall separating a chunk of rock at the end of the half-acre field fronting the cottage. Whatever's down there, glints silver. 'What's that?'

'The pool.'

'How deep is it?'

He shrugs. 'Twenty or thirty feet in the middle.'

At least three people know we're staying here: the housekeeper, whoever Humphrey tasked with collecting from and delivering the Sprinter to the garage, and the MOT tester at Sinclair's in Cardiff. The first person that police will suspect if Humphrey decides to try walking on water while drunk late at night is his wife.

Perhaps drowning him isn't such a good idea.

The bedrooms are either gloomy-looking or too pale. Whoever designed the décor couldn't decide whether they wanted Edwardian or post-war features. The fireplaces are the main focal points to a mismatch of rooms containing elaborately detailed plaster cornices, stained glass, leaded bay windows, velvet upholstery, dado rails, herringbone designed tiles in glaring red, green, yellow and blue, geometric wallpaper, parquet flooring, art deco ornaments, monochrome cupboard door handles and Clarice Cliff vases.

'Ours is down the hall.'

The master bedroom has a vaulted ceiling with a central skylight directly above the Georgian bed. A steep set of steps in one corner lead to a mezzanine where there is a Windsor chair and telescope.

'I didn't have you down as a star-gazer.'

'There's a lot you don't know about me,' he winks.

I turn away from his penetrative gaze to avoid witnessing him mentally undress me.

The original furnishings, outdated as they are, seem to fit the old-fashioned property. Yet the contemporary additions give it a complex, bleak vibe.

'There's something I'd like to show you,' he says, steering me to the stairs. We descend along the hallway to the back of the cottage, walk past the utility room, and through a set of French doors to a patio. There is a veranda above us I hadn't noticed as my eyes flitted towards the windows while opening and hastily closing the doors to peer into the upstairs rooms. Along a passageway there is a raised hot tub with a view of the glade I imagine is impressive in daylight. The acres of undisturbed land, only part of which can be seen from what little light the house projects onto the rich grass makes the existence of the formal gardens redundant.

He points east and puts an arm over my shoulders, leaving a slobbery kiss on my temple as he squeezes me. 'The sunrise here is one of the best.'

'I don't intend to get up early enough to see it.'

'I've planned a little excursion tomorrow. A visit to Dolbadarn Castle followed by a romantic meal at The Heights riverside hotel.'

I paste on a superficial smile and remove his arm from my neck. 'That sounds lovely.'

He wraps his arm round my waist. 'Tuesday we're going to trek through Dinorwic slate quarry. I thought we could check out the museum and miner's hospital.'

He's got to go. I can't feign interest in a trip to a fucking museum long enough to avoid stabbing him with a piece of flint.

He senses my reluctance and holds me tighter. 'Wednesday, we're heading for the Caernarfon coastline. We'll follow the footpath, hike the wildlife trail, see the castle lit up at night.'

'You've written an itinerary without my input.'

'Anglesey Sea Zoo Thursday. And—'

'Let's play it by ear, huh?' I drag his hand off my hip and recoil as his fingers brush against my thigh.

We eat, watch a film, and as the big hand on the face of the enamelled brass carriage clock aligned centrally to the opulent candlestick holders on either side of the mantle nears 11 p.m., I pour us both a Pinot Noir. I drop one capsule's worth of Rohypnol into Humphrey's glass, stir it with a cocktail stick to incubate the clinking, and hand it to him with indifference.

I lay beside him on the sofa, my head on his stomach, feeling the beat of his heart against my arm and his breath on my head. Once his muscles have relaxed, his pulse has slowed, and he begins to snore I switch off the Zanetti Murano parrot lamp and the TV, and head outside, closing the door quietly behind me.

I unlock the car, gritting my teeth from the echoic *click* of the central locking that sounds louder in the obsidian dusk, and close the driver's door gently to ensure the parking lights go out in case the glare they cast wakes Humphrey.

I flick through the dials on the steering wheel to disable the Tracking Control System on the Electronic Stability Program, to validate the impression something is amiss with the vehicle in the unfortunate event he survives the fatalistic crash.

DI LOCKE

Then

The Newport Butcher's method of mutilation was similar to the way in which Jane Doe had been cut up.

His victims had all been between the ages of twenty-five to thirty. He selected them off the streets on impulse. Drove them to a quiet location. Raped them. Hacked them into pieces. Wrapped each body part in a bin liner. And buried them in different locations along the Marches Line that runs south from Manchester to Newport then west to Fishguard harbour.

Each of the women had been stripped of their clothes and possessions before they'd been butchered. Each wrapped segment had been deposited along the disused banks of the south western railway that covers nine miles from Pontypool, through Carleon to Newport East. The only differences were that after decapitating them the Newport Butcher had separated their heads from the rest of their bodies by burying each body part a few feet away from the

75

last so that it was still possible to identify the women. And none so far had been discovered inside a suitcase.

We thought he'd been operating for about a year by then, and believed he'd committed his first murder in 2016. Although we knew it was likely he'd killed before and had honed his craft through practice but until Dr Ward had confirmed our suspicions regarding the weapon used to mutilate the women, we had nothing to prove our theory. But now we suspected the same individual was responsible for Jane Doe's murder. And when Jones saw that Rick Kiernan's vehicle had been flagged up on ANPR cameras, close to the crime scenes of two other body dumps, we thought we'd found their killer.

MELANIE

Then

Rough hands scooped me up off the comfy chair where I'd been curled like a foetus into its sunken womb of ripped fabric.

'Come on, sleepyhead. Time to wake up. Your mother's here with a car.' My gran's sloppy voice roused me, but my numb limbs refused to cooperate with my fuggy head as I was lowered to my feet.

'For fuck's sake, Mel!' My mother inhaled sharply then let me go.

I dropped, and a sudden pain shot through my lower spine, jolting me awake.

'You didn't have to do that, Sam. Can't you see she's tired?'

I blinked one eye open and looked up at Gran. She was dribbling.

'I didn't send her here to sleep.'

'No. But we both know why you did.' Gran's eyes were half-shut as she spoke.

I rubbed my back and felt myself wobble as I walked. My mother grabbed my arm to march me out of the house and the circulation in my lower extremities slowly returned.

A car horn blared from the roadside. I looked down from the stepped walkway to the pavement at the white car I recognised from the park two days prior.

Jason sat behind the steering wheel, moving a cigarette from side-to-side between his teeth. He took one long drag then threw it onto the tarmac, rested his arm over the open window, and wolf whistled. 'Exercise those legs, ladies.'

I glanced at the time on the dashboard – it was almost 9 p.m. – and caught a flash of Jason's teeth from my rear-view seat as we set off. He smiled at me while kneading my mother's leg. I averted my gaze to focus on the road ahead, resting my face against the cool window as we cruised along the street, the glass vibrating my skull.

When we arrived home, Jason parked the car in front of the house, turned off the engine and followed us to the door. He entered the gloomy living room behind us and halted in the doorway at the sight of my parent's wedding photograph in the silver-plated embossed frame attached to the wall.

My mother wrapped her arms round his waist, but he pushed her hands away and turned to me. 'Hadn't you better get to bed?'

She lowered her eyes. 'Yes, Mel. He's right. It's late. Off you go.' She batted the air in a half-hearted wave.

'Where's Dad?'

She glared at me. 'Gone.'

'Is Jason staying the night?'

'Yes,' they said in unison.

'Where are you going to sleep?'

He looked at my mother. 'Sleep?'

Her unease disintegrated and she chuckled as he trailed his fingers down her arm, her hip, and lowered his hand to the back of her dress, which rose slightly before she shrieked. She slapped him lightly on the chest and his features hardened.

He grabbed her arms and pulled her close. 'Go, M—' she said, as he swallowed the rest of my name from her mouth.

I climbed the stairs, dragging my feet as I neared my bedroom. Something downstairs fell, furniture was scraped across carpet, wood knocked against wood and my mother giggled. I closed the door, sunk onto the bed, squeezed my eyes shut, clenched my fists until my nails dug into my flesh and fell asleep to Jason giving my mother a private lesson in aerobics.

When I awoke, sunlight was streaming through the wide gap in the curtains and onto my face. I turned away from the heat, my hair knotted and damp, skin sticky, the bedsheet twisted around my legs. But the blazing sun followed me to the edge where the mattress gave way beneath me as I stretched my leg out. I pressed my foot down in time to prevent myself from falling onto the thinly carpeted floor as I slid off the bed and stood.

Downstairs, my mother, wearing the T-shirt Jason had arrived in the night before, whistled as she slept, one arm dangling off the sofa. The coffee table was adorned with empty bottles of Smirnoff Ice and Coors Light.

Jason was in the kitchen singing along to the radio while

stirring steaming coffee in the Tommy the Tiger cup my father had traded for his Esso tokens. He dropped two slices of bread into the toaster and pushed the lever down. Then he turned around and put the teaspoon onto the counter with a clang. 'Morning.'

'You don't have kids, do you?'

He frowned. 'Why'd you say that?'

''Cos if you did, you'd know not to walk around the house in your underpants.'

He looked down at his bulge then leaned forward and lowered his voice to a whisper. 'When my name is on the lease, I'll do what I want in it.'

I caught the hint of menace in his tone and felt my stomach lurch.

As he straightened, he smiled over my shoulder. 'Morning, Sam.'

It was a strange juxtaposition because he looked genuinely pleased to see her, yet I now knew he was only after her money. And would have to stay with her long enough to oversee her divorce settlement if he was planning to spend it.

I turned. My mother was leaning against the doorframe, rubbing the sleep from her good eye; the surrounding skin of the other was still flecked purple and green. She wore a lopsided smile that dropped when she saw me. 'What are you doing out of bed?' She poked my ribs with her bony finger as she passed me. 'It's still early.'

'I'm hungry.'

'Go and sit at the dining table and I'll bring you in a bowl of Frosties.'

I spun round and left the kitchen. 'What are you telling

her that for?' My mother hissed as she closed the door on
their conversation, not bothering to quieten her voice.

'What?'

'*When my name is on the lease, I'll do what I want in it*,'
she mocked.

'There's no flies on her, Sam. I think you should sit her
down and explain the situation.'

'What do you mean?'

'She knows what *he* did to you, why he's not here, and
why *I* am.'

'That may be true, but what's your point?'

'Young minds adapt easily to the circumstances they're
presented with but that doesn't mean they aren't affected
by them.'

'She's resilient is what you're saying. So, what do you
propose? That I tell her he's never coming back? That her
dad punched my face in then walked out on us because she
told him I left her alone in the park to hook up with you?'

'You can't guard her from the things she's already aware
of.'

I shoved open the door and it hit something.

My mother screamed. 'Fuck!'

She limped over to the freezer, flung the door open so
violently that it almost bounced shut, removed an ice-cube
tray, bashing it onto the counter and tipping blocks onto the
floor. She grabbed a shard of ice before it swum away and
rubbed it over her bloody toenail, eyes clamped shut, teeth
grinding. 'Stupid girl. I told you to wait in the living room.'

'It was an accident,' Jason said.

Her eyes didn't leave mine. 'You're not having any
breakfast. Go to your room and stay there until lunchtime.'

'Don't be harsh with her just because you're in pain.'

'Don't tell me how to take care of my own kid.'

'Go on up, Mel. Leave me to speak to your mum.'

My pulse quickened and I stomped my foot. 'No.'

'Mel?!'

I ignored my mother and held Jason's gaze. 'You're going to hurt her.'

He startled, reached out, lay his hand on my shoulder and squeezed. 'I don't know the extent of everything that happened here between your mum and dad, but I promise you I never have nor would I ever raise a hand to a woman.' As he stepped back, he stuck his little finger out and motioned for me to do the same. Then he curled it round mine, so they were hugging. 'Pinkie promise.'

My mother's face softened. She blinked, flicking tears onto her chest which she wiped away with a trembling hand. Then she knelt to collect the remaining ice-cubes from the lino, threw them into the sink, and left the room, limping. I retreated into the living room and switched on the TV.

Minutes later Jason placed a bowl of cereal onto my lap and handed my mother a cup of coffee before he went upstairs to shower.

Dale Winton pushed a shopping trolley down the aisle of a supermarket. A man and woman were shoving as many items into it as they could before their time was up.

My mother blew on her cup and sipped the liquid slowly, eyes focused on the TV screen. 'Jason will be good to us, Mel.'

I shrugged, crunching and swallowing the last mouthful of Frosties. Then I sprung off the sofa, dumped the bowl on the kitchen counter, and went upstairs.

Jason was exiting the bathroom as I reached the top of the staircase, a towel wrapped round his waist, hair sticking up at angles, face flushed. I watched a rivulet of water gliding down his bare chest and when I raised my head to look at him, he wore the same expression he gave my mother right before he dragged her into his arms.

BETHAN

Now

Humphrey stands poised beside the open passenger door, the car keys hanging from his forefinger, his face etched in shadow.

'Traipsing through a village of slate houses in the rain is my idea of hell.' I cross my arms and push my tongue against the back of my teeth, jutting my chin forward in defiance.

'I'm not going on my own.'

And I'm not getting into that death-trap with you.

'You refused to accompany me to the castle, to take a stroll along the river, to eat a meal... I insist we visit the quarry. The views are fantastic.'

I sigh loudly and turn my head to the squawking of a red-billed Chough high up in a birch tree lining the pond.

Thick grey clouds fill the sky and wind whips my hair in front of my face. The weather is perfect. The car is prepped. I just need Humphrey to get behind the steering wheel, lose control and speed through a three-foot high wall and into the Llyn Padarn to prove the E-Class can't be driven off-road.

I smile, visualising the car plunging into the river, Humphrey's fearful shrieks emitted as a gurgle that is drowned by the air-tight, water-logged cabin of the sinking vehicle.

'I love it when you smile.'

My grin falters. Keeping up the façade of the respectful, caring wife to my dull, rich husband is exhausting.

He approaches me, face sulky, crunching gravel beneath the soles of his Thom Browne brogues. I look down as he takes my hands in his, presses his thumbs into my palms, circles them. 'Bethan, darling, please join me?'

'A day of climbing steep, moss-covered steps without handrails to wander through cold, windowless sheds or watching re-runs of *The Real Housewives of Orange County* while gorging on Godiva chocolates in front of the log burner? Choices, choices...'

'Clean air, good food, old films, and lie-ins... Bethan, we need this break.'

'What do you mean?' I tug my hands free and his drop to his sides.

'We rarely spend any time together unless it's in the company of others.'

'If you didn't arrange social gatherings to appease your old business associates, we'd have plenty of time on our own.'

And I'd get to spend more time in a tracksuit than a ballgown.

A fat droplet of rain lands on his nose. He shakes it off and looks up at the gathering mist curtailing around the treetops. 'I don't want to stand here arguing with you. Go and get your hiking boots on and a warmer coat.'

'I'm going back inside for a warm drink and to laze in front of the TV. *You* can do as you please.'

'How about a truce?'

My pulse is quickening, my hands shaking.

Just hurry up and fucking die, old man.

'We spread our excursions out over the week.'

'You go and do whatever you want.' I turn back to the house.

He tugs on my sleeve, but as I try to shake him off, he spins me round to meet his stern gaze and something inside me uncoils, an unwanted memory. I draw my arm back but before my fist connects to his smug face, he catches my wrist in a vice-like grip and moves towards me, forcing me to step back. 'Don't ever raise your hand to me again.'

'Or what?'

His eyes blaze with a fury I've never seen him possess. 'Do you really want to find out?'

'Don't threaten me.'

'Don't test me.' He eventually releases me and shoves me away, so I stumble on the slippery, pebbled path. Then he turns and walks in the direction of the car.

'Hey! Where are you going? Oi! Don't walk away from me!'

He turns and I panic, thinking he's going to change his mind, return to me and strike me. Or worse, apologise. But then he shakes his head.

'You're pathetic,' I spit.

'When you've calmed down, we'll talk. I'm not prepared to take any more of your crap, Bethan. And I won't be threatened with violence by anyone, especially not from the woman I've chosen to spend the rest of my life with.'

I feel the weight of his words relieve the tension in my muscles and stare after him in disbelief as he drives away, to his death.

DI LOCKE

Then

I stared at the clock on the wall and began my n^{th} pace of the room.

'You're going to wear a hole in the floor, Emma.'

I turned sharply to Detective Chief Inspector Evans. 'I wish I was cuffing the bastard.'

'Me too.' He stood.

'Where are you going?'

'To watch the bastard being brought in. It's the next best thing,' he said.

The bastard being Rick Kiernan AKA the Newport Butcher. Dubbed thus due to the way in which he tortured the women he paid to have sex with.

My team were responsible for getting the sick specimen of a human being off the streets. I wanted to witness him being escorted into the building too, so I followed Evans from the incident room, down the corridor and outside to greet him.

It was my second case with my new team. My first

had been a cold one. The disappearances and subsequent murders of several girls two decades before. The killer had recently died. His daughter had inherited his farm. It was during renovations that she'd discovered the bones in the paddock. I'd been asked to lead the investigation as I had experience working missing persons, specialist training in sexual offences, and when I'd requested a transfer from Avon and Somerset Criminal Investigation Department it was the first case I'd been assigned since my promotion to detective inspector.

Evans stopped abruptly and I almost walked into him. I stood aside, backing into the wall to allow Winters and Chapman the pleasure of escorting Rick through the door and into the custody suite.

He didn't raise his head until he reached the desk. And when asked to confirm his name and date of birth he tilted his head back and spat in the custody sergeant's face.

MELANIE

Then

I took one final bite of the warm, crispy doughnut, squashed the crinkly paper bag into a ball and tossed it into a nearby bin. Then I licked the sugar from my lips and wiped my greasy hand on the lilac- and lime-coloured leggings my mother insisted I wore, leaving stains on the thin fabric that didn't prevent the whistling wind from seeping through and coating my legs with goose bumps.

Jason strolled a few yards ahead, beneath the weak sun, occasionally turning around to ensure I was following him.

We passed a meat van, a stall selling half-price videos, a tarpaulin covered table containing sweets and another filled with knock-off perfumes.

Jason stopped in front of a woman marking up items on a clothing rack and started chatting her up. I pretended not to notice and sifted through rails of bright patterned jumpers and nylon trousers, fuzzy with lint from where they'd been handled.

'What do you think of this, Mel?' said Jason, holding out a royal blue belly top.

I screwed my face up and fingered a mid-length chiffon dress in light rose, but it was snatched away from me in an instant. Jason dumped it on top of a rack of long grey, cream and brown skirts and held out a lemon-coloured five-piece outfit on a hanger. The hairband and purse on a string that came with it caught my eye and I took it from him to closer inspect. 'It's nice.'

'It'll look lovely on you.'

'How much is it?'

'It doesn't matter. Do you want it?'

I nodded.

He handed the woman a ten-pound note and swerved towards an aisle of black heeled boots.

'You know Mum won't let me wear those.'

'It's a good job she's not here then, isn't it?'

I smiled.

'What size are you?'

'One.'

'Adult size one?' As he spoke his voice rose in mock surprise.

'Yeah.'

He looked me up and down. 'You're becoming a little lady.'

My face warmed and my limbs tingled.

When we got home, my mother was Sellotaping balloons emblazoned with the number ten to the gate. And when we entered the house, I could see two of Jason's friends already seated, drinks in hand, in the living room. In the background Take That were singing through the speakers, Gary Barlow's voice overpowering the other four members of the band as he sung about love and regret.

My mother carried through a tray of sausage rolls and placed it on the dining table. The steam rose off them and made my mouth water but the second I reached out to grab one my mother swatted it from my hand, and it dropped on the carpet. She gave me a disapproving look and tutted as she turned back to the kitchen.

I knelt to retrieve the small parcel of meat, stuffed it into my mouth and brushed away the crumbs decorating the newly vacuumed carpet.

When I stood, Jason was right behind me. I could feel his breath lift my fringe. 'Here's the birthday girl,' he said, dumping a plate of miniature pizzas beside the tray and snatching a handful of crisps from a bowl. He ate them in one mouthful. 'For you,' he said, as he chewed, passing me a cupcake and winking.

I smiled.

Your secret's safe with me.

Then, aware of my wonky teeth and wanting to hide them, I shoved it into my mouth. The sponge was thick and dry and stuck to the roof of my mouth like chewed up paper. I swallowed a hard lump of unmixed flour and it clogged in the back of my throat.

My mother returned with the dish full of cheese and pineapple skewered onto cocktail sticks that no one, but she, ate. She swayed to her own tune while the music pumped from various sized speakers dotted around the room. The sound surrounding us vibrated the table containing dishes of food that were becoming drier and staler as the guests became looser and more slobbery.

As the evening wore thin, I began to wonder if the party was more for the adults' benefit than mine. The music grew louder, the men rowdier, and my mother's high-pitched wailing more slurred.

She stumbled across the room, leaned to one side, her head tilted, eyes heavy and thick with eyeliner that had smudged into the creases of her crows-feet. 'My little girlie. Are you enjoying yourself?' She held onto the wall for support, stopping in front of me.

I shrugged. 'It's okay.' And inhaled the pungent fizz she'd been drinking all evening.

Her face twisted into a scowl. 'You ungrateful—'

'Hey, Sam. Come on, let's dance,' said Jason, snatching my mother's hand and tugging on the bell-shaped sleeves of her snake-print top. He turned her to him, pulled her close and winked.

I smiled back and watched him lead my mother round the room to the theme tune of her favourite chick flick. But it wasn't my mother's eyes that had Jason enthralled, it was mine.

I trod up the stairs, crept along the hall and landed on my bed yawning soon after. Beneath the duvet I listened to the hazy music and the muffled voices of late arrivals. At some point during the night I drifted off into a noxious doze.

I awoke with a jolt. The smidgen of sky visible between the curtains was ebony, the weight of the man sat beside me heavier than the air.

I recognised Neil, Jason's friend as he kicked off a shoe

and it thudded onto the floor. I bolted out of bed and whacked my elbow on the frame of my chest of drawers.

'Oh, hey, sorry to disturb you. Your mum said I could sleep in the bedroom.'

'This one's mine.'

'I can see that. My mistake,' he spluttered. He collected his shoe from the floor and pushed his foot back into it. He turned but stalled. 'Did you have a nice time?'

'What?'

'Your party. Did you enjoy it?'

'Fuck off.'

'What did you say?'

'I said—'

'No guess as to where you inherited your mouthiness from,' he said, heading for the door. He opened it and the glaring light filtered into the room and trailed up to my bedside.

The bathroom door opened, and my mother's silhouette stepped out onto the landing, bare-footed, eyes glistening, face flushed, hair stood on end. Her features changed rapidly as she absorbed Jason's friend leaving my bedroom.

I scooted along the wall as she darted towards me, wide-eyed, and leapt on Neil.

My mother, the panther – wild, feral, mesmeric – wrapped her hands round his throat and pushed her thumbs into his windpipe.

He choked, grasped both her hands and tried to prise them apart, but she just squeezed harder, until he slumped onto the floor.

She stood there, staring at the body on the carpet, her arms outstretched, curled fingers trembling.

Jason's footfall roused her from our shared frozen silence, and she screamed. His feet hit the top step and rounded the staircase. He looked from my mother to me, to the man who lay unmoving at her feet. 'What the fuck happened?' He knelt, pressed two fingers to the underside of Neil's jaw. 'Neil? Get up! Neil, can you hear me?'

Time drifted and sped simultaneously.

Jason stood, spun me round, and shook me until my teeth chattered, my head felt slack, and my vision blurred. 'Mel, what have you done?'

My mother's eyes flit from Jason to me to Neil then she pierced her pin of hatred through my bubble of security. 'Mel?'

Neil looked pale. His skin mushroom-white, lips blue.

'He's not breathing,' said Jason, his fingers digging into my flesh.

'No!' my mother howled, a piercing cry that shattered the fragile atmosphere.

Everything was louder, brighter, edgier.

'Sam, how long has he been like this? What happened? How did he...?' Jason's voice died as he noted the bruising that had formed around Neil's throat.

My mother's hands fluttered behind her. 'Tell Jason what he did to you.'

'He didn't do any—'

'Tell Jason why you had to strangle him,' her lips quivered.

'It wasn't m—'

'Who killed him?' Jason glanced at my mother.

She shook her head, pressed her lips together and looked away.

Then his eyes settled on me.

BETHAN

Now

I wait by the window, peering through the glass at the atlas-blue sky. The sheer drop to the river below shimmers crystalline from a pale slice of weak sun that splashes through the bare trees lining the dry-stone wall. A heron's call splinters the late evening air, swoops down, then crouches in the undergrowth. When it reappears, it's carrying a mouse in its beak. The rodent tries unsuccessfully to scramble away. I note the complex juxtaposition of the imminent birth of the moon and the cycle of death as the bird beats its prey about the head in the boggy rushes bordering the garden then swallows it whole.

Impatient for the phone call from police: *Can you confirm your name and place of residence? We're sending officers to your address.* Followed by the knock on the door: *can you confirm your husband's name? We're sorry to inform you, he's been found unresponsive at the scene of an accident.* I watch the delicate hands of the clock on the mantle turn, 7, 8, 9, but by 10 p.m. my eyelids begin to shutter, and I feel the weightlessness of peace wash over me until I am submerged in it.

I awake from a collage of images: Neil's pale complexion eclipsed by my mother's towering form, intermingled with Humphrey's battered face and body. Their corpses jarring me from sleep.

A thud and a cough send me spiralling from the bed, tripping over my slippers, and sprawling out of the room. I stand at the top of the staircase, heart racing, looking down at the empty porch shrouded in darkness, positive someone has entered the cottage.

There is a crash from the kitchen. I thunder downstairs. When I hit the bottom step, I swear there's a hint of damp air weaving its way down the hall. The whisper of a coat zip tapping against granite.

I tip-toe into the living room, grab the poker from the fireplace, and like the victim from a detective novel I'd yell at for such dim-witted behaviour, I kick the kitchen door wide-open and switch on the light.

White hot fear stabs me in the chest. I drop the poker on my sock-covered foot and inhale the yelp. My ears ring with the heavy burden of confused rage that filters between the cracks of my Fabergé-like existence.

Humphrey's erect posture belies his unsteady gait. 'Sorry I woke you.'

'Uh...' I point at his arm, a cast wrapped around it, held against his torso with a sling, my mouth agape while I try to process the fact he is here, injured but alive. 'What the fuck happened to you?'

'The brakes failed. I drove into a hawthorn bush. Dislocated my shoulder forcing the door open to get out. Got a taxi back from Ysbyty Gwynedd, ten miles away, which is the nearest A&E hospital. The car's a write-off though unfortunately. I scraped the side of it on a wall at forty miles an hour. I'm tired. I'd like to hit the sack. Will we be sharing a bed, or shall I sleep on the sofa?'

'Um...'

'I apologise for the way I spoke to you earl...' He studies his Rolex. 'Yesterday. It was wrong of me to say those things. I'm sorry. I've done nothing but reflect on our fight. I hope you can forgive me?'

'Yes, sure.'

He sighs, his unharmed shoulder dropping an inch. 'Goodnight, darling.' He pulls me into him, crushes me against his chest and kisses my forehead.

'The car?'

'With a garage. The insurers will investigate the damage and decide whether it was caused by negligence or mechanical malfunction.'

'Oh.'

'They'll want to know what happened. Why a perfectly good car, barely two years off the forecourt of a dealership, suddenly and inexplicably failed to stop and almost killed me.'

My limbs go rigid yet feel unsupported. 'I'll be up in a minute. I'm going to get a glass of water.'

He nods.

I wait for him to ascend the stairs and close the bedroom door before I release the pent-up frustration building to a crescendo inside me by punching the wall so hard my knuckles burn. I scrape my fist against the rough exposed brickwork as I withdraw it. Then I stare at the bloodspots rising to the surface of my skin until the tension in my muscles recedes.

I sip ice-cold water from the tap over the kitchen sink, sploshing droplets of it from the rim of the glass and onto my throbbing foot. I stare at the pendulum light fixture until my jagged breaths even out.

I hobble upstairs in a trance, my foot already starting to bruise, and lie staring at the ceiling, watching the room light up inch-by-inch as the sun rises, Humphrey's lips vibrating as he snores.

I check the time on the Westminster bedside clock and give up on the idea of sleep, hopping back downstairs before even the birds have begun to chirp their morning welcome.

I sit at the dining table still wearing the scent of beeswax. The lacquer is shining, the edges solid against my palms as I tap the hardwood with my newly manicured nails.

I boil the kettle, swig strong bitter coffee, pour another. It's the aroma of my second cup that arouses Humphrey.

He enters the kitchen just after 7 a.m., yawns and stretches, rubs his unharmed hand through his thinning hair, and refills the kettle with stubborn difficulty. 'How did you sleep?'

He's never asked me that before. His head must have bounced off the headrest at the point of impact during his collision with the hawthorn bush.

'Awful.'

'Same.' He attempts a smile which belies his disconcerting gaze.

He opens a cupboard door, closes it again. 'We'll dine out for breakfast. I'll reserve a table.'

'I don't think—'

'I insist. We need oxygen. And we haven't left the cottage since our arrival.'

'But we haven't got a c—'

'My insurers have arranged for a hire car to be delivered here at 9 a.m.'

'You've got it all sorted, haven't you?'

He winks, and for a split second I see Jason and the other half-dozen stepfathers who, after The Incident, walked into and back out of my childhood once they'd got what they wanted from my co-dependent mother.

I nibble on honey roasted cashew nuts – all I could find in the cupboard – while I watch the time creep ever-closer to the moment the doorbell chimes and a lad who looks too young to drive hands Humphrey the keys to his temporary ride. He gets him to sign an inventory and introduces him to the mid-life-crisis-red open-top S-Class with an aerodynamic spoiler and giant Bola dish alloys.

'You'll have to drive.' He raises his elbow and winces motioning for me to get a move on.

I snatch the car keys off him and march out of the door, foot aching with every step, not bothering to give Humphrey or the naïve-looking man a second glance.

Behind the steering wheel I hold the power to ram us both into a ditch or enjoy a warm carb-concentrated meal. My foot automatically hits the accelerator as we reach a tight bend and Humphrey grips the door for support.

Dancing with death somehow makes me feel more alive.

We park in front of the grey stone façade of The Heights,

stood erect beneath a backdrop of lime-green, slate-grey, and rust-coloured mountains, drizzled bone-white at their peaks.

Inside, there's a walnut-panelled bar, varnished floor and ceiling beams, and the walls above the dado rail are seafoam-grey. The wide windows allow warm puddles of light to fall over small square tables where a glass vase containing decorative pebbles and a peony floating inside sit centrally on each.

We're shown through an archway and into a snug with a distant view of the river running alongside the far end of the gardens. We sit on teal-coloured cushions in silence until our food is brought to the table: eggs benedict on brioche muffins with maple cured bacon and hollandaise sauce. The rich aromatic coffee awakens my senses enough for me to enjoy the sweet and savoury food, momentarily forgetting it will be our last shared meal.

I do not intend to wait any longer to intervene in ending his life.

Humphrey leaves the table while I visit the bathroom, pee, reapply my lipstick, smack my lips together and smile at my reflection. This is it. The end of the beginning.

In the car, I'm not paying attention to the signs, the too narrow road I've taken leading us out of Llanberis and further north, away from the cottage. I'm focused instead on all the things I will buy, and do once Humphrey is gone, until I feel his hand on my thigh. 'You've taken a wrong turn.'

His phone buzzes and he answers swiftly, eyes frozen on the chunky rocks, the wisps of fog hazing the hillside. I stiffen my shoulders at the deep masculine voice emanating down the line, 'ABS,' and feel my limbs locking, breath hitching as the conversation becomes more intense, the explanation more mechanical. 'Fuse blown?'

I frown, keeping my eyes on the road ahead.

'What do you mean?' Humphrey says.

I don't catch it all, but the word 'deliberate' weaves its way across to me. My knees lock, my hands go rigid and when I glance into my side mirror, I see a frozen expression, hard impenetrable features and a spark of cold anger visible in my ice-blue eyes.

'Leave it with me,' he says.

My throat constricts and a spasm of uncertainty creeps down my spine.

He glares through the passenger window at the low-built wall, the hedgerows becoming denser and the river edging closer. 'You should've turned left, back there.'

'Who was on the phone?'

He sighs heavily. 'The garage.'

'What's wrong with the car?'

'Someone tampered with it.'

'Why would anyone do that?' My laugh jettisons out like cracked glass being stepped on.

'I don't know, Bethan. Perhaps you could enlighten me.'

DI LOCKE

Then

I looked Rick Kiernan in the eye. The screen was paused on his face while Detective Sergeant Jones rummaged through his man-bag for the Jaffa Cakes I'd insisted he buy me from the petrol station shop, to make up for the coffee he forgot in Greggs.

'Happy now?' he said.

'Ecstatic.'

If you didn't know it was banter, you'd think he was being disrespectful to his superior. But that was just how our relationship worked. We bounced our energy off each other until one told the other to fuck off. In all honesty, it was usually him having to bring me down a notch.

He dumped the box on the desk in front of me with a satisfied smile sliced across his face, displaying his pearly whites.

'You're looking pleased with yourself, Dylan.'

'I haven't eaten a Jaffa Cake in years.'

'That's a shame,' I said, ripping open the box.

He sat beside me and hovered his hand over the remote.

I motioned to the television. 'This is the best bit of the film,' I said, tearing into the wrapper and shoving a biscuit into my mouth.

'Are you going to hog them?'

'Press play,' I said as I chewed.

He hit the button. Then he leaned towards me and stretched out his arm.

Without a second's hesitation I'd elbowed him away and fixed my other on the back of his hand, trapping his thieving mitt to the tabletop.

'That's assault, Emma.'

'And that's theft,' I said, snapping up the box and returning the opened stack of cellophane-wrapped Jaffa Cakes beside their companions, unable to look away from the screen now that Rick was staring back at me.

'I bet you wish you'd bought me a coffee now, huh?' I retrieved another biscuit and bit it in half.

Rick was of average height, average intelligence, and scored no significant findings on the personality inventory he volunteered for when his boss introduced psychometric testing to increase work productivity and wellbeing, that could have alerted anyone to the red flags typically identified in serial killers. He had no criminal record, had never displayed a propensity to violence, had a stable childhood, a secure relationship, a job he'd held onto for over a decade. There was no obvious reason to suspect he had the compulsion to murder.

I believe that was how he'd got away with it for so long.

MELANIE

Then

Neil's spine arched, his feet wrestling with the skirting board, while his face slowly turned towards me. His eyes were bloodshot. Burst blood vessels had turned patches of his cheeks purple, and his pallor retained an unhealthy hue even after he spluttered, 'Thank you.'

My mother's expression displayed her disgust at Jason for having conducted mouth-to-mouth to bring Neil back to the land of the living. She turned to face the man who, only minutes before, she'd tried to murder. 'What were you doing in my daughter's room?'

'You said to crash in the bedroom,' he croaked, clutching his sore ribs. 'I didn't know... I got the wrong room.'

'Why didn't you say something before I—'

'Pounced on me and began to choke me? I didn't get a chance, did I?'

'Well, I—'

'Like mother like daughter.'

'What do you mean by that?' Jason puffed out his chest.

'Impulsive, irrational.' His eyes flicked down to me. 'Aggressive.'

'Get out of my house and don't come back.'

'Sam?' Jason reached out to my mother, but she elbowed him off. 'Don't touch me.'

Neil hoisted himself up off the floor. He almost sank back down but Jason shunted him along and he grappled with the wall until he was stable enough to walk without aid.

'Go back to bed, kiddo,' said Jason. 'Me and your mum need to talk.'

My mother's last words to me still rung in my ears as I trod the stairs: 'Tell Jason why you had to strangle him.'

'I didn't,' I'd wanted to say, but my vocal cords froze.

I closed my bedroom door and listened, like I always had, to my mother yelling and Jason trying unsuccessfully to keep her calm. 'You should have left him to die.'

'You're not serious?'

'Deadly. I wanted to kill him.'

'It was an honest mistake.'

'The word *genuine* and *Neil* don't go together, Jason.'

'You don't really believe he's *that* way inclined?'

'Why else would he wander into Mel's room?'

'Accidentally? He's a mate, and I trust him.'

'You're useless.'

'Don't say that.'

'Fucking useless.' Her voice rose an octave.

'Sam, don't.'

'Waste of fucking space.'

'Sam!' The thud, the crack, the faint murmur of, 'Now look what you've done,' and I felt we'd done a three-sixty, returning right back where we'd come from.

While Jason slammed the door and revved his engine, and my mother sobbed, I sat on the windowsill with my face pressed against the glass.

When Jason had gone, I crawled back to bed and huddled beneath the duvet with a pillow over my head to block out my mother's whimpering. Sleep found me just as the birds began their dawn chorus.

I opened one eye, shrank back into the gloom of my duvet to hide from the dull rainy morning, roused by the kitchen door rattling against the frame directly below the floor of my bedroom. A cold blast of air forced me out of bed, downstairs and into the kitchen where I found my mother, hollow-eyed, hair a tangled mess, an unlit cigarette dangling from her mouth, lips stained red from the wine she'd drunk the night before.

She flicked the lighter, pulled on her cigarette, exhaled a puff of smoke and continued staring through the open window at a sparrow pecking at the rooted bark of an alder in search of food.

I filled a bowl with Frosties, poured half a pint of milk on them and scraped a chair back to sit at the table beside her.

She paid no attention to me as I ate, washed the bowl, left it on the draining board and collected my rucksack from the coat hook in the hallway. But when I opened the front door, her voice came rough and thick. 'Go straight to your gran's after school.'

I nodded in acknowledgement as I slammed the door behind me.

★

Stacey greeted me at the school gate. 'What have you got for lunch?'

I shrugged and poked the bottom of the bag on my shoulders. 'Whatever it is I'm not eating it.'

Maddison hovered behind me, staring at the ground. She was a couple of inches taller than me but stood as if carrying a heavy load on her back.

The bell rang and the playground became a frenzy of rushed parents and unhurried kids. The adults continued chattering to one another as they sauntered to the exit and the learn-shy children dispersed from their huddled groups and swarmed into neat rows outside the classroom doors. Stacey was among them, but Maddison made no move to follow.

I tilted my head up to the sky as the first droplets of rain began to fall which I welcomed by sliding my puffer jacket off over my head and snapping open the poppers while I waited for the teacher to call us in.

I don't know how many minutes passed, but my hair was wet, and my polo-shirt soaked through when I felt someone tug on my arm. I turned slowly and met Maddison's worried face. 'They've all gone in.'

I snapped my head round. The playground was deserted except for us. I moved towards the building, but Maddison stepped out in front of me, eyes pleading. 'We can't go in now. We'll get into trouble for being late.'

I glanced back to the gate. The caretaker hadn't yet locked it. 'Let's go to the park.'

Her eyes followed mine. Our teacher's shadow darkened the blinds inside the classroom. 'What if we get caught?'

'We won't.'

We exited the playground and traipsed the hill, scuffing our shoes along the pavement as we walked alongside each other, so close our hands almost touched. When we reached the railings and scooted through the kissing gate and onto the weed-riddled grass – covered in a blanket of autumn leaves that crunched underfoot: blood red, canary yellow, and tawny orange – we ran. The soundtrack to the changing season crackled beneath the soles of our Kickers as we neared the park.

I picked peeling paint off the metal frame of the slide while watching a group of kids my own age crowded round the swings, moving in time to the wind, braiding each other's hair with multicoloured yarn. Maddison whistled and tugged on the sleeve of my jacket and said, 'Race you to the pond.'

I hadn't been down there since the summer. The grass bordering the pond was overgrown. The mud squelched beneath my feet and splattered up the backs of my legs as I ran to reach the dark, still water before Maddison.

I recognised the girl instantly. She wore the same doe-eyed expression on her perfect alabaster face as she had all those years ago. And I knew she remembered me because she instinctively reached for her nose and swung away from me, noting the flash of my smile.

Maddison knelt on the dew-covered grass verging the playing fields. She collected a pile of stones at her feet, looked up at me, then turned fast and began pelting them at the hazel trees where the girl who'd fallen from the slide and onto her face five years previously fell onto her backside, arms crossed over her face to protect her adult teeth.

The girl and her friends kicked leaves and mud up in the

air as they ran, ascending the hill like a flock of frightened geese.

Maddison bent over, giggling so hard she snorted. She stood, her shoulders shaking, holding her stomach until she caught her breath.

The rails rattled as a train passed behind the dense grove of trees behind us, causing dust from the grit path to swarm through the air. 'Come on.' I grabbed Maddison's hand and she pressed her fingers between mine and squeezed tight. 'We're a team,' she said.

I had an ally.

We spent the rest of the morning running along the railway line and jumping off the moment the tracks started to vibrate, indicating that a train was imminently approaching. We made it as far as the River Usk then retraced our steps and headed back to Liswerry.

Gran was peeling potatoes when we entered the kitchen. She ripped off a piece of stubborn potato skin with her teeth and chewed, then threw the vegetable over her shoulder. It bounced off the bin and skidded across the floor, landing beside another two that had made the same journey.

'Why don't you cook them?'

'They're bad.' She began to sing an out-of-tune Celine Dion and I guessed that was all the explanation I was going to receive.

She was so absorbed in her bizarre ritual of peeling then throwing away her fourth potato she didn't notice Maddison in the doorway until she cackled. Gran twisted round, aimed the knife at me and barked, 'What's got into you, girl?'

I shrugged and frowned, glanced back and saw that Maddison had disappeared.

I followed the sound of her footsteps and found her in the living room, flipping through the pages of a yellowed newspaper perched on top of a pile of dubious-looking bottles half-filled with murky water the colour of piss.

'Stop chewing your nails.'

'I'm hungry,' said Maddison.

I huffed, turned my head to the door and yelled, 'Gran, have you got any sweets?'

'No. But the sausages and mash will be ready soon, so you won't be eating anything until you've had your dinner.'

Maddison pulled a disgusted face.

'You said the potatoes were rotten.'

'I've got instant,' she replied.

'Maddison doesn't like mashed potato.'

Gran stomped down the hall and peeked her head round the open door. 'Well, *Maddison's* going to have to learn to eat what she's given then.'

'Can I go to the corner shop?'

'Have you got any money?'

'No. But you still owe me fifty pence for the weeding I did for you on Saturday.'

She sighed, turned, and called out over her retreating shoulder, 'Top drawer of my bedside cabinet. There's a couple of pounds in there. Buy some chips.'

'Thanks, Gran.'

I went upstairs in search of money. I found the dosette box while rooting through the cabinet. There were four days' worth of pills still secured behind the individually labelled foil. I closed the drawer and heard a commotion outside. I stood at the window and looked down onto the garden where Gran was throwing potatoes at a pigeon.

My face burned.

I used the bottom of an ornamental vase of flowers to crush some pills into a tissue, stomped downstairs, poured a cup of tea, tipped the powder into it, binned the tissue and handed the cup to Gran. I watched her sip it tentatively then I grabbed Maddison's hand, and marched out of the door.

The wind whipped my hair in front of my face as I hurried along the pavement. I stopped at the end of the road and poked Maddison in the chest. 'If you tell anyone Gran was arguing with pigeons, I'll kill you.'

She mimed zipping her mouth shut.

I grabbed her arm and dragged her across the road towards the chip shop. The queue snaked from the doorway and stopped two houses past the chippy. When we got to the front of the line I glanced at the clock on the wall above the counter and saw that half an hour had already passed since we'd left Gran's.

'What can I get you?' said the woman serving.

'Two small bags of chips.'

'Salt and vinegar?'

'Yes, please.'

'One pound eighty pence,' she said, eyeing the customer behind me.

I handed her the coins, took my change and held out my hand for the two paper-wrapped parcels. The smell made my mouth water. I inhaled deeply as I squeezed past several men wearing high visibility jackets gathered in the doorway.

A tin can rolled along the road and a carrier bag flew into a red-leaved tree. The wind seemed to follow us back to Gran's where we found her staring vacantly at the TV, her mouth hung wide like a Venus fly trap, dribble running down her chin.

Maddison sat on the other end of the sofa while I checked on the food. On the counter beside the lukewarm kettle there was a pile of thick white dust that looked like plastic shavings in a bowl that I guessed was instant mash, and an unopened packet of refrigerated sausages well past their expiry date perspiring inside their wrapper.

Gran's chest was rattling when I re-entered the living room and Maddison was frowning at her. I turned the volume of the TV up and, noticing Gran had fallen asleep, switched the channel over to catch *Sweet Valley High*.

I was midway through the episode when my mother burst through the front door, giggling, cherry-red lipstick smeared across her teeth. A car horn blared behind her and my stomach knotted when I glanced over her shoulder at the man seated behind the steering wheel of a Ford Escort. He honked the horn again and gave my mother a salute. She fanned her eyelashes, blushed, and held the wall to support her legs. Once she'd regained control of her muscles, she swept down the path to open the passenger door for me to get inside. 'Come on, Goldilocks. Time to go.'

I heard footsteps behind me and turned to find that Maddison had already reached the gate.

My mother was resting her chin on her elbow as she leaned on the top of the car door, tapping her faux talons against the green paintwork of the roof as I approached. I could smell the Lambrini on her breath, noted her dewy complexion and the tremble in her fingers as she straightened my hair with her damp digits.

She was hesitant to offer me affection but willing to lust after a man I guessed she'd only met earlier that afternoon in the pub.

I caught the man's smile. 'Hello, poppet,' he said, eyes focused on something ground level. He wore the rest of my mother's lipstick on his moustache.

My mother nudged my arm. 'Say hello to Tony.'

Maddison rolled her eyes.

'Gran's making weird noises.'

My mother's smile dropped. She huffed, turned to the house and sauntered inside. I followed her into the living room and stopped in the doorway.

Her legs buckled and she released a shriek. 'Mum! Oh god. Mum!' She rushed towards me and pushed me violently in the direction of the phone. 'Call an ambulance.' Then she knelt at Gran's feet, holding her wrist to check for a pulse like Jason had done after she'd strangled Neil.

I picked up the phone, blew dust off the earpiece, and felt the grime on the buttons coat my fingertips as I pressed 999. There was no dial tone. I held the cord out to her. 'Shouldn't this be plugged in?'

She was shaking Gran and trying to rouse her. 'Tony! Give next door a knock. Her breathing's laboured and she's unconscious.'

He'd already stepped out of the car and rushed to my mother's side. He ran back down the path and hurried up to the front door of Gran's neighbour's house.

As the minutes passed my mother grew more frantic. Tony rubbed her arm and bit his lip. Neighbours opened windows and doors to get a better view. Blue lights flash and sirens wailed. Paramedics donned in green carried Gran out on a stretcher. The ambulance sped off. Tony steered me to his car, and I hopped into the back. He strapped me in, jumped into the front, started the engine, and drove away. I stared at Maddison's emotionless face through the glass and pressed my hand to the window.

She didn't wave back.

BETHAN

Now

If my high-pitched cackle doesn't indicate my lie, the seconds it takes me to recalibrate must, but Humphrey's confused expression remains unchanged. 'Why would anyone want to harm you?'

'Money,' he says in a dejected tone.

My faux smile falters. I reach out and lay a hand on his thigh and squeeze. He threads his fingers through mine like Maddison used to, moves my hand back to the steering wheel and indicates for me to concentrate on safely navigating us around a cyclist.

'Turn right onto High Street then left past Padarn Country Park,' he says.

I steer one-handed passing Joe Brown's, a gift shop, the honey farm and winery, and follow the road as it merges onto the A4086 over the bridge, my attention pulled to Electric Mountain's aquatic power station ahead. The hill of slate above it shimmers like a silver fortress from a ray of sunlight piercing through a bunch of puffy clouds.

'Follow the sign for the slate museum,' he says.

'You're determined to see me stumbling across the fucking stuff, aren't you?'

He tuts and blinks, his jaw tightening at my lackadaisical comment, then signals for me to turn into the car park. 'We'll walk to the quarry from here,' he says, directing me into a space at the far end, close to the miner's hospital.

I slam the car to a stop, pull on the handbrake and rip the key out of the ignition. 'You came here with your ex-wife.'

'Is that a problem?'

'No.' I unclip my seatbelt, spring from my seat and slam the car door behind me.

He guides me down a tree-lined path, through dense woodland where I trip over gnarled roots hidden beneath thick undergrowth. We eventually hit a patch of spacious land that curves and dips like grassy waves in various shades of green and brown.

The mud sparkles soot-black and crunches underfoot as we ascend the path. The surrounding lime, gold and charcoal-grey landscape leads to rock formations the colour of dirty steel. 'There's a viewing spot near the pumphouse.'

'Did you take her there?'

'My deceased wife, yes.' He stops mid-stride. 'Are you going to continue this act of jealousy in the hope of starting a fight or are you going to zip it and pretend you're still in love with me?'

I turn on Humphrey so violently I stumble. He reaches out and grabs my arm to prevent me from falling. I shrug him off the moment I gain traction on the uneven ground, limping and wincing until adrenaline overpowers the pain that's added to my already injured foot.

We walk for hours along the riverbank, past the desolate rail-line, zig-zagging uphill in a steady ascent until we reach the tramway. I stand at the bottom of the steps looking up at the rusted ancillary works.

'I forgot how far it is,' he says, panting.

'Do you want to head back down?' I rub his arm and smile sadly.

It has the desired effect. 'The barracks are up there.' He continues walking with renewed vigour.

When we reach the summit, the sun blinks behind the quarry walls, bordering them in a dusky orange glow and casting shadows under the hollows. I shiver. Humphrey wraps his arms round my waist.

We stand in silent observation. I judge the possibility of anyone hearing him scream while darting my eyes across the horizon in search of the best item to hit him over the head with. He turns me to face him, pinning me in place with his hands on my elbows, and I calculate the amount of time it will take him to tumble down the steep drop just a few yards behind us, where aside from the waterlogged pits the land is as barren as our marriage.

Though the buildings have been neglected since the mine closed in 1961, tourists visit the hiking trail all year long. Except today there is no one to witness Humphrey fall.

He releases me, then does a slow circuit to absorb the view while I walk towards the ledge to scan the treacherous earth below, wondering if slate can slice through skin and how much pressure must be applied to pierce a main artery when Humphrey emits a yowl.

I spin round but don't spot him immediately. His grey trousers are the same shade as the stone carpet beneath him.

He's lying several feet down from a chain-link partition. A few feet in front of him is a deep ridge where there is a rusty piece of machinery including a spiked wheel positioned directly underneath.

I run to him, giddy at the sight of blood running into his ear and down his neck as he sits and tries to steady himself on one leg.

I let him lean on my shoulder until he's standing. 'You've cut yourself.'

He rubs his temple, smearing blood into his stubble before inspecting his hand.

I push his head forward so that his chin rests against his chest to examine the wound. 'It's just a gash.'

'Be careful,' I admonish him. *For every injury you acquire will need explaining.*

'We should have come prepared.' Noting the look of confusion on my face he adds, 'The first-aid kit's in the E-Class at the garage.'

'Right. I suppose you want to turn back?'

'I should clean this cut up.'

I'm not returning to the cottage with you.

'I thought you wanted me to experience the "spectacular views"?' I quote the air.

'I hit my head hard on that—'

'It was your idea to come here. I wanted to stay in the cottage.'

'Yes.' He smiles, clasps my hand, squeezes my fingers and together we trudge carefully onward.

By the time we reach the highest point the sun has dipped, the air has cooled, and Humphrey's gait has changed to what I'd expect a man much older to exhibit.

He stops for a moment, clutching his head.

'What's wrong?'

'I feel a little dizzy.'

'Are you okay to carry on?'

Say yes.

He nods then closes his eyes as if to refocus them from the movement.

He fumbles inside his coat pocket, the wind blowing his hair upright so that it looks as if he's been electrocuted. My pulse quickens at the thought of having to rig such an accident when a gust of wind sweeps the phone Humphrey has managed to retrieve from his hand. I catch it before it hits a sharp piece of slate jutting out from a mound of clay peat at a brilliantly dangerous angle.

'Take a photograph of us, right here.'

I sigh, ignoring the tremor in his voice, snatch the phone, sidle up to him so that we're almost touching, turn on the camera and aim it so that we're both centred in the frame. His positioning shadows the dark, claret-coloured stain above his ear as I paint on a smile, snap the picture and hold the phone out for him to collect. But he doesn't take it. He's shielding his eyes from the glare of the sun with one hand, entranced by a bird flapping through the sky.

I shove the phone in front of his face, our image fading before being replaced by the screensaver. 'Do you want to see it?'

He dismisses my question with a swipe of his hand, almost knocking the phone from mine. 'Look at the way the light casts a golden halo around the Peregrine Falcon.' His face is lit on one side, his enthralled expression one of joy.

I pocket the phone. 'Come on, David Attenborough, let's shift our arses.'

He laughs, steps forward and points ahead. 'We should go back before it gets dark and we have to call mountain rescue. This route takes longer but it's flatter terrain.'

I cross my arms and bite the inside of my cheek. There is a slope ahead. 'I'm going this way.' *In search of somewhere to push you off.*

Humphrey's footsteps grind behind me as I scramble down the track of slate that shifts beneath my feet with every step. Midway through our descent, he stalls to take a breather. 'Are you trying to kill me?'

I smile and stride on.

Nearing a lower portion of the hill he appears at my side. 'Tread carefully. There are potholes and...' He falters mid-step, kicks the air behind him, falls on one knee and I involuntarily reach out for him in a feeble attempt to offer my support, but grasp only air as he lands face down with a loud crack, his bandaged arm snapping from the weight of his body.

I lean over him. 'H-Humphrey?'

I take a deep breath, exhale it with a long moan and tug his shoulder until he turns, his face with it, slack features covered with blood. A large flap of skin hangs from a dent in his forehead, the open flesh above his right eyebrow glistens like cream in the semi-darkness. The blood that oozes down his nose and trickles between the gaps in the slate has the consistency of thick strawberry jam.

Brain matter?

'You idiot!'

How am I going to explain two head injuries and a broken arm, as well as the car accident that caused it, especially when the police investigate Humphrey's eventual death and discover the E-Class was tampered with just like the Sprinter?

His pulse is faint, his heart is still pumping blood round his body, albeit slowly. Although there's not enough blood surrounding the skull to cause him to bleed out there is a substantial amount of it spreading through the cracks in the slate, creating a marble effect across their surface. It's then that I notice the impact of his fall has reopened and worsened the cut he received to his head earlier; there's bone now visible beneath the slice.

I don't want to be stuck caring for him. But I can't leave him here to die. Yet if I call him an ambulance as he's only just been discharged from hospital the staff will view his medical records, become suspicious over the amount of injuries he's acquired in such a short space of time, and notify the police who'll want to question me about them.

I have no choice; I must keep him alive.

But as soon as I've made this decision he begins to gurgle, and I notice blood seeping from his ear. I'm not medically qualified but I've done enough research to know that's a classic sign of brain injury.

I force my shaking hands to still and regain control of my hammering heartbeat so that I can drag Humphrey by his feet to a more suitable, less conspicuous site. Except he weighs fifteen stone and my lung capacity proves I'm too unfit to do so. Instead I move the slate and gritty mud to surround him in a way that suggests he fell, and the slate will shift into position around and over him during the storm we're expecting, so it'll prove harder and take far longer for someone to discover him. Then I stand, inhale a short burst of relief and survey the scene before me, reassuring myself no one can see the inch-wide gap displaying his pale nose or the protrusion of black where the toe of his scuffed shoe peeps out.

The wind whistles through the trees as I jog across the stone path in near darkness, the underside of my fingernails clotted with blood and grains of soil. I take a wrong turn, teeth chattering, movements stiff. My surroundings black against onyx, with just a sliver of moonlight to guide the way.

An hour or more later I reach a clearing. I stop to collapse on the ground, rest my spine against the exterior wall of a slate-built hut and laugh until I cry.

Six months I've meticulously planned Humphrey's death, choosing the perfect method, place and time, and he goes and dies in an accident.

I pull his phone from my pocket, swipe the screen to unlock it – grateful it's not password protected – and my pulse ratchets up a notch at the photograph on the screen: the last shot of us together.

In the left-hand corner, between two pine trees there is a distinctively humanoid figure standing with his or her head and torso bent forward as though watching and listening to us.

Did the individual witness Humphrey fall and my subsequent cover-up?

I jump at the rustle of leaves and the caw of a crow.

Dizzy with exhaustion, calves protesting, I run. Snapping twigs and catching my clothes on protruding branches, nettles ripping through them and clawing at my skin. I emerge opposite the car park, covered in scratches. I glance back as I reach the locked cast iron gate, see that only my conscience is chasing me. Now I'm presented with another unforeseen problem: how to get the car through a bollard as stealthily as possible.

DI LOCKE

Then

It was the third time I'd watched the remotely recorded interview between Winters and Chapman, and Rick Kiernan. But no matter how many times I saw those soulless eyes meet the camera lens he clocked in the corner of the ceiling of Interview Room Three, they never ceased to cause my skin to prickle.

I remember watching a horror film with my mates as a teenager and one of them – Craig, I think – said, 'That's what evil must look like.' His words were aimed at the bad guy whose face remained expressionless as he tore his hooked hand through his female victim's neck and watched her splutter as blood poured from the hole in her throat.

I knew what Craig meant. I was staring at evil now.

He might have appeared and acted normal but if you knew the signs as I did, you'd know there was something not quite right about the way Rick looked at you. Or more specifically the way he looked at women. Like Winters. Who we knew was his type. Thick, dark hair, toffee-coloured eyes and pale skin. Having her as well as Chapman interview him was deliberate. I thought it would bring out his predatory side. And it did. Unfortunately, so did the defence.

I'd made a conscious decision to influence Rick's behaviour during his interview. Something his solicitor couldn't prove without admitting his client's guilt. Which meant I couldn't be accused of allowing my personal grievances to impact my objectivity.

Allegations of entrapment could be used to discredit an investigation when a suspect was facing a life term, and as Rick was facing an indefinite sentence, his solicitor had all the more reason to try everything he could to fight the prosecution.

We had Rick locked up, the evidence against him stacked, and the gun barrels that were the Crown Prosecution Service and his only living victim aimed at him. What we didn't have was a forensic profile linking Rick to the murders of all five women.

Even though the circumstances surrounding their deaths were similar, the way they'd been killed was the common denominator, and some fabric CSIs found in the hair on one of the bodies resembled the colour of a sweater in Rick's chest of drawers. We were relying on the one who'd got away to get him put away.

MELANIE

Then

My mother's brow was creased, and her mouth hung open. 'Overdose?'

'Yes,' said the doctor.

'You're saying it was deliberate, that she wanted to die?'

'When she regains consciousness, I'll arrange for the psychiatric nurse to speak to Elin. We'll need to assess her risk of self-harm before she can be discharged. And as the medications she's been prescribed are controlled substances it's likely she'll be referred to the Community Psychiatric Team for a monthly depot injection, for her safety.'

'This is so out of character.'

'The depression?'

'No. Attempting to take her own life.'

He nodded lightly. 'She hasn't exhibited signs of suicidality in the past according to her medical notes, but the depression could be an unwanted side-effect of the anti-psychotics. Which would explain her apparently sudden decision to end her life.'

'You think she planned to kill herself with my daughter in the house?'

The doctor glanced at me then back to my mother. 'That's something only Elin can answer.'

'Can I see her?'

The doctor nodded and said, 'We've given her a boost of noradrenaline to counteract the sedative effects of the drugs she took but she's still unwell and will be for some time.'

We followed the doctor from the office and into the corridor. My mother stopped halfway down the slope, turned to me and said, 'You can't come in.'

The doctor gave me a weak smile and said, 'There's a waiting room down there,' then led my mother towards the lifts.

I went back the way we'd come until I reached the waiting room. I dismissed the idea of sitting beside a woman who stank of piss and a man who was talking to himself and continued to the café where I sat on a hard, plastic chair in the corner.

There was a pile of comics on a shelf above my head. I picked one up and flicked it open, scanning the pages without absorbing the words. I was midway through the third paragraph when my mother tore the magazine from my hands. 'Up and out.'

She didn't speak until we were yards away from the grey painted walls of the ward. She grabbed my arm and swung me round to face her. 'You gave your Gran too many pills.'

A car reversed out of a parking space. Its headlights beamed through the small rectangular sash windows, dazzling me. I turned away, blinked.

Her fingernails dug into my arm. 'She almost died.'

A tune began in my head.

She tilted my chin up, forcing me to meet her gaze. 'You crushed too many tablets into her drink, stupid girl.'

The music got louder.

'When will you ever learn? You're just like your father… Jason left because of you.'

The singing in my head stopped. The voice that came out of my mouth sounded unlike my own.

'No, he didn't.'

My mother released me with a shove. 'What did you say?'

'Jason left because you strangled Neil.'

'Shut up,' she said through gritted teeth, smiling as a couple neared us.

I waited until they'd passed. 'You thought you'd killed him, so you told Jason I'd attacked Neil in retaliation for something he hadn't even d—'

She pressed a trembling finger against my mouth and the words died on my tongue. The couple stopped mid-stride just a few feet away from us. The woman shot me a look of incredulity, then tore her eyes from me as her husband coaxed her away and guided her down the corridor.

My mother steered me to the wall cornering the fire exit to our left where two concrete steps led out to a pair of double doors and lowered her voice to a whisper. 'I was protecting you. I thought he'd touched you.'

I pushed her hand away. 'You misinterpreted it.'

'You stood and watched. You didn't try to stop me from—'

'Almost killing him.'

She took a step back, shook her head slowly, and smiled. Her eyes flashed with anger, then glazed over with tears of sadness.

'Jason left because you lied to him. You tried to blame me for something you did. He was going to help you cover it up.'

'Hah.' She turned and stormed off, out of the hospital. I had to run to catch up with her. I met her at the car where she stood with her shoulders slumped and her head bowed.

Tony sat bug-eyed in the driver's seat eating a Snickers bar he'd bought from the vending machine in the entrance to the hospital. 'Everything okay?'

'She'll live,' said my mother, tilting her head back and flicking me a disdainful look. 'No thanks to her.'

He glanced quickly into the rear-view mirror, caught me picking at the frayed edges of the seatbelt and swallowed the last mouthful of chocolate. He started the engine, wound the window down, dumped the wrapper in a bin at the edge of the car park as he passed it and drove us home without a word.

When we got there, he followed us from the car and into the house. He stayed that night and the next. And remained living with us for four years.

I came home from school one Friday, about two months after he'd moved in, to find an eight-year-old girl sat on the end of my bed combing the hair on the Barbie doll my father had bought me the Christmas before.

'Who are you?'

She looked up at me with startled eyes and dropped the doll. 'Caitlyn.'

'What are you doing in my bedroom?'

'Dad said it was mine.'

'Tony?'

'Yeah,' she smiled.

I turned towards the door and yelled down the stairs. 'Mum?!'

'Alright, Mel,' she said, pounding up the staircase.

'What's the matter?' said Tony, appearing behind her seconds after her feet hit the landing.

I pointed at Caitlyn. 'She's not having my bed.'

My mother frowned. 'You're sharing.'

'No way. She can have the spare room.'

My mother glanced from Tony to Caitlyn. 'She can't. Your gran's going to have it.'

'What? Why?'

Tony put his hand on my shoulder. 'She's moving in so we can keep an eye on her.'

'Because she took too many pills?'

My mother shook her head then looked away. Tony sighed heavily. 'Because while she was in hospital your mother collected Gran's post and found out she hadn't paid her rent for almost seven months.'

'Can't you pay it for her? You've just got your half of the proceeds from the sale of your house.'

'Divorce doesn't work like that, Mel. I had to give my ex-wife child support to pay for Caitlyn's upbringing.'

'But if she's living here with us you don't need to.'

He smiled at his daughter. 'Caitlyn's only going to be here weekends.'

I turned to face my mother. 'You can work it out that she's here while I'm with Dad, so we never have to share a room.'

She widened her eyes at my comment. We both knew that was an impossibility. I hadn't seen my father since the wedding. I didn't know where he and his wife lived. Hadn't yet been invited to visit the newly built home they shared with their honey-coloured Labrador.

BETHAN

Now

My hands are shaking so much I can barely hold the steering wheel. My limbs have locked into position, my foot is juddering on the accelerator and my right eye is twitching as I reverse out of the parking space, stopping in front of the swing gate to decide on my best exit point. Without bolt cutters the only way I am going to be able to leave the car park is to drive into the barrier and hope it doesn't do too much damage to the hire car.

Does it have a tracking device fitted to it as per the rental insurance agreement?

The tremor in my hands builds as I back up, put my foot down to rant the engine, and prepare for the collision. I get the car up to thirty-five miles an hour, close my eyes and...

The parking sensors ping, there is a brief crunch of metal as first, the front bumper, then the bonnet hits the hollow steel arm of the barrier. It bends, snaps off and lands on the concrete several feet from the car with a *ding*. I brake as I open my eyes, faced with another set of headlights, piercing through the night-time gloom.

The car swerves round too fast for me to catch sight of the driver or any passengers as it turns and speeds off, but the dim orange glow of the only nearby streetlight allows me to read part of the distinctive personalised number plate: GTY.

Guilty.

I follow the narrow road round the bend, the car that left ahead of me long gone. I zip over the bridge, along past the river, and hit the familiar line of trees. Taking the slip road down the steep incline, I turn a sharp left to travel the rest of the uphill journey through the town to the cottage.

I jam my foot down on the brake pedal and screech to a stop the second I hit the gravel drive. I jump out, slam the car door behind me and reach inside my handbag for the key as I storm down the path. I drop it from my stiff trembling fingers the first time, and merely graze the lock the second. By my third attempt at opening the door, tears of frustration are prickling the backs of my eyes. I jab it into the lock, give it a twist and fall onto the tiled entryway.

My pulse is pounding so hard there is a whooshing in my ears. I shut the front door behind me then enter the living room where I switch on the light and catch my reflection in the ornate mirror above the mantle. I can see my chest expanding and retracting in short quick bursts.

I turn, exit the room and head for the kitchen where I pull the half-open bottle of Pant Du rosé we bought on our journey here from Goldcliff from the fridge and glug it straight from the bottle until it's empty before throwing it into the bin where it thuds against the stainless-steel side.

I wipe my mouth with the back of my hand. It stings as I withdraw it; cut and bruised from shifting heavy lumps of slate to part-bury Humphrey's body.

I stomp upstairs to the bathroom. Mud clings to the ridges of my knuckles and dried blood stains my fingernails. Under the shower the soil rubs off easily, leaving clumps of red clay peat and orange dirt soil to slide down my legs. The blood runs pink between my fingers and onto my feet. I shake it off and stare at the murky water filtering down into the plughole. I scrub my skin so raw I must turn down the dial and rinse off the last traces of his DNA with cool water.

Giddy from the heat and exhaustion I stumble out into the hall wearing a towel, another wound round my head like a turban. I dress robotically, gather all the cleaning products I can and scrub the bathroom until my torso aches. I bin the cloths and bottles and my dirty, bloodied clothes, planning to burn them in the morning on the fireplace. Then I traipse downstairs and sit on a stool at the rustic kitchen table where I retrieve Humphrey's phone from my handbag.

I hadn't foreseen the accident at the quarry. I hadn't prepared for this eventuality. I'm totally screwed.

If I switch my phone back on and the police, for whatever reason, learn of Humphrey's death, wonder why I didn't report him missing, and decide to investigate they'll not only discover that someone tampered with the brakes on his car, causing him to crash and break his arm the day before he fell and hit his head twice, they'll know I returned to the cottage afterwards.

I've kept Humphrey's phone on so I can pretend he's alive to anyone who calls him. Besides, even if I deleted the photograph I took of us together at the quarry it won't eliminate it from Google Drive and if I'd left his phone in the pocket of his trousers it would be discovered when his body is recovered, and the police would be able to retrieve the photograph, would know I was with him minutes before he died and removed the only piece of evidence proving it. I'd be the first, the only person, suspected of his murder when the search history suggested I tried to find out where the nearest phone mast was situated while he lay cold and stiff up a mountain rather than call for help.

Plus, I must learn the name of the housekeeper who minds the cottage, and I need to contact her to ensure she doesn't come snooping round. I don't know how close her relationship to Humphrey is, was, or how often she visits to clean the place, tidy the window boxes, meet the gardener or speak to her employer, but I need to find out.

Something blinks in my peripheral. A red dot. The alarm system. She'll no doubt know the code, the one I plan to reset when I leave.

I scan his list of contacts but find only names I recognise and none of them live in north Wales. He doesn't appear to send text messages and when he does, they're all to me.

It's all too much. My forehead hurts, the pain gnawing across my skull and down my neck. The reassuring lick of locally brewed wine loosening its hold on me as my hand begins to shake, my steady grip on the future fraying at the edges.

I need a top-up. I want liquid oblivion. I'll deal with this mess tomorrow.

*

I sleep fitfully like a gripey infant and wake two hours post dawn, mouth dry, temples throbbing, stomach growling and churning in equal discontent.

There's no booze left, and we didn't get to the supermarket so there's nothing to eat. I haven't yet decided what to do about the woman who will be arriving in just a few days to keep house but finding out exactly how much Humphrey is worth might provide the clarity I need to choose my next course of action.

So I've decided: I'm going home.

DI LOCKE

Then

There's a long-held theory that killers return to the scene of their crime. And it didn't surprise me that once we had Rick in custody, we could place him in close proximity of the area where the suitcase was found as recently as thirteen days before, by the GPS tracker built into his mobile phone. And on the same day Katrina Leonard was walking home from her shift in the residential home where she worked as a care assistant.

She fit the same profile as the other five women. Except for the fact she didn't work in the sex industry and she'd survived.

'I usually left work at 3 p.m. but one of my colleagues was on maternity leave, another was off with a virus and I needed the overtime so I stayed on for the evening shift after dinner which I ate with the residents.

'It was midnight when I clocked off. Dark. Quiet. I drove. Even though I only lived half a mile down the road. There weren't any spaces on my street. I did a U-turn and parked on the main road. It was cold so I walked quickly round the corner. I heard footsteps and when I turned, I saw a man dressed all in black. Or at least his clothes were so dark they looked black. There was one streetlight between us. No cars on the road. But I was sure that if I screamed for help someone would hear me. He slowed as he crossed the road. He seemed to have come out of the lane leading down to one of the entrances of St Cadoc's.

'I stuffed my car key between my fingers and clenched my hand into a fist, fully intending to jab him in self-defence if I had to. But I didn't realise he was carrying a rock.'

She began to cry. And I felt my eyes water too.

'He slowed as I entered my road. I was in front of the street sign when he struck. He'd already slammed the rock into the side of my head by the time I swung round to stop him.'

She shook. But continued. She was a warrior.

'He grabbed me from behind, wrapped his arm round my mouth to muffle my screams and dragged me backwards. I couldn't get a grip on the pavement and no matter how much I tried I couldn't prise him off me, so I went limp, thinking that if I didn't do anything to make him angry, he wouldn't have any reason to hurt me.'

Tears met snot, but she soldiered on, recalling the horrific event.

'He... had a knife. Long blade. Like a miniature sword. Up his sleeve. He pressed the pointed end against the top of my neck and told me to walk through the hedge, down the verge, onto the tracks, and along the rail-line. Then he stopped, turned me round to face him, and told me to strip. He said that if I did what he told me to he'd let me go, let me live.'

Her ragged breaths came fast and shallow and I could feel the fear and humiliation that was pouring off her. But she showed no sign of relenting. It was all or nothing. She wanted to purge herself of the memory as quickly as possible to begin the long arduous healing process.

'I thought… I was going… to die.'

He held the blade against her throat and raped her. Afterwards, he told her he was going to slice her head off, chop her into pieces and bury her in several different locations so no one would ever find her.

That's when the sky above them lit up and the unmistakable sound of a helicopter broke through the trees. The civilian seated beside the pilot was assisting with the search of a group of youths who'd robbed a convenience shop. Rick hesitated.

'I took the opportunity to raise my foot in the air. I had one chance to kick the blade from his hand with as much force as I could gather and run.'

Which she did.

'I got home, dressed and called the police.'

That's when she says her ordeal really began. The two PCs that arrived drove her to the Sexual Assault Referral Centre for a forensic medical examination. She gave the police officer her statement in the presence of a crisis worker. She was assigned an Independent Sexual Violence Advocate who planned to visit her at home within the next three days to provide emotional and practical support. After that, she was offered trauma-focused counselling. Her first appointment was booked in for the following week.

Her attacker might have been an opportunist, but he wasn't sloppy. He'd worn a condom. And as he'd ordered Katrina to remove her clothes there was minimal DNA transfer and what there was wasn't significant enough to create a forensic profile. It seemed Katrina was never going to get the justice she deserved for what had happened to her, unless by some chance her attacker repeated the offence, and the thought made her sick.

Then Katrina recognised Rick's face on the screen of her phone while scrolling through Facebook and realised what a close call she'd had when she read the words:

NEWPORT BUTCHER CHARGED WITH THE DEATHS OF FIVE SEX WORKERS.

She picked up the phone and called the detective who'd been assigned her case. DS Choudhary called the senior officer leading the investigation into the Newport Butcher's crimes. I answered that call fired up on all cylinders.

We had a credible witness. The CPS were satisfied we could hold Rick on the rape charge while we continued making inquiries. Katrina was our saviour. We just had to hope the jury thought so too.

MELANIE

Then

Gran was in the garden when I returned home. She wore a tracksuit, her dark roots topping a head of dyed hair that looked more yellow than blonde and reminded me of the straw wig of the scarecrow, Worzel Gummidge. Tony was pouring her a glass of iced tea from a pitcher. Mint leaves retrieved from the potted herbs that lined the kitchen windowsill were tossed on top of the shit coloured liquid he handed her to add a touch of class to what otherwise looked like pond water. Caitlyn was upstairs on my bed doing her homework, a lone tear trickling down her sullen face, upset because she had to redo the essay I'd thrown in the bin after my mother, who was ironing Tony's shirts and singing along to Robbie Williams' latest hit, had threatened to ground me if I didn't tidy my bedroom.

No one was expecting what happened next. The event resembled an episode of *EastEnders*.

The car screeched to a stop opposite. The man who exited the vehicle was indistinct. If it weren't for his hasty movements, furious eyes and red face I wouldn't have given him a second glance. I watched him through the side gate as he looked up and down the road, checking the door numbers of our neighbour's residences before his eyes fell on our house and zoned in on Tony.

Tony caught the man's gaze, a moment of acknowledgement flashed between them, then the pitcher flew to the ground, the glass shattering on the hard, dry, grassless lawn. Gran coughed iced tea down her front and jumped off the deck chair. The front door bounced back open as it hit the backpack I'd dumped there as I'd entered, returning from my second day as a year ten senior. Tony brushed past Caitlyn as he legged it upstairs. She thundered down and met the stranger at the bottom.

'You can't hide up there forever, Tony. When I get my hands on you, you'll be leaving this house breathing through an oxygen mask.'

My mother reeled him towards her, holding the iron at her waist with a protective grip. 'How dare you threaten my partner in front of our daughters? Who the fuck do you think you are?'

As he moved closer to her, she raised the weapon. He held out his hand in invitation to shake hers and through gritted teeth introduced himself. 'Barry Isles. Debbie's husband. The one your boyfriend's been shagging behind our backs.'

My mother's mouth fell open, then snapped shut as she lowered her hand, closed her eyes and whispered something unintelligible under her breath. Her eyes were wet when she opened them, and her cheeks were warm. She spoke with an air of superiority and frightening emotional control. 'I don't know who you are or what your game is, but you will not harm my family with your accusations. Now get your arse off my property or I'm calling the police.'

'You want proof?' said Barry. 'Here!' He flung a brick-sized mobile phone at her.

She caught it in her palms, which were trembling with forced calm, and narrowed her eyes to read the message on the screen.

I can't stop thinking about you. x

I stood at my mother's side, read the text over her trembling arm, felt the heat of anger emanating off her in waves. She inhaled, passed the phone back to Barry and turned towards the front door, hesitant to cross the threshold as she shouted up the stairs. 'Tony! Get your lying, cheating arse down here now or you'll be leaving here in a body-bag instead of wearing an oxygen mask.'

Barry gave me a half-hearted smile. I stared back at him until his eyes fell to his scruffy trainers and the oily stains at his shins. I suspected Barry's wife was a grade above him in looks and social status. That's why my mother had snuck around behind my father's back with Jason. My father didn't care much what he wore and she knew she was far better looking than either of them.

Now she was the one being cheated on.

Karma.

A sound drew my attention to the first floor, or more specifically the open bathroom window, at the side of the house where Tony's legs dangled precariously from the full height of the building.

My mother's eyes followed mine. She put her hands on her hips and called up to him. 'Where did you meet Debbie?'

He caught the hurt in her expression and his foot slipped as he scrambled to get a foothold on the ledge. 'Is she an IT consultant at your place of work?'

Barry scrunched his face up while she, oblivious to his disgust, continued airing their private problems as if seeking public scrutiny. 'Did you sleep with her here, in our bed?'

The woman who lived next door peered through the net curtains blowing in the breeze of a downstairs window. An elderly man walking a Springer Spaniel caught my mother screech 'traitorous cunt!', tugged on the dog's lead and dragged him out of earshot.

Neighbours gathered, each pretending to admire one another's gardens, brickwork or cars. Passers-by, unable to avoid my mother's ranting, stopped to listen. Some disguised their interest by whistling up at the clouds, checking the time on their watch or simulating the removal of a stray leaf from the sole of their shoe. Others made it obvious. And it wasn't long before we had a large audience.

There were plenty of witnesses to Tony's fall.

Gran rushed to his side first, kneeling to check his pulse, and Barry joined her to survey the extent of Tony's head injury. My mother gasped as he sat up, neck twisted at an odd angle, spitting blood as he gurgled through a loose jaw. Caitlyn dialled the ambulance. And I stood on the periphery of the mayhem, numb.

Tony's recovery took longer than anyone had predicted. He never apologised for or excused his dishonest behaviour. My mother refused to forgive him. Caitlyn didn't visit for the entire duration Tony received occupational rehabilitation provided by his private health insurers. My mother only learned he'd been discharged from hospital when speaking to one of the nurses from the brain injury ward she recognised while waiting for the bus to work.

She sat at the dining table slugging back Blue Nun. Tears and snot had glued her hair to her damp sorrowful face.

Gran sat beside her, stroking her matted tendrils in consolation. 'You've never had a problem finding a man.'

Mum reached for Gran's hand. 'I know,' she sighed. 'But I really thought he was the one. That I'd got it right this time. That Tony was my knight in shining armour.'

Gran laughed; her fingers stopped smoothing Mum's hair. 'You've got to be in distress to attract one of those. And you're *no* damsel, Sam.'

I stopped writing, placed the pen between the pages, and considered what my narrative suggested regarding my childhood experiences. Was my mother the victim or the perpetrator?

I used the pen as a bookmark, closed the notebook and read the inscription embossed across its front:

LIVE YOUR STORY BEFORE YOU TRY TO INTERPRET IT.

My case worker bought it from a gift shop in the village near the hospital. She was the first to visit me, five days after my admission to St Cadoc's. She said it would help me to understand myself better if I reflected on the years that led to the day I was sectioned. And it had.

I recalled what she said when she handed me the diary she'd bought.

'There's an experiment psychologists use to assess an individual's sense of selfhood: identity, beliefs, aspirations, motivations etc. Unlike quantifying an individual's characteristics to define their personality type, thematic analysis qualitatively dissects the underlying themes within the discourse used by an individual to narrate their lives.'

I squinted, leaned my head on my closed fist, elbow on the table, an act of defiance against my mother who wasn't there.

'If I have your permission I'd like to read and analyse your journal, so together we can explore what led you here.' She glanced around the room at the crisp white walls.

My eyes followed hers to the sterile, peach-coloured linoleum, the high-backed chairs with blue leather covered seat cushions placed into a perfect oval inside the communal room that stank of pine scented cleaning fluid. Then back to the window I'd been gazing through for the past forty-eight minutes. 'Sure.' My eyes stayed fixed on the lime green lawn brushed lightly by the breeze on the opposite side of the glass.

I'd have agreed to anything if it meant I'd be released sooner than the mandatory twenty-eight days I'd been admitted for.

BETHAN

Now

Iopen my eyes and stare at the digital alarm clock on the cabinet at my bedside until the blurry green numbers unmerge into four separate units. It's noon. My face is damp against the pillow, my stomach crampy. I stand and immediately tear my eyes away from my reflection in the full-length mirror centred between my own and Humphrey's wardrobes.

My hair is a mass of greasy waves, there is a ring of red wine tattooed around my lips and my breath tastes of ash. I use the wall to hold myself upright as I cross the room, light-headed. When I reach the bathroom and tug my knickers down to sit over the toilet bowl there are spots of blood on the gusset.

'What a great start to a miserable day.'

I wipe, flush, wash my hands, take a swig of water from the tap to rid my cottonmouth and rub my mascara-clogged eyelashes with a tissue until it's smeared charcoal-black.

I exit the bathroom after a shower, my face heavily made up, hair glued to my scalp with enough hairspray to fuel a housefire.

I hold my cigarette away from me while I light it as I step outside the cottage, and gag as I blow smoke into the grainy mist. I shiver and rub my temples with a thumb and forefinger.

Rain bounces off the steel-cladded roof of the disused barn to the side of the property. I pull hard on my cigarette and walk to it, squelching through the mud in my Balenciaga's, place my palm on the pebbledash wall to feel the texture of something solid, and a fleeting movement between the trees behind the building causes me to swallow and cough the smoke out from between my lips.

Someone moves beyond the branches, presses his or her foot onto a twig. It snaps, and another one, higher up the bark, rebounds near to where I stand, flicking water onto my face. I spin round and run, leaving a spray of backwashed mud across the otherwise pristine white barn exterior.

And then I see him.

His handsome face arced by a dash of sunburst through the drizzly skyline. A tall, solidly built mass of lean muscle and aged intelligence. He gives me the eye, nods, then turns and strolls away.

My cigarette hangs limply between two fingers, browned and soggy, my hand shaking so much I release it, watch it fall onto the puddled ground. I laugh in awe. Then find I can't stop. I'm howling and bawling and soaked through, tears and rain streaking my cheeks, when, crossing the thin path of windblown deadening grass, a woman holding a set of leather reins comes bounding towards me.

'I'm so sorry but Cad,' she points to the stallion that had frightened me to tears of nervous laughter, 'he's escaped the field. He wouldn't jump at Chepstow for the Welsh Grand National, but he's got a bloody hair under his tail about rabbits.'

'Cad's an unusual name.'

'Cadwalader. It's the name given to a battle leader. Befitting as he's also a bit of a rogue, as you can probably tell. Although he was an untamed beauty when we, that's me and my partner Joya, bought him. We renamed him when we took him on. He was known then as Arawn.'

'Unrestrained wildness.'

'That's right,' she smiles. 'Didn't do him justice.' She studies me for a moment, points at the hedgerows, then says, 'Do I have your permission to slip through there into the field to fetch him back?'

At my nod she bounds forward, pulls on the chicken-wire fencing separating the surrounding wilderness from the garden, where there is already a gap, and tugs on it until it rips wide enough to glide through. She calls to her horse through the hedge, pushing aside the Sycamore branches as she trudges onward. 'Cad? I'm coming to fetch you.' He snorts a reply from somewhere nearby and I exhale a heavy breath.

First world problems.

My own involves a possible witness to my husband's illegal burial if not also his death for which I failed to provide help, and another individual – the horse-owner

– who can attest to my upbeat character twelve and a half hours afterwards.

'Fucking marvellous.'

I skid and slide in my designer trainers through the thick slimy mud to reach the front door. As I pull it open a gust of wind attempts to wrench it from my hand. The wind is as volatile as my mood: calm one minute, furious the next.

Once I start to pack our belongings, my unstable temper is replaced with excitement. And by the time I've filled the boot of the car with our suitcases, coats and spare shoes I'm focused exclusively on the wealth I am about to procure.

The drive home to *my* estate is unencumbered but without Humphrey to argue with I spend the three hours and fifty-seven minutes of it listening to Kiss FM and swearing at the radio presenter every time he cuts a song off to discuss how much he likes it or to offer a competition the contestants never seem surprised or overly pleased to have won. After another rendition of Ava Max's 'Psycho', I switch it off and drive the final few yards in silence.

It's as I'm parking that I really absorb the magnitude of everything I've inherited, how far from that emotionally neglected child I've come.

'You're the Lady of the manor,' I sigh with a smile as I exit the car.

I picture my name listed on the land registry. Owner/proprietor: Melanie… No, Bethan Philips.

Melanie… where did that come from?

I need a drink. I'm rattled. I can't let my guard slip.

I stare up at the annex of the large building, filled with

antiques and family heirlooms. Collectors editions of art, books and music.

I have so much to do.

I dump the evidence of our holiday at the foot of the staircase. I don't give myself time to rest before I begin to explore the house for proof of Humphrey's worth.

I start in the attic and work my way down to the top floor, rooting through boxes of paperwork, files of accounting records and shoe boxes stuffed with photographs. Some black and white, some coloured, most taken with Canon's, and all printed by a photography company no longer in operation. There are a few images of his first wife, their wedding, their families, mutual friends and acquaintances.

The ceremony was in 1980, five years before I was born. The men have unruly hair, porn-star moustaches, and wear tuxedos. The women have perms or boyish pixie-cuts, their jewellery is gaudy and their clothing floral with shoulder pads and puffy sleeves. The bride wears a string of pearls and a hideous ivory dress that reminds me of the toilet roll doll cover my gran had in the bathroom of her council house.

I continue flicking through the photographs until I find the familiar leather album with the gold embossed lettering on the front, titled 'Our Wedding'. I skip it, not wanting to remind myself that it was all a farce. But I can't entirely avoid our 'special day'.

There are loose images of my fatherless walk up the aisle – Derek had to act as his stand-in, giving me away with a faux smile plastered over his smarmy face – along with the marquee, the cake, the banquet and the wedding night, stuffed between pictures of Humphrey as a toddler and a few of his long-deceased childhood pets: a couple of dogs and a cat. Me, posing for the camera in a hotel room at the Celtic Manor Resort. Some sexy shots. Then a bed sporting a sheer velvet duvet cover I don't recognise, a pair of legs waxed to a shine that are much too slim to be mine. I flip the final two pictures over. There is a braless blonde woman in one, Humphrey's hand over the lens of the other. Not us. Not his ex-wife. A rebound fling? A mistress?

I continue my mission – pulling out drawers and throwing linen and books onto the floor in my haste to uncover Humphrey's hideaway – until my arms ache and my legs are cramped.

Why did Humphrey keep his most precious documents hidden away from me, his wife?

It takes me all evening and most of the night to find what I'm looking for: a stack of aged, tabbed manila folders, the fronts of which are written on with black biro and dated April and whatever year they were filed – tax returns for the various business investments Humphrey made throughout his life. When I do, I choke out a sob of despair. Because there is evidence too, that he lost as much as he gained from his pyramid selling, timeshares and livestock.

I flick through the self-assessment forms which are handwritten to begin with, then typed, then faxed. Some more recent ones are photocopied. And the most up-to-date ones are scanned. As I'm returning the folder dated 5th April 2018–4th April 2019 a piece of paper folded in half flutters onto my lap. The envelope for the typed letter is stamped with a local postmark, dated three months ago.

Maenor Blodau Gwyllt,

Goldcliff,

Casnewydd,

Gwent.

FTAO H. E. Philips,

I write to regrettably inform you that your recent loan application was declined by Sceptre Universal Bank. I was unable to secure the funds of £25,000. This decision was based on information acquired from the following sources: credit scoring, credit history, personal banking, business income, company expenditure, retirement funds, and the current value of shares.

In relation to our recent discussion concerning your financial investments, both in the UK and abroad, I advise you to transfer any remaining monies, including foreign dividends, to your personal account and withdraw them before instigating its closure.

Best regards,

J. T. Hughes (ACCA)

What did their conversation entail? Why was Humphrey advised to withdraw all his money? And if his foreign property, dividends and investments still exist, then where's the cash?

I thumb the screen of my phone to Google Johnathon Timothy Hughes Associates and learn they are a Gwent-based accountancy firm located in the centre of Newport.

The faint purr of a car engine draws my attention to the doorway. I drop the folder to the floor at my feet, tread across the room and cock my head towards the top of the staircase to where a light tap has begun against the ancient wooden front door below. Too heavy to be rain. Too early to be the post. Muriel wouldn't dare show her face here after being laid off.

I tip-toe down the stairs, peer through the leaded window to the side of the porch where a shadow shifts from side to side as though the person is leaning his or her weight onto one foot and then the other.

Impatient for me to open the door or feeling violent?

'I know you're in there. The car you've got parked out here is rented under your name.' Gravel shifting beneath booted feet. 'And it looks like you hit something. There's a dent across the bonnet.'

I don't recall the man's deep voice or his Gloucestershire accent.

'Humphrey? I'm not going away. This isn't going away. You must pay up.'

He paces, his footsteps scuffing the dust and dirt from the drive that's blown onto the concrete step in the wind. 'Tomorrow. Los Reyes tapas bar. 7 p.m.'

The Kings Mexican restaurant, eight miles from here,

and if he came from Gloucester much further from anyone who might know the man.

He hovers a while, turns eventually and strolls away.

I rush into the living room and press an eye to the net curtains. He closes the door of the Bentley he's just got into, which reverses slowly before reluctantly edging out of the courtyard and away from the house. I mentally note the vehicle's registration to file in case it becomes relevant one day, then tread into the kitchen where I pour a rich Domaine de la Romanée-Conti into a Waterford goblet. I sip the rich, fruity red while I try to create a logical explanation for Humphrey's deceit.

Why would a man with his wealth need a loan? And why would he borrow money from someone I've never met? Unless...

The idea that he could be broke is absurd. He owns an estate worth over £1.5 million. He considered his twenty-two-thousand-pound E-Class – before he wrote it off – a run-around for fuck's sake.

I swallow the last dregs of wine from my crystal glass. It tastes bitter.

The garage will be trying to contact Humphrey about his accident with the hawthorn bush. The insurance from that alone would be enough for me to afford to live in luxury for the next twelve months. Except I can't access it without his permission or his debit card, which is in his wallet, inside the pocket of his coat, on his back.

I must find out where he stashed the money he withdrew from those accounts as a matter of priority.

DI LOCKE

Then

A courtroom is like a place of worship. Everyone bows down to the judge as though he is a godlike spectre. But the trial is like a theatre. Everyone reading their lines, weaving together a story that fits their own agenda. It's the jury's job to figure out which actor is playing the hero.

And it quickly became apparent our star witness had gained not only the jury's sympathy but also that of the accused's wife who wasn't seated in the public gallery to support her husband. We learned why before the second day's hearing when the exclusive interview she'd given to a journalist was published online.

By the third day the entrance to Cardiff Crown Court was so swarmed by press, riot police were required to maintain order of the crowds.

We knew the evidence was slim, so we had all the more reason to celebrate when, five days after proceedings had begun the judge declared Rick Kiernan guilty of murder times five.

LOUISE MULLINS

The prosecutors were at one end of the bar, the defence drowning their sorrows at the other end, I was standing in the middle ordering mine and Jones' drinks, not sure how to feel.

'I hope he rots,' said Mrs Kiernan, slamming her handbag down on the counter and downing the glass of gin the barman had just handed her.

She clocked me and thrust her hand out to me. I backed into whoever was behind me, and mumbled an apology, staring at Mrs Kiernan's swollen fingers, adorned in gold, silver and gemstones every colour of the rainbow. 'I want to thank you, Emma, Mrs Locke, Detective, for making sure that bastard ex-husband of mine is no longer prowling the streets.'

I took her hand and shook it. 'You're welcome. But I was just doing my job.'

Though right then I didn't feel as if I had. Because although we'd been able to prove that Rick and the Newport Butcher were one and the same there wasn't enough evidence to tie him to the murder of Jane Doe.

MELANIE

Then

I met Cai in my final year at Hartridge High School. The building, cracked and damp and damaged by concrete cancer, has since been demolished, rebuilt and renamed Llanwern. But the school, when I was enrolled there, was situated within walking distance of the estate where most of the fathers who worked the steel mine and the mothers who remained at home tending to their younger children and completing the household chores before their teens returned for dinner, lived. It was during one lunchtime between exams that I ended up seated beside Cai. We fell for that young naïve love the songwriters from the romantic playlist he'd recorded for me on a cassette tape from the Top 40 charts sang about.

I'd chosen to study art, history and Spanish. He was in my compulsory English, maths, and science classes. He sat geography and French with Maddison.

She'd chosen home economics for one of her GCSEs, so we only got to spend the occasional break between lessons together. And it was during one such day, when our tutorials didn't allow for us to catch up with each other while smoking behind the bike sheds during recess, that I first spoke to Cai. He asked me to light his cigarette.

I slid my hand down the sleeve of my coat and stood close enough to him that I could smell the washing powder on his clothes as I lit the end of his Mayfair. The spark of flame protected from the wind caused his eyes to sparkle and I felt my face warm.

'Thanks,' he said.

I smiled because if I'd opened my mouth, I'd barely have been able to splutter a reply.

One year later we were partway through our finals. Cai smiled at me then sat at his desk, two spaces to my right and within my line of sight. I winked back and wrote my name, student ID and form number at the top of the piece of A4 paper in front of me, waited for the clock to strike 1.30 p.m. then turned over the page of the booklet to begin my English literature exam. I noticed Cai hesitate, take his time to choose a pencil, drop it and collect it from the floor while he removed a folded chewing gum wrapper from the underside of his desk and slid it beneath his exam booklet.

He didn't need to cheat. He excelled in spelling, grammar and punctuation. But he was easily distracted, chronically bored and would rather have been doing something other than writing with his hands. Shakespeare to him was like football was to me: although I couldn't understand the rules, I was good at scoring a goal. Cai didn't read for pleasure. He couldn't unpick an author's work and decipher the hidden meanings behind their words. But it was our opposite abilities that glued us together.

It wasn't a physical attraction. It was spiritual. We read each other's mood and often communicated with just a look or a subtle movement. Which was why when at the school leavers' disco, he took my hand and regarded me with a lengthy look I squeezed his in return and we walked out of the hall, down the tree-lined path, across the A-road, through the estate, past the green and into Ringland woods.

We scrabbled around in the dark looking for rocks and kindling to create a fire. Then, cuddled against each other beneath the hood of a tree, we watched the embers flutter in the breeze while sharing a pre-rolled joint.

When I returned home, an hour past my curfew, I ate a twelve-pack of cheese-flavoured tortilla crisps, twenty-four chocolate biscuits and drank a litre bottle of coke. Even after they'd been washed in powder and ironed, the woodsmoke clung to my clothes.

When I got caught by a teacher leaving the school by climbing a hedge while attempting to bunk off, I dipped my chin and fluttered my eyelashes at him and got away with a sharp rebuke. From then on, I readily embraced my femininity as experience taught me it softened men to my whims.

While I hadn't bothered with my appearance before bunking off school to climb trees and investigate derelict buildings with DANGER: KEEP OUT signs attached to the mesh fencing fronting them, I started to care about the cut and style of my hair and began to wear makeup. My tomboy image was replaced by designer sportswear in shades of pink, lilac and cream instead of unknown branded turquois, orange or green.

Cai said it made me look gentler, that I could get away with almost anything.

Except with him. He saw through me.

Cai hid a part of his personality too.

His thick, dark hair curtained deep hazel eyes that flashed an amber warning when he was angry. The first time I witnessed him lose his temper was towards our biology tutor.

Mr Hudson hadn't been our teacher for long. He appeared mid-term and left soon after his altercation with Cai. His fault: he stuttered as he spoke, his voice was so quiet you had to stand close to hear him speak, and he never seemed able to look anyone in the eye. I don't know who started the rumour, but it spread rapidly.

'Mr Hudson's a paedo,' the kids chanted as he walked into the classroom.

Cai was leaning over his textbook. He'd been struggling with the terminology for the different sections of a neuron for over ten minutes and was grumbling with impatience. Mr Hudson passively repeated the names of the individual structures of the cell: nucleus, soma, dendrite, axon, myelin sheath, synaptic terminals – each time duller than the last until his voice was barely illegible.

'Yes, but where does each label go?' said Cai, his jaw tense and eyes narrowed.

'It's your job to work that out. That's what you're being marked on.'

Cai's foot was tapping the table leg and his exhalations were getting increasingly louder.

'If you're struggling, perhaps you could read the diagram pinned to the noticeboard and—'

Mr Hudson stopped talking as Cai stood, the legs of his chair screeching against the tiled floor. He thundered across the classroom to the front, ripped the picture off the wall, screwed it up and threw it at Mr Hudson. It landed at his feet.

'I don't think... that's not... please calm down,' said Mr Hudson, arms outstretched, palms up in surrender.

The other kids remained seated. A few gasps and a snicker could be heard from one side of the room.

Cai thought they were laughing at him rather than with him. He picked up the heavy wooden chair from behind Mr Hudson's desk and threw it. It landed on Mr Hudson's foot.

His high-pitched squeal was heard down the corridor by the headteacher, and the school inspector who was walking alongside her. 'Couldn't you have waited until the Estyn report had been written before violating the rules of appropriate behaviour?' she said.

Cai was suspended for the rest of the day and the next. We spent it together. We met at the end of my road in the morning, caught a bus into town and walked, holding hands, to the station. We jumped on the next train to Cardiff, hiding in the toilets to avoid paying for a ticket. We ate pasties on the bay, and pick 'n' mix on the grass in the centre of the castle walls.

'What does your dad do?' he said.

'Blondes.'

He laughed. 'What does he do for a living?'

I shrugged. 'Haven't seen him in a while.'

'Nor mine. He's in Iraq.'

'He's a soldier?'

He shook his head. 'He *is* in the army, but he's a caterer so less likely to get blown up.'

'What does your mum do?'

'Auburn-haired wasters,' he said.

I nodded. 'Same.' I looked up as a fat raindrop fell onto the crown of my head. 'Do you have any brothers or sisters?'

'Yes, but she left home last year to go to college. You?'

'I did. Her name was Caitlyn. But when my mum split up with Tony she stopped coming over.'

'Is he your step-dad?'

'Was. Sort of. He didn't stay around long enough for them to get married.'

'If you don't have any other plans and my mum doesn't find out about my suspension and ground me for the weekend do you want to hang out tomorrow?'

'Sure.'

I waited on the corner for three hours, but he never arrived. He wasn't in school on Monday, and I didn't see him for the following fortnight. When he eventually returned to school, he ignored me. So when he caught my gaze and smiled at me from his desk inside the hall a month later I was pissed off and intent on revenge.

I cornered him in the corridor and shoved him on the shoulder.

'Hey, what was that for?'

'I thought you were my friend.'

'So did I.'

'Then why didn't you show up that Saturday? And why have you been ignoring me for the past four weeks?'

'I couldn't. My mum... she had cancer...' He lowered his head with his voice.

'She died?'

He raised his head and a lone tear trickled down his face. 'She was getting better... I thought she was going to be alright... she didn't tell me how bad it was. I wasn't expecting her to... she wasn't supposed to...'

'Why didn't you tell me? Explain? I thought you didn't like me anymore.'

'I wanted to, but it was difficult to say the words. I couldn't believe she'd actually gone.'

'She hasn't. We don't.'

'How can you know that?'

'Because I still see my best friend.'

He wiped his bleary eyes and waited for me to expand.

'Her name was Maddison. We were the same age. We went to playgroup together. My mum babysat her while her mum went to work. We were practically inseparable. Then one day, when we were four, Mum left me in charge, and she slipped and fell into our swimming pool and drowned.'

'That must have been tough,' he said.

'It was. I always felt guilty for not being able to save her.'

'You were just a kid. Your mum shouldn't have asked you to look after her.'

'I was jealous of her. Her parents spent time with her, bought her nice clothes. Mine were always busy and skint.'

'You weren't to blame. It was an accident.'

'I wished it.'

'What do you mean?'

'Right before she fell, I almost wanted her to. I think that's why she haunts me.'

'You can see her?' he said, incredulously.

Maddison stepped out of her class and leaned against the wall, waiting for me to walk home with her.

I turned my attention back to Cai, saw the curiosity in his dilated pupils. 'All the time.'

Dr Watkins' office was at the end of the long corridor of the Glen Usk wing. My bed was in one of six dormitories on the Adferiad Unit. Those who were counselled in the Outpatients Day Care Department were considered no risk to themselves or others, and that was where I continued to meet with my clinical psychologist for eight weeks of intensive psychotherapy after my release. I had no home to return to once I was discharged, so my keyworker was in the process of organising supported accommodation for me. My landlord didn't wait longer than one missed payment before starting eviction proceedings.

Dr Watkins had lots of letters after her name I was uninterested in enquiring about and several certificates recognising them were hung on the wall above her desk. She had long, wavy, natural blonde hair that fell to just above her elbows. She wore flowing cotton fabrics that disguised her thin frame, and bangles on her wrists that jingled as she moved. Last time we spoke she'd asked me what metaphors I could see in the text of my journal.

'Are there any underlying themes that stand out to you?' When I bit my lip and allowed my eyes to wander across the room towards the snow framed window, she tapped a page of the notebook I was using to write in and added, 'For instance, here, you mention your father fleetingly as though he had a secondary role to your upbringing.' She flicked the pages back and her hand dropped to another, her finger tracing a line of words she'd highlighted. 'And here, you do the same for Tony. Yet he lived with you and your mother for four years.'

I shrugged.

'I'm interested to know what impact these men that your mother dated had on you while you were growing up. Neil and Jason too.'

My teeth found the inside of my cheek and began to chew on it until I tasted blood. The salty metallic flavour had an instantly calming effect on me. 'They were there then they were gone.'

I watched her circle the words she'd written on the notebook spread open on her lap:

Men – Disposable.

She didn't pursue the subject. Not then.

'And your relationship with your mother. Would you think it fair that from your depiction I'd consider it strained?'

'My mother's behaviour is self-destructive. She's unhappy on her own.'

Dr Watkins circled the words:

Insecure and Co-dependent

She smiled. 'Abandonment comes in many forms. While your physical needs may have been taken care of, your emotional needs were often neglected.'

'I thought we were talking about my mother?'

'We learn from our elders. We repeat the patterns of behaviour they express. Which they recite from their own parents.'

'My mother was conditioned to act that way because of how her mother behaved towards her?'

She nodded. 'Perhaps because of your gran's struggle with poor mental health.'

'Or her father.'

She tilted her head conversationally and motioned for me to expand.

'My grandad was a sea fisherman. He worked away for weeks at a time and he died young. The vessel he was on capsized. He and his brother were onboard. They both drowned.'

'Perhaps you understand then, how a lack of both physical and emotional attachment can affect a child.' When I didn't reply she continued. 'For example, here,' Dr Watkins tapped a sentence three quarters of the way through my story, 'you wrote that you would "go mad with loneliness." And here,' she shifted her fingertip across the page to another paragraph, 'that your mother "feared she'd inherited the genetic predisposition for mental illness" that your gran exhibited: paranoia, delusions etc.'

'I'm here, aren't I?'

'You had a breakdown, Mel. You suffered an unimaginable trauma and placed immense pressure on yourself to avoid processing your grief.'

'You don't think I'm crazy?'

'Not at all. Your first experience of bereavement after the death of your friend Maddison when you were a pre-schooler impacted the way you deal with loss. Denial is a normal part of the grieving process, but for you, it has become a defence mechanism.'

'Like my mother. Men became *her* crutch.'

She smiled again. 'You can break the cycle, Mel.'

BETHAN

Now

The thick heavy wood lands with a thump on top of the pile of loose upturned floorboards, three-feet-high. I scoot back until the heels of my shoes hit the wall, lean over the next and, with the nail-puller grip, tug the nails out before raising and throwing the board onto a bare patch of floor where the rest will follow. The room is filled with dust and I sneeze as I continue ripping up the floorboards until there are only the edges of the joists left to step onto, which I use to tip-toe out of the room.

My clothes are lagged in underfloor dirt. I wipe my grimy hands on the knees of my Yves Saint Laurent jeans and gag when I detect the scent of body odour emanating from my armpits.

After I scoured the house for the money, I decided it must be in one of the crawlspaces between floors but, aside from flakes of dried lead paint in primary colours that had slipped through the cracks from the decorating of years past, and coins no longer of legal tender, there were just a few buttons and an ice-lolly stick. No stacks of notes to be found.

I'm red-faced, my skin is hot and damp with perspiration, and I'm breathless when I head down to the basement to collect a bottle of wine from the store. The angry thudding starts almost as soon as I pass the front door. 'Humphrey?! Time's up. Keith wants his money. Answer this fucking door now or I'll get Pablo here to knock it off its hinges.'

I move quietly into the cellar, the recesses of the house cold and dim and musky smelling now that Muriel is no longer filling the rooms with Vranjes Firenze reed diffusers or Jo Malone candles. I pause on the bottom step, the space lit from above by low wattage spotlights in an ambient blue, eyes fixed on the axe mounted on the wall above a bag of chopped wood. I blink away the memory of smoking sweet pungent cannabis beside a fire in the woods back when I hung out with Cai as a youngster.

It makes me feel old.

I bypass the ruby and white bottles of expensive vino, their labels faded with age, and unhook then yank the axe off the bolted iron sleeve attached to the unevenly plastered wall. Its weight forces me to carry it with one hand on the knob of the handle and the other close to the sharp metal head.

I walk slowly back up the concrete steps in time to hear the first scuffle of shoes on the mat outside, the mumbled arguing, and the resultant scrape of a shoulder against the oakwood as one of the men – Pablo I presume – tries to nudge his way through the steel-plated door.

I considered sitting in the dark of the car park at Los

Reyes tapas bar yesterday, waiting for Mr Unknown to arrive to find out how much money he lent Humphrey but I was too drunk to drive and I had no cash, couldn't even have afforded to order a glass of house red.

I step over dirty laundry strewn across the floor and spot, through the open doorway, the dishes piling up near the kitchen sink as I reach for the doorknob.

I've ransacked the place. It looks like it's been burgled.

I open the door and speak through the chained four-inch wide gap. 'Can I help you?'

'You must be his wife.'

'Yes,' I say, though it's not a question.

'Go get him.'

'Humphrey's not here.'

'His hire car is.'

'Yes, it is.'

'He's run off.'

The first rule of lying is to allow the recipient of the lie to fill in the conversational gaps. That way all you're doing is omitting the truth.

'I don't know where he is.'

I'm not aware of the exact coordinates of his location.

'Look sweetheart, you call your husband and tell him to come home with Keith's money or—'

'How much are we talking about?'

'With respect, Mrs Philips, it's none of your business.'

I smile, flutter my eyelashes and step back while producing the axe I'd kept behind me. 'My husband is… indisposed. You'll deal directly with me.'

'What did you do, bury him under the patio?' he sneers. Halted by my unamused face, his expression turns serious.

'He owes The Man twenty grand. He wants it back by the end of the week or he'll be seeking payment via other means.' His eyes travel the length of me, up from my naval, pausing on my bust, and settling on my face.

A flash of anger gut-punches me, but before I can think of a comeback he turns and strolls away. Another man – Pablo, I presume – shorter, stockier, olive-skinned and wearing as expensive attire as his boss steps out of the shadow cast by the porch and follows.

I swallow my regret at not being able to reply quickly enough, hesitating due to my lack of sleep and the physical exhaustion of my increasingly desperate search of the house, and find my voice only as he nears the rear passenger door of the Bentley, held open by Pablo. 'What's your name?'

'The Messenger,' he yells, not bothering to look back over his shoulder at me as though I'm not worth the effort of eye-contact.

I wait until the car is a smudge of onyx and chrome in the distance before I close the door, leaving the chain in place, reset the alarm, and return to the basement to collect a bottle of locally distilled merlot.

I sit on the rug in front of the stone-cold fireplace, sipping cognac in a port glass and eating extra mature cheddar smothered with plum and caramelised onion chutney on seeded crackers, dropping crumbs on the handwoven rug. It was bought from a pilgrimage to India, or so Humphrey told me. Though I'm disinclined to believe a fucking word he's said because I haven't found a single note anywhere in the house.

If *I* had a few thousand pounds to stash I'd keep it with my passport, birth certificate, National Insurance card and vehicle logbooks, but I can't find those either.

If I knew where the V5 was, I'd sign the car over to myself, fake Humphrey's signature and send it to the DVLA before the insurers post the cheque to my dead husband. I could cash it in at The Money Shop in town.

The fridge, freezer and cupboards are filled with food, but it won't take me long to empty them. Without an income I'm going to need to source some finances from somewhere, somehow.

I empty the glass down my throat, pour another, barely tasting the spiced violet and black cherry flavours the discoloured wine label boasts, bite on a thick slab of sharp crunchy cheese, chew fast and swallow it too soon. I cough and splutter as I absorb the contents of the room. The glassware alone costs more than the average worker's annual income so I won't starve yet.

I'm seeing double and feeling nauseous when I climb the stairs, tripping over first edition hardbacks and discarded vinyls as I cross the landing to reach one of the guest bedrooms. The door is jammed so I kick it until it opens, splintering the wood, snapping the lock and landing face-first on the carpet.

I've only been in this room once – when Humphrey gave me a tour of my future inheritance the morning after the night I'd passed out on the sofa during a game of Rummy.

We met at the bar of a nearby golf club. I was on the prowl for a wealthy, elderly gentleman. I was about to leave when I caught Humphrey's eye. He offered to buy me a gin and tonic. I thanked him, slugged back the one in my hand, slammed the glass onto the bar counter and pushed it towards the barman for him to refill. Humphrey said he liked my forthright attitude and asked if I'd ever had sex on a beach.

He paid the tab he'd acquired during the business meeting he'd attended with a wad of notes from a Cartier wallet. I gave him a seductive smile, downed my drink and followed him out the door. We drove back to his. He ran inside the moment we arrived and reappeared moments later carrying a bottle of champagne which we drank in his convertible classic Aston Martin with the roof down, watching the rough waves smashing against the boulders lining the sea wall, the exterior security light bouncing off the metallic bonnet.

He received a call on his mobile phone, looked annoyed when he answered, walked into the house to talk, and apologised when he returned. 'My godson,' he said. 'He's fallen out with his father, again. He and his *partner* need somewhere to crash.'

I guessed from the fallout and his pronounced vocabulary the lad was gay and his parents – Humphrey's friends of twenty plus years – didn't approve.

'Friends and family first.'

'It's late. I'd drop you home but—'

'You've been drinking. I'll order an Uber.'

'I so wanted to bend you over the bonnet and—'

I was saved by the sound of tyres on gravel. The godson. He stepped out of the car and in seconds his smartly groomed boyfriend was at his side.

Humphrey turned to greet them, and I swallowed down the nauseating thought of the white-haired, wrinkled man whose clothes stank of whiskey and cigars, old enough to be my grandfather, pounding away on top of me.

'Hiya,' said the godson, waving at me as if we were old friends. His boyfriend nodded hello.

I introduced myself. Humphrey acted like we knew each other, and I played along. I liked the idea that I hadn't met Humphrey after I'd just left a client's hotel suite needing a piss, and had only used the golf club's toilets to avoid being questioned by the receptionist seated behind the desk at the entrance who'd seen me dressed in two different outfits arm-in-arm with two different men in the same vicinity twice in one day.

We played card games, drank expensive wine and ate pre-cooked food that Muriel had prepared then stored in the fridge. When his godson and his partner called it a night and went upstairs, Humphrey and I stayed up late eating yogurt-dipped fruit pieces until I pretended to fall asleep on the sofa.

He spread a chenille blanket over me, his hot breath grazing my cheek as he retreated without attempting to steal a look beneath my low-cut taffeta dress, then the door clicked closed behind him.

The moment his feet hit the top step of the staircase I got up and hunted the room for valuables. I Googled the value of several items and realised he was worth far more than I'd imagined and I lay back on the sofa, closed my eyes and fantasised about the kind of life I could have if I lived in a house like the one Humphrey owned.

I survey the room now.

The hand-carved French oak headboard, the Tibetan wall

hanging, the Aztec-style throw folded on the linen chest, are all familiar yet untouched.

I stand, and wobble to the bed where I land on the soft, Egyptian cotton covered duvet and close my eyes to stop the room from spinning.

When I awake it's dark and frost has gathered at the corners of the windows where the glazing meets the sill. It sparkles in the moonlight.

I rub my arms to warm them as I descend the stairs and enter the utility room to turn the heating dial on the boiler up high. I wait for the reassuring hiss that indicates the valve has opened further before I close the door to muffle the noise being emitted from the clunky old pipework.

There are a couple of envelopes on the doormat. I collect them as I cross the hallway, scraping my fingers on the stiff, coarse, boar hair mat inside the porch as I do.

I read the letters while I wait for the kettle to boil. The first is an itemised bill for Humphrey's mobile phone contract. The second is an arrears notice from American Express. Both must be paid within twenty-eight days.

I dump the letters in the sewing drawer that closes with a smooth, soundless subtlety that Humphrey's debt collector lacks.

I turn to the window. 'There's a door, you know.'

'You'd invite me in?'

He forces the open kitchen window wider, hoists himself up, and with one foot in the sink and the other on the draining board he clambers through, trampling on the crystal ashtray filled with the distinguished butt-ends of cigarettes I don't remember smoking the night before.

We stare at each other for a moment, neither one of us willing to look away first. When he raises an eyebrow my lip twitches with the wish to smile.

I quash the idea of his wallet in my hand by pouring boiled water over the tea strainer filled with loose Darjeeling. I pour in thick creamy milk, deposited on the doorstep each morning by the farmer who tends to the cows and sheep surrounding the land I now own. I add a teaspoonful of sugar and, as I stir it into the cup, I recall the dusting of snow that fell onto the car park outside the window of my psychiatric suite.

The sky was a pure Icelandic-white, the leaves on the trees had ceased to rustle, the birds no longer chirped, and I could see my breath in front of my face as I fell on my knees at the news that the man I loved was dead.

My uninvited guest clicks his fingers in front of my face. 'Earth calling Mrs Philips.'

'What?' I snap.

'Your husband. I need to speak to him.'

Keep up that attitude and you'll be fucking joining him.

'Why does Humphrey owe you money?'

'Don't play games with me.' He steps forward.

'I'm not.' I move towards him.

He huffs and shakes his head in mock disbelief. 'You're going to tell me you don't know how Lord Fancy-Pants earned all this,' he indicates the room, 'despite sharing his bed?'

'He doesn't include me in his business ventures and I don't enquire.'

'Don't tell me, you spend his money blissfully unaware of where it comes from, never dig into his private affairs, never ask how he became so wealthy in such a short amount of t—'

'He said he'd inherited the manor and made the rest of his fortune buying and selling property, stocks and shares, and... Why are you shaking your head?'

'He sold up, moved his funds and put them into high interest savings accounts years ago which he told me he'd recently withdrawn. This house isn't even his.'

'W... what?'

'It was his ex-wife's. Belonged to her father.'

'She's dead.'

'Yes, and he's been living off her private pension for the past three years because he only has a state funded one of his own.'

'How do you know all this?'

'His ex-wife's sister inherited the house.'

'How do I know you're not making all this up?'

'The deeds are in her name. Check it out for yourself if you don't believe me.'

'Fuck.'

'Why not?' He winks, goes to remove his coat. I shove him in the chest. He doesn't even blink but a smile curves one side of his mouth. He grabs my wrist, removes it from its upright position in preparation to attack and eases it slowly down to my side. 'Where is he, Mrs Philips?'

I gaze into his penetrating eyes until I feel my cheeks warm.

'He's done a runner, hasn't he?'

'If he has, he never informed me of his plan to do so.'

'You expect me to believe you have no idea of his whereabouts?'

'Think what you want. It's of no concern to me.'

He looks me up and down. Goose bumps follow his eyes as they trail across my skin. My stomach flutters.

He stares at the only wedding photograph of Humphrey and me that is on display. It sits inside a sterling silver gilt frame on the mantle. He moves away from me, picks it up, examines it, puts it back down. 'What does he do for you?'

'I love him.' I can't disguise the inauthentic inflection that's entered my voice.

'You love the *idea* of him, of this.' He gestures to the room, lowers his voice. 'I warned him off you. When he told me he'd met this young, busty, blonde bird. I told me that a woman of your *pedigree* could only be interested in his money.'

'I love him.' The words, this time, come out through clenched teeth.

He leans in close. His woollen jumper smells of tree bark and his mouth of spearmint. 'You,' he points at me, 'have a problem.'

I turn my head, feel his breath kiss my chin.

'You'll be panning the river for gold before you get a pound out of him.'

'Maybe.' I turn back to face him, reach for his shirt collar, tug his face towards mine and headbutt him.

There is a crunch of bone. He wears a stunned expression on his face. Slick blood instantaneously drips from his nose, down his mouth and slides along his jawline before landing on his sleek camel-coloured shoes. His dark eyes bore into mine. Then he has one hand covering the exposed jagged cut that the impact of my forehead has caused to his otherwise handsomely sharp features and the other round my throat.

I inhale a whine, reach for his fingers to tear them away but he presses them harder until my pulse is thumping like bass in my ears and the room spins. He lets go just as I begin to fear he won't, and I gasp and inhale as much oxygen as I can.

With his palms flat on the wall at either side of me and his eyes pinning me to it he licks a droplet of blood from his mouth, so close to mine I can almost taste it. His temple is throbbing, his breath quickening against my own. He pushes himself back, leaving a bloody handprint smeared across the matte paintwork. He turns away and retreats to the bathroom.

I follow, stopping in the doorway.

He grabs the large box of Kleenex from the cupboard below the sink, tugs a handful of tissues out, scrunches them in his palm and presses them against his nose.

He grunts as I appear behind him, roll some tissues into the shape of a sausage and take the opportunity to shove it up one of his nostrils, where the most blood has gelled to his upper lip while he's folding more, those in his hand already soaked through.

He grabs my wrist, presses his thumb into the two pressure points there and jerks my hand away. 'Don't touch me,' he says, nasally.

I bite my lip, watching his biceps flex while he washes his face. He looks up, catches my reflection in the mirror above the sink, sees me staring at him, reaches back and says, 'Pass me the hand towel,' his voice calmer. He dries his face with his eyes set on mine.

'How well do you know Humphrey?'

'A lot better than you it seems.'

'Yet you've no idea where he'd hide out.'

I take the damp towel from his hand, a spark of static from his woollen jumper sends me backwards as though I've received an electric shock.

'I don't need to.'

He steers me out of his way and side-steps a pile of laundry parked in front of the bathtub to exit the bathroom.

'I don't understand.'

He sighs, turns around. 'I'll make it clearer for you then, sweetheart. You're going to find your husband.'

'And if I don't?'

'You will.'

'But what if I can't?'

'As his wife the debt will fall on you.'

'No.'

'Is that a *no I won't look for him* or *no I won't pay it back*?' he scowls.

'I'll pay you.'

'It's a lot of money Mrs Ph—'

'How much?'

'The Man lent him twenty grand.'

'I'm sure I can find enough objects within this house to cover it,' I say, eyeing one of the paintings in the hallway. 'How long have I got to…? Why are you shaking your head?'

'Your husband baulked, Mrs—'

'Bethan! Please, call me Bethan.'

He raises his chin, nods once. 'Humphrey disrespected my uncle with his disloyalty.'

'How much more money do you want in compensation?'

'With interest I'll see if I can get it down to thirty G.'

'And that's it? You'll leave us alone?'

'*You'll* have no fear of reprisal, Mrs P.'

I guess he intends to harm Humphrey, so I suppose it's a good job he's already dead.

DI LOCKE

Then

Rick Kiernan was sentenced to an indefinite life sentence for the murders of five women, plus ten years for raping Katrina Leonard at knifepoint. He would never be released. But nothing could satisfy the itch to find that one missing link in the chain of evidence we had on him that would nail him for the murder of Jane Doe. Which was why I was on my way to HMP Berwyn to pay him a visit.

Although I'd led the team who'd investigated, arrested, interviewed and collated the evidence against Rick that would lead to him getting locked up, we'd never met. I was hoping that my dark hair and fair skin would increase the likelihood of eliciting a confession from him.

I entered the building, dropped my car key and phone into the plastic box, and did the airplane pose while a security guard scanned me for metal. The rod bleeped until I removed my wedding ring. Then I waited in the visitors' room until my name was called.

There was a boy playing with a duck toy that quacked

every time he slotted a shape into its stomach. The girl sitting on the floor next to him, who I suspected was his sister, squealed with glee every time then passed him another shape. They repeated the game several times before the girl grew bored and crawled towards the bookcase to grab a copy of Spot the Dog which she began to chew the corner of. In a plush leather chair, a woman sat and read. And a man sighed and stared out of the window.

A woman entered the room, apologised for the wait, and escorted me down the corridor and into the community hall. It wasn't like any prison I'd been in before. There was no queue to get in, the staff were dressed as informally as the residents, and negative terminology such as prisoners, prison officers and cells were considered as bad as curse words.

She showed me to a sofa cut off from the other six by a partition that made it appear as if it was stationed inside a lounge that looked like it belonged in a hotel.

I paused midstride when I saw a familiar face staring back at me from another.

I mouthed 'what the fuck?' before my escort turned to usher me towards the man I was there to see.

As I sat opposite Rick, a coffee table containing two cups, two plates and an open box that housed several packets of biscuits parked between us, I couldn't shake the fact my mate Craig was sitting on the sofa two back from mine.

What's he gone and done now?

MELANIE

Then

After Tony, came Owen, followed shortly by Ian, then Robert, and a series of others I cannot name. My mother's bedroom door was a revolving one and each man who crossed the threshold was as revolting as the last.

One swindled money out of her bank account then left hastily to visit his sick cousin. When my mother reported him missing the police told her his name and age didn't match anyone registered on the electoral roll. Another punched my mother in the face and split her lip when she questioned why he'd brought a man he'd met in the pub who'd just been released from prison back with him, to our home. And yet another broke the valve inside the cistern with ounce bags of cocaine he was storing there, causing the overflow inside the toilet to... well, overflow. Adrian was the one she married.

His imprisonment, their subsequent divorce, and my mother's depression is how I ended up living alone with Gran.

Every failed relationship drained my mother's empathy more. She stopped swearing and weeping when teetotal Adrian, wearing chinos and a shirt he'd ironed himself, and carrying the keys to his BMW, moved in.

He walked out of the living room and stopped to survey my legs. 'You've grown two inches since you last wore those. Come on, I'll take you into town to buy some new clothes.'

I rolled my eyes and my mother saved me the embarrassment of explaining why that would be uncool. 'She's sixteen, Ade. Give her the money. She can go with her friends.'

He packed picnics for us to eat during day trips to Tintern Abbey, the Wye Valley, or the Brecon Beacons, and listened to my problems when I fell through the front door drunk and my mother was too angry to discover why I was set on 'pissing my life away'. He offered to pay for me to continue my studies at Cardiff University and didn't argue when I left my veterinary degree six months into the course to 'shack up with a man too immature to have any prospects'.

He drove us to Pembrokeshire for a caravanning holiday and kept my mother's wardrobe up-to-date without protest.

'I should have known,' said my mother afterwards, her head buried in Gran's neck, clinging onto her like a child who'd woken from a nightmare. 'He was too good for me, for us.'

The signs were there, but we didn't know what they were.

I returned from my mid-term waitressing job early one day and caught Ade – as he preferred to be known – watching porn on a DVD. I continued past the part-open living room door, jogged up the stairs and sat in my bedroom and tried to block out the muffled moaning that radiated from below by plugging my earphones in and listening to Clubland Xtreme at full volume.

Another time I recognised his car parked near the primary school as I raced to the bus stop. Other than his obviously healthy sexual appetite and the fact he'd pulled a sickie from work there was no indication he was anything other than the calmly confident gentleman he portrayed himself to be. He was quiet, well-spoken, well-mannered, and well-educated. I never felt uncomfortable in his presence, had no inkling he was a sexual predator. Because he wasn't interested in me.

I was in my bedroom reading the latest edition of Mizz magazine when I heard the letterbox flapping vigorously. I thought it was Gran in a panic because next door's cat had chased her down the path again, but when I opened the front door to two police officers my stomach somersaulted. I knew Ade appeared too good to be a truly honest man. He'd fooled us both.

I called my mother in from the garden where she sprang up on the sun lounger, tipping the glass of ice-cold lemonade down her tanned bikini-clad chest. She turned to look at me. 'What have you done?'

'Not your daughter, Mrs Hale. Your husband,' said the tallest of the two men.

The other officer's eyes found Ade's. 'Adrian Hale?'

He looked defeated and nodded.

'I'm arresting you on suspicion of communicating with a child whom you have been grooming with the intent of meeting by arranging and facilitating the commission of a child sex offence, sections 14, 15, and 15a of the 2003 Sex Offences Act...'

My mother jumped off the sun lounger, mouth open in

the shape of a scream that took a while to extend from her brain to her vocal cords. The glass flew at his face before she collapsed at my feet, almost bringing me down with her, where she sat, hugging my legs until Gran dragged her off me and led her into the house.

'We're going to the central custody suite,' the officer directed at Ade, whose face was cut and bloodied. 'They're only surface wounds. We'll get you cleaned up.'

The other held a piece of paper in his hand that said:

WARRANT TO ENTER AND SEARCH PREMISES.

I watched as Ade was escorted through the house, out the front door, and into the police car parked in front of the gate.

I waited until he was gone before I turned back to the house. My mother was stood at her bedroom window, tears streaming down her face, eyes hard. I wasn't sure if she was mad at me for wearing an I-told-you-so expression on my face or Ade. She retreated from the window before I could decide.

Two casually dressed detectives arrived in an unmarked car. They seized a Dell computer, a few floppy discs and Ade's porn stash.

I'd never had a strong relationship with my mother but Ade's sudden departure, the reveal of the sick secret he'd kept from us both, acted as the catalyst that inevitably widened the gap between us further, causing a chasm that couldn't be refilled. Not even when she met Paul.

★

Dr Watkins tilted her head, mirroring me. 'Your mother began to exhibit symptoms of depression,' she summarised.

'I think she blamed herself for Ade's behaviour.'

'You think she felt responsible for Ade's actions because she wasn't there to oversee them, to supervise him.'

'That and, there I was flaunting my relationship while she mourned the loss of another.'

'You think she was jealous.'

'I was with Brandon most of the time. We were inseparable. After Ade was arrested my mother looked at me with contempt.'

'You think she envied you.'

'I left home to move in with a man to spite her.'

'Your grandmother was there.'

'It was my fault Gran overdosed and stopped paying her rent and had to live with us.'

'It was an accident. You were a child.' She paused, leaned forward to reflect my own defensive stance. 'I'd like us to explore why you feel obligated to ensure other's happiness.'

I uncrossed my legs.

She uncrossed hers. 'Why you're so willing to take the blame for things that are out of your control.'

She softened her voice. 'Why you're convinced you murdered your boyfriend.'

I lowered my gaze.

Brandon took the duffle bag from my outstretched hand and offered my mother a nod and a weak smile goodbye, that became one of relief the second he turned his back on her.

I followed him down the path to the Cosworth that was half-packed with my belongings and stared vacantly through the tinted passenger window at my pale-skinned, greasy-haired mother as we drove away. Gran waved at me over her shoulder.

I felt Brandon's hand on my thigh as we neared the junction and I turned to look at him. 'I'm never going back there.'

'Not even for Sunday lunch?'

'I don't ever want to see her again.'

He patted my thigh. 'I can roast potatoes.'

I swatted him away and turned back to the window to hide my smile.

We met in the college canteen. As soon as our eyes met after I'd walked into the tray he held in his hands, spilling tango over his oily overalls, and he raised his eyebrows, told me to buy him another drink, I knew I'd met my match.

He smiled as he took the can I proffered and thanked me. Then he asked, 'What are you doing tonight?'

I shrugged. 'Nothing.'

'Would you like to do nothing with me?'

It was the cheeky glint in his eyes that led me to say, 'Sure.'

He picked me up and drove us to Blaencuffin canyon where we spent the evening stargazing, eating the picnic he'd prepared, and getting to know each other.

From our suburban levelled abode there was no view of the fiery reds and blazing oranges of the setting sun. Just an oppressing, overcast sky that meant we had to flick all the lights on the second we entered his two-bedroom townhouse.

He carried my bulging bags upstairs to the bedroom we were going to share while I searched the kitchen cupboards for enough food to create a meal with that portrayed me as the mature little wifey I was glad to act the part of.

I heard Brandon opening and closing drawers, imagined him placing my folded clothes into neat piles inside the unit that lined the wall of his bedroom.

He came downstairs and sat at the table while I dished up. He raised his nose and sniffed. 'Tomato, basil, garlic and… is that beef?'

'Meatballs and pasta.' I put a plate in front of him and motioned to the candles. 'Romantic.'

He nodded his approval and I sat opposite.

He stopped me before I could raise a forkful of food to my mouth and took my hand in his, stroking the back of it with his thumb. 'I know you're weirded out by the lack of tension in our home but I'm hoping you'll get used to it.'

'I don't start arguments, Brandon.'

I finish them.

'That's good because I've taken the initiative to choose which side of the bed I'll be sleeping on – the right. You get the left, nearest the radiator.' He leaned over his food, his sleeve skimming across the blood red sauce.

'Anything else I should know about?'

'The house is old so it's likely someone died here once so it could be haunted.' He darted his eyes around the room.

I flicked a spoonful of pasta onto his face. 'Liar.'

He plunged a finger into his food and smeared sauce onto the tip of my nose.

That's how the fight started.

Oasis played in the background from the stereo hidden

behind a plant almost as tall as Brandon. Its large, dark green leaves looked waxy and smelt of plastic, but he insisted it wasn't.

'It's not real.'

'I'm telling you it is,' he laughed as I dusted it.

'Do you water it?'

'Yes, but not for a while. And now that you've moved in it's going to be your job.'

'Oi!' I threw the duster at his head. 'Your turn to act the role of Stepford Wife.'

'Do I get to wear your sexy maid's outfit?'

I studied his lean muscular form. 'It won't fit you. Your arse is too fat.'

That first night in my new home ended in bed before we'd got halfway through the meal. Too high on excitement and unfamiliarity to eat, Brandon lying beneath me, my thighs clamped against his hips. My face resting on his heaving chest, his hot breath on the crown of my head.

He threaded his fingers through my tangled hair, stroked then turned my chin up, forcing me to look at him. 'I love you, Mel.'

I pushed myself upright and pressed my damp, hungry lips against his.

I thought that was the way to express my feelings.

My mother taught me that.

Brandon was a hands-on man. He had to have a tool in one hand and the other in my knickers. But when we weren't fucking each other senseless we were partaking in a screaming match. The only contestants in a power-play, neither one of us willing to surrender control, both too stubborn to admit when we were wrong and accept defeat.

Our passion didn't fizzle out, it exploded in the most horrific and violent way.

When Dr Watkins therapised me into altering my perceptions to the events in my life there was one thing her textbook counselling sessions got wrong.

I *did* kill Brandon.

BETHAN

Now

I throw kitchen towels and tampons onto the conveyor belt and slam a checkout divider down to separate my items from those belonging to the gruff-looking old fart that smells of chicken soup, stood too close behind me. I remember the washing powder as I glance down at my low-cut jumpsuit – the only item of clothing I could find this morning that didn't require washing – deciding against hurrying down the aisle to grab a box and holding the queue up.

'That'll be £118.57 please,' says the cashier.

I slide my card into the machine, distracted by a familiar car pulling into a space at the front of the supermarket. 'Your card has been declined. Do you have another one you can try?'

Try? It's not a fucking game show.

I remove the card, take a different one from my purse, shove it into the machine, and tap in the pin number.

The shop assistant frowns. 'That one too, I'm afraid. I don't suppose y—'

'I've got about thirty more, but I don't intend to stand here and try them all. Your machine is obviously broken.'

'Okay,' she says, lengthening out the word as though she's being asked to go above and beyond her job description of sitting on a stool and hitting a few buttons with her pound shop gel-painted nails, clicking out a rhythm that almost causes my hands to involuntarily reach up and strangle her.

'Support required at till number four please?' she calls out through the microphone, her bimbo-voice echoing across the spacious shop and hitting the ears of the youngest, spottiest assistant manager – according to his nametag – I've ever had the displeasure of speaking to.

'What's the problem?' he says in a high-pitched, boyish voice.

'Your card reader isn't working.'

'I'll fix this, Stella.' He plants a hand on the shop assistant's till and rubs his crotch against the back of her chair to take the third card I'm willing to try before giving up from my hand.

The woman behind Mr Chicken Soup sighs, the two men behind her share an eye-roll.

'Insufficient funds,' says Mr Spotty-face, wearing a false smile.

He has a sheen of sweat building on his upper lip that makes me heave. I feign a coughing fit and turn my sight back to the car park to watch the male driver vacate the vehicle I recognise and head towards the supermarket entrance.

'Forget it.' I grab the now sticky card off Mr Spotty-face and envision him wanking himself off at the back of the storage depot, cleaning his hands on a wet wipe from a packet he keeps inside his locker, leaving his hands damp when he's forced to assist the cashiers on the shop floor. I feel the bile rise to my throat.

'Don't worry about the food. We'll return it to the shelves for you as a goodwill gesture.'

I head for the exit.

'Bethan!' A shrill voice drills through my head.

I pause, paint on a subtly surprised expression and turn around to see Roberta unhook her arm from Gerald's and wave at me.

He gently touches her elbow and whispers into her ear. She lowers her arms and strolls over to me, eyes sparkling, cheeks flushed.

'Don't show your husband up.'

She grins.

'He's let you off your leash?'

'Don't,' she says, slapping me lightly on the shoulder. Her eyes dart from her husband then back to me. 'I promise not to make a spectacle of myself like last time.'

'The party?'

'You didn't get too drunk, did you?'

'Oh, no...'

Coked-up.

'*You* held your composure well despite being pissed out of your skull and having the lips of a blowfish.'

Roberta gasps and presses the back of her hand to her mouth then cackles. 'Oh, you're so funny.'

'Bertie?' Gerald calls from a few yards away, pointing at the trolley he no doubt expects her to push round the shop.

'Alright,' she says, rolling her eyes. 'I'm coming.'

'Don't keep him waiting.'

The shock of my unfiltered words split Roberta's lips apart into a wide grin.

Gerald is at her side in an instant. He gives me a wry smile. 'Bethan,' he nods in greeting.

I smile to reciprocate the endearment. 'How are you both keeping?'

'Good. We've just returned from a visit to our villa.'

'The one in France?'

'You look surprised.'

'Isn't it cold there?'

'No worse than here at this time of year. I wanted to collect the last of the wine from the vineyard. We're clearing the place out, to sell.'

'Oh, that's a shame.'

He shrugs. 'Holiday lets aren't money magnets, and we're of an age now where we must start living sensibly. Cut down on the number of holidays we take each year for instance.'

I nod, not sure how else to respond.

'Humphrey wanted some Pinot Noir. I'll bring some crates over?'

I smile evasively. 'It's lovely to see you both but I must dash. I'm in rather a hurry.'

'See you tonight,' says Roberta.

Gerald spots the confusion on my face which I manage to reign in before his wife notices.

'Dinner,' he says. '7 p.m.'

'She doesn't need reminding, Gerry. Bethan is a marvellous hostess. Her culinary skills are the best.'

'Far greater than your attempts,' he laughs.

I feel my muscles clench. His voice fades and I find myself staring at his fat pompous mouth spouting misogynistic shite that I fear Roberta's self-esteem is so low she no longer hears.

Gerald stops talking, glances down at my empty hands and gives me a questioning look. 'You're not carrying any shopping.'

'I'm getting it delivered.'

'What's wrong with the car?'

'It got hit.'

'Ah, that explains why I didn't see it parked out there,' he says, motioning to the exit.

'Uh, yes.'

'Humphrey's collecting you?'

'Um, no. I'm getting a lift from… oh, there she is.' I raise a hand and wave at an elderly woman whose typically British reaction is to wave back then appear confused as she tries to work out who I am.

Gerald looks amused but Roberta, embarrassed that I've witnessed such an intimate act of sexism pass between them, can barely look me in the eye.

'I'd better go. See you both later.'

I glance over my shoulder as I make my way over to the hire car to ensure Gerald isn't watching to see me unlock the door, sit, belt up and start the engine. As I reverse out of the parking space, my eyes on the side mirror, the registration plate on the front of the vehicle I recognised before I spotted Gerald and Bethan comes into full view. I slam my foot down onto the brake so hard the discs squeal.

The black Jaguar directly behind me wears the letters: GTY. It's the car that sped off ahead of me when I left the National Slate Museum three days ago in Llanberis.

DI LOCKE

Then

Craig was right when he said I'd know evil when I saw it. As Rick stared at me across the coffee table I felt as if he was peeling layers off me. And that was before he spoke. 'Emma.'

I didn't like the sound of my name on his lips.

'Hello, Mr Kiernan.'

Recognition dawned on his face. 'You were at the trial, Inspector Locke.'

'I was.'

'DCI Evans is your boss?'

'That's correct.'

'That's correct, yeah. Well, you certainly sound intelligent, Detective. So tell me why you need my help.'

I didn't, of course. Giving information pertaining to an ongoing investigation to a suspect would make sure anything he told me about Jane Doe would jeopardise the entire case and end my career. Instead I asked if he could tell me anything that might help me to understand him, the crimes he was convicted for, in the hope of furthering my understanding and inform my future work.

He volunteered a lot of information I already knew and was surprisingly honest in his responses. Which is why when he said the women he was convicted for killing were the only ones he'd killed I suspected he might be telling the truth.

I left HMP Berwyn feeling deflated. But as I crossed the car park, hidden from view of the open windows of the prison that looked even from the outside like a hotel, my despondent mood turned to elation.

Craig was leaning against the side of my car, hands in the pockets of his jeans, wearing a huge grin. 'I was visiting my cousin.'

MELANIE

Then

This had been going well. So well in fact that perhaps that's why I was so pessimistic. Knowing how my mother's relationships had ended I'd convinced myself my own wouldn't last. I was too busy searching for faults that I missed what was right in front of me.

The door closed on the whistling wind. Brandon shook off his rain-soaked jacket and dumped his shoes beneath the coat hooks in the narrow hallway. He swept through the house, deposited his wallet and keys on top of the kitchen counter and bent to kiss me. Rivulets of water ran onto his mouth from his wet hair and his stubble grazed my forehead as I turned fractionally so that he almost face-planted the stove where I stood stirring a pan of creamy peppercorn and garlic sauce, watching the simmering potatoes in the other.

'What have I done now?' he said.

'What haven't you done?'

'Why are you still mad at me?'

'Hah,' I huffed and pulled the wooden spoon from the pan so fast it sprayed boiling hot sauce across his arm.

'Shit!' He turned sharply away and ran his arm beneath the cold tap. 'What's got into you?' he winced.

I poured the boiling hot water from the pan of potatoes into the sink, forcing Brandon to back away fast to avoid another burn. 'I should ask you the same thing.'

He stared at me, shook his head, said, 'I don't know you right now.'

'Not as well as you know her.'

'Who's *her*?'

'Don't pretend not to know who I mean?'

'I don't even know *what* you mean, Mel.'

'You've been screwing your apprentice.'

'Not this again. She's seventeen, Mel.'

'I was her age when *we* started dating.'

'So was I.' He grabbed his keys and wallet off the kitchen counter, left the room, stuffed his feet inside his Doctor Martens and dragged his jacket off the coat hook, slinging it on as he reached for the front door handle. 'You're going to have to get used to me working alongside women. There are loads of female engineers, Mel. There's my fucking boss for a start.'

'Don't swear at me.'

'I don't need this shit the second I get home.'

'Stop swearing!'

'I'll swear if I fucking want to. It's my fucking house.'

'Oh, it's your house now, is it?'

'What's that supposed to mean?'

'I'm surprised you remember where you live considering you're rarely here.'

'Fuck this again.' He slammed the front door so hard the pendant lightshade that hung from the passageway ceiling swung from side-to-side.

I stomped down the hall and flung the door open. It was dark and misty. Rain bounced off Brandon's helmet. 'Where are you going?' My words battled against the wind that whipped my hair from my face.

He spun round on his twin turbo low-rider to face me, and I caught the disappointment I'd often seen in my father's eyes. He kicked down and turned the handle, sparking his precious Harley Davidson into life.

The chrome wheels shone from the orange glow of the streetlight above him. I watched until the roar of its exhaust was swallowed by the fog.

The sky flashed then crackled as I entered the house, turning my back on the storm that was about to descend upon our home.

I lay awake for hours waiting for Brandon to return, convinced he'd gone to *her*, to spend the night in her bed.

I answered the door angrily when I heard someone thudding on it with their fist.

My stomach somersaulted when I met the police officer's stoic demeanour. 'Can you give us your name?'

'Mel. Melanie Driscoll.'

He was accompanied by another officer, slightly shorter, who was taking note of the garden fencing fronting the house, that now shuddered on the ground where it had blown down in the gale.

'Do you live alone?'

'No. I live with my boyfriend, Brandon.'

'Can we come inside? We need to speak to you.'

I stood aside and let them in. My feet heavy and my heart strumming overzealously against my ribcage as I led them into the lounge.

One of the officers tapped a photograph pinned to the corkboard I'd nailed on the wall to prove Brandon wrong when he'd argued there were cables running up behind the plasterboard.

When I'd ignored his warning and hammered the nail into the wall he'd said, 'It's a good job there aren't any, or you'd have been thrown across the room.'

'Who's this?' The officer drew my attention back to the photograph.

'That's Brandon. He's who you've come here to speak to me about, isn't he?'

Not a flicker of emotion passed between them.

'Does he drive?'

'A motorbike.'

'Do you know the make and model?'

'Why are you doing this?' my voice broke. 'He's had an accident, hasn't he? He shouldn't have left in this weather. He was angry. I tried to stop him—'

'We've recovered a motorbike registered to a man named Brandon Miller, who according to the Driver and Vehicle Licencing Agency lives at this address.'

'Is he hurt? Where is he? What hospital did they take him to?'

His colleague stepped forward and reached out to catch me as if he knew I was going to collapse when he spoke. 'I'm sorry, Mel. Brandon didn't make it.'

The next few days were a blur. I declined the invitation to say my final farewell at the chapel of rest despite the chaplain's assurances that I could. The funeral was held by a vicar in Newport Cathedral. The eulogy written by his Catholic brother, who blamed me for Brandon riding to his death because I was the last person to have seen his younger sibling alive and, 'should have stopped him from leaving the house'.

The wake was held in a small parish hall in St Woolos. There was a buffet spread and a gathering of sixty people – my mother counted – I'd never met, who were eager to stuff their faces with salmon and goat's cheese sandwiches and miniature fruit salads while I stood alone.

Brandon's father signed the house over to me and continued to pay the mortgage to ensure I didn't become homeless. His mother gave me a character reference to secure a waitressing job in the pub where she worked as a barmaid.

But the inquest is the only event I can recall with any clarity during those long winter months. The words in the low solemn notes of the coroner's voice played on a loop like an unrhyming poem until I sought solace from them in the same way I had when Maddison died: by pretending he was still alive.

'Brandon left the house on his motorbike. It was dark. It was raining heavily. There was thick fog, and strong winds. Brandon was an experienced driver who was driving within the speed limit, but his vision was compromised. His braking even more so. We cannot say with any certainty what caused Brandon to lose control of his motorbike, but the wet tarmacked road meant that when he did the tyres span and he skidded beneath a heavy goods vehicle. One of the large wheels on the articulated lorry drove over him, and he tragically lost his life.'

When the coroner read out the post-mortem report, I felt my legs buckle, the room tilt on its axis.

'Brandon's organs were crushed. He suffered several fractures: to his pelvis, ribs, shoulder, leg, neck and skull. The most damaging injury was the excessive trauma to his head. Along with internal bleeding to his stomach and the collapse of his left lung, there was evidence of severe haemorrhaging to the brain, consistent with the rupture of the major artery that runs from the base to the top of the spine, the cord partly severed.'

He was almost decapitated.

I don't remember being driven home, curling up on the sofa wearing Brandon's sweatshirt that no longer smelt of him, or playing Puff Daddy's version of 'I'll Be Missing You' on repeat, but that was how Gran found me a few days later. Hair matted to my head, face blotchy, eyes red, breath stinking of vodka, the room smoky and cluttered.

'I'll run you a bath,' she said.

She eased me off the sofa, steered me upstairs, poured Radox into the tub, rolled one sleeve up and tested the temperature of the water with her elbow like my mother had done when I was a child. She helped me to undress because I didn't have the energy to, and retreated downstairs.

I listened to her tidying things away, temporarily distracted as I sank beneath the water and inhaled it through my nose.

I awoke to the sensation of choking. I coughed. My throat was sore, and my chest felt bruised. I opened my gritty eyes to a brightly lit room painted white. The curtains were red, and the bathtub had turned into a bed. I shifted onto my side, hit my arm on a metal safety rail. Gran was sat beside me in a blue hospital chair.

She blinked then sprang from her seat and grabbed my hand. She looked over her shoulder and yelled for my mother. 'She's awake!' She leaned over me, kissed my forehead. 'You're awake.'

Her tears soaked through my hair and her grip tightened until my fingers tingled. 'You don't want to die. You just want Brandon back.'

My mouth went dry and my chest tightened.

How could I explain to her that he was stood at the side of the bed holding my other hand?

'Your grandfather died at sea before you were born. I'd never replaced a fuse in a plug before my husband died. I was too frightened to live alone, and the Valium removed my ability to feel.'

Gran studied my reaction and I nodded my assent for her to continue.

'I stood over the M4, the wind lifting my hair, and tasted the salt from the Severn Estuary in the air…' She licked her lips as if the memory of it remained on her tongue.

Mum gave her a sharp look and stood straighter as if she'd predicted what Gran was about to say.

Gran squeezed my hand. 'I wanted to die, but your mother stopped me. She started crying. I'd left her in her buggy with the brakes on at the other end of the bridge so it wouldn't roll into the road and so someone would find her. A car zoomed past and I ran to her, saw the worry in her little eyes.'

My mother's jaw clenched. 'She doesn't need to hear this, Mum.'

'Yes, she does,' she snapped. 'You're both at risk of depression because my illness is hereditary. My psychiatrist said you could have a genetic predisposition to mental health problems.'

I glanced at my mum who confirmed it with a nod.

Gran sighed. 'I gave myself until your mum was eighteen to live. But then she met your father and I had a wedding to attend. Then she had you, so I gave myself until *you* were eighteen. And I expect I'll have to hang on now to see you get married and have kids.'

Brandon wove his fingers through my hair and stroked my chin with the back of them.

I brought his hand to my lips, kissed his knuckles. 'I love you.'

Gran tilted her head, and my mother narrowed her eyes. 'Who are you talking to?' they said in unison.

'You two, of course.'

Gran smiled but my mother refused to take her eyes off me for the duration of her visit.

'Don't ever do anything like that to me again,' she said before they left. 'Don't you realise I already have enough crap to deal with from your grandmother. I can't have you trying to take your own life too.'

I didn't remind her that it was my childish attempts to get Gran to take her pills that had caused her to overdose.

'I didn't. I fell asleep.'

'Bullshit.'

'It's true. I was tired. I must have slipped into the water.'

The hospital psychiatrist tasked with assessing my risk of attempting suicide agreed, handed me a leaflet about Talking Therapies, and I returned home twenty-four hours after my admittance to a cold, dark house that no longer felt like home.

I spent that night on a bar stool drinking Pinot Noir, and the following morning throwing up the kebab that the man I woke up beside had bought me before hailing and paying for the black cab that had brought us to his rundown house-share.

I opened the front door of his Georgian abode to a dazzling sun that cast a reflected beam of light off the wing mirror of his neighbour's Mazda and onto the zip of his Calvin Klein jacket which hung on the bannister. I leafed through his bulging Burberry wallet and stuffed a wad of notes into the pocket of my jeans.

I couldn't afford Tommy Hilfiger, but my one-night-stand wore *Levi's*. He wouldn't miss £380.

I walked the backstreets in case he woke up and decided to come looking for me. I didn't know if he owned a car or had a propensity to violence so I caught a bus from Malpas into the centre of town and through Bettws to get back to Maes-Glas, stopping in an off-licence for wine and cigarettes on the way just in case he was following me.

I ate, tidied the house, showered, dressed into my finest attire, poured and drank a couple of glasses of wine for courage, took the train to Cardiff, then hit the swankiest looking nightclub I could find. There I met a nameless man who kept my glass topped up and insisted on taking me somewhere quieter 'to get to know me better'.

He ensured my plate was full at the French restaurant his

friend owned and gave me my own door key to the hotel room paid for by his company. I stayed for the weekend, visited the spa and jacuzzi during the day while he worked, and ate with him in a diner before watching a romantic film that night. I put the film on his tab just like I'd done with the daily facials, massages, fine food and wine.

'Thank you for a wonderful evening.' I kissed him on the cheek as we left the restaurant on what was to be our final evening spent together, and, feeling generous, let him guide me into his room. We had hard, fast sex that filled a void I didn't know was there then he paid for my taxi home.

When the driver dropped me off, I took the bus from the address I'd given to the man I'd fucked all weekend to the house he didn't know I lived in.

I dumped the Chanel handbag I'd stolen from a stuck-up bitch who'd turned her nose up at me while I struggled to open my locker in the sauna earlier that morning onto the bed and shook the rose-gold Breitling watch down my wrist. I unclasped it and wrapped it carefully inside the silk scarf I'd nicked from an elderly woman who'd tutted impatiently at me while I'd emptied the face creams and body oils from the gift bags into mine just before I left the hotel.

I sold the watch and the proceeds covered the council tax, gas, electricity and water bills for the next three months. I used the sale of the handbag to gain entry to expensive nightclubs and the theatre where I met older men seeking companionship and sex. Most were too drunk to perform by the time we reached the hotel room. Others wanted to meet for lunch the following day or asked me to accompany them to business conferences. I robbed most of them subtly, but some got rough.

Sean was one of those men.

He pressed his arm against the top of my chest as he pushed me up against the wall, adding enough pressure to prevent me from escaping but barely touching me so it couldn't be classed as assault. 'Where's my money, Mel?'

His forehead sheened with sweat.

'That's not my name.'

He smirked. 'You can't bullshit a bullshitter, *Mel*.'

'I haven't got your money.'

'You took it,' he said, motioning to where a small camera looked down on me stood beside the till, from the ceiling above the bar where I worked serving food and drinks to the unemployed who after collecting their giro's crossed the road from the Job Centre to enter the pub to get drunk, play pool, and sell stolen merchandise. It faced the only games machine that wasn't alarmed.

'I needed it for food.'

'Don't I pay you enough to eat?'

'I got kicked out of my house.'

He looked down at me with pity. 'What did you do?'

'It was my boyfriend's house. His parents inherited it, paid the mortgage so I could stay there. They saw me with a man and—'

'They made you homeless for daring to move on after their son's death. Want me to pay them a visit, break his dad's legs?'

'No! Who the fucking hell are you?'

'I could buy the house off them.'

'No. It's not the same without Brandon there.'

'We'll redecorate. You were happy together, weren't you?'

'Yeah.'

He took my shoulders in his hands, squeezed them. 'Where are you staying?'

'A B&B.'

'Check out, bring your stuff here. I'll come back with good news.'

'I'm guessing I don't get to keep my job?'

'You stole from me. You're a hustler. I can get you plenty of work, but it won't involve handling money.'

That's how I ended up the owner of my deceased boyfriend's parents two-bedroom house, working as a social escort for a gangster named Danny Newall.

The long working hours and the constant demand for my attention from men old enough to have fathered me meant I tired quickly. I had to keep up-to-date with the news, sports and fashion. Regardless of my mood I had to wear a smile, listen to their boring stories, laugh at their unfunny jokes, and let them paw me as if I was a prize filly.

One day during break I followed one of the women who worked in the strip club Danny owned from the bar to the toilets where I found her snorting coke off a CD case she removed from her cosmetics purse. 'Do you want some?'

'What does it do?'

'It's like a strong caffeine hit.'

'Sure.'

I took the straw from her hand, bent and sniffed. My surroundings brightened, my heart began to beat faster, and my muscles contracted and a rush of heat like a hug spread from my head and down to my feet.

Danny ran a clean ship. Drugs, weapons, personal grievances between members of staff – on or off the books – pets, and of course kids, were prohibited from his premises.

The security guard flung me out of the door and stood like a soldier poised for battle at the entrance.

'My bag's in there?!'

'It's not yours.'

He was right. It didn't belong to me. I'd stolen it from Debenhams.

'What am I supposed to do for money?'

He shrugged.

That's how I ended up in a sleazy backstreet pub, offering my 'services' to a rugby player I envisioned would become my sugar daddy.

An hour later I was in his bedsit kneeling on threadbare carpet, having my hair tugged from my scalp, and my skull squeezed in a vice-like grip as I gagged.

When I returned home, I gargled mouthwash until my throat stung and scrubbed my skin until it burned.

I stared at my reflection in the bathroom mirror until the desire to smash it overwhelmed me.

My reflection split in two. One side of my face remained intact, the other was broken, distorting my features so that a part of me had become unrecognisable.

BETHAN

Now

I slam the door and sink against it, the oakwood flooring cold and hard against my soft buttocks.

I didn't see the driver of the Jag. I don't know who saw me dispose of my husband. But whoever it was is taunting me.

I stand and hobble down to the basement to grab a bottle of Domaine du château de Martigues – wine from Roberta and Gerald's vineyard. I drop it from my shaking hand, spraying dark crimson liquid across the floor and up the wooden shelving unit engraved with vine leaves. I tread over the shards of glass to collect another, take it up into the kitchen, and pop the cork, ducking as it bounces off the ceiling, missing the lightbulb by an inch, hits the floor then rolls into the kick-board.

I rinse out a used goblet and pour in the wine almost to the brim. It tastes sour and woody. There are particles of cork bobbing along the surface of the five-year-old French red.

I neck it, wiping the drips that descend from the corners of my mouth with the sleeve of my jumper.

I pour another which I sip while searching through the fridge for something to cook. I find eggs, haddock and the cheese Humphrey bought in Snowdonia.

I'm plugging in a pair of pearl earrings when the first set of headlights beam across the lawn.

I open the front door with half a glass containing the last of the bottle of red in one hand and my lipstick in the other. 'Roberta, it's so good to see you. Come on in.'

Gerald frowns as she air-kisses me and holds me too tight when he draws me towards him for a stiff hug when it's his turn to be greeted. He pats my arm as he steps back and holds my gaze for too long.

Pinpricks of unease leave gooseflesh to coat my skin.

I totter down the hall in my heels and bounce my hip off the doorframe as I lead them into the dining room where I've left my iPod attached to the Bluetooth speakers. The sub-woofer is parked on top of the eight-foot-high unit that contains brassware – too high for anyone to reach and detach without using the stepladder I returned to the shed preventing anyone from changing the music. The remote control is in my pocket so only I have the power to turn it down. This is my night; I'm listening to what I want at the level I choose.

'There are appetisers on the dining table. Dinner should be ready in twenty minutes.'

'That'll give your girlfriend time to arrive.'

'Sorry?' I tap my foot absentmindedly to the beat of a catchy tune I often sing along to in the car while running errands.

'Kim's late. Perhaps she's had another falling out with Derek.'

'I thought they were solid.'

'Looks can be deceiving, Bethan.' He glues his eyes to mine a second longer than necessary.

Roberta sighs and reaches for a bottle. 'They're not having marriage problems, Gerry.'

He turns, links arms with his wife and leads her away from the champagne. 'Not tonight, Bertie. We don't want a repeat performance of your karaoke skillset.'

I vaguely remember handing her a microphone at one of our gatherings but I don't remember her using it. Perhaps I was drunker than I remember being then too. Has only two weeks passed since our last soirée?

'Where's Humphrey?'

'I'm to apologise for his absence, but he's had to visit a business associate abroad. Something to do with the contract for one of the properties he sold.'

'I see,' says Gerald.

'Which one?' says Roberta.

'No idea.'

'I thought he'd sold them all?' says Rupert from behind me.

I shrug.

'Did he give you an estimated time of his return?' says Gerald.

'No. I'm afraid not.'

I serve poached haddock with cheese sauce, and boiled, buttered potatoes. I sprinkle a mixture of finely chopped lemongrass, chives and dill from what's left of the frost-covered herb garden on top of each plated slice, and sway to Ava Max's 'So Am I' while downing the last dregs of wine from my goblet.

We eat and drink and feign pleasantries, and by midnight Kim and I are seated on the arbour, huddled beneath a fleece blanket, swigging wine from champagne flutes. Her eyes refuse to leave Derek.

'How did you meet?'

'France,' she says, without reverting her eyes from her husband. 'I was on a friend's hen night. He was conducting business with a bar owner. We got talking and, voilà.'

'He was marketing Gerald and Roberta's wine?'

'I believe so,' she laughs. 'It's a small world, huh?'

We clink glasses, share a look that instantly warms my thighs, and minutes later we're running upstairs to the bedroom, and we're fumbling to remove each other's clothes.

There are damp lips on skin, hot mouths on flesh, fingers exploring, and tongues gliding before we reach euphoria.

I'm sat behind Kim, clasping on her white lacy bra when Gerald walks in.

Kim's face turns scarlet. 'I was trying on one of her dresses.'

He surveys the crumpled bed.

'It didn't fit.'

He nods and leaves, slamming the door behind him.

How long has he been skulking around upstairs for?

Derek's voice calls up the stairs, 'Are you expecting anyone else?'

I slide my hands down her smooth arms and walk to the window. The headlights of a vehicle hit the brickwork below, to where the kitchen is situated.

'I've got to go and deal with this.' I kiss Kim's full lips. 'Don't move.'

My heartrate has ratcheted up a gear and my feet betray me as I stumble down the stairs to face the lone policewoman who stands in the open doorway, Gerald holding the door wide, wearing a creased brow.

'Kirsty Richardson?'

DI LOCKE

Now

I close my car door and immediately see Jones stood waiting for me at the entrance of Cwmbran CID. He motions for me to follow him from the car park, into the building, down the corridor and across the incident room to his desk.

He taps the top of his computer monitor. 'Nightshift handed this over to us.'

I speed-read the report made by PC Malone at 2.09 a.m., my pulse building with every word.

Neighbour who wished to remain anonymous
called 101 to report noise disturbance at
Wildflower Manor, Goldcliff at 12.15 a.m.
Neighbour was advised to call the council as
it is classed as a civil dispute. Neighbour
rang back at 12.27 a.m. and said community
warden line was engaged and warned they
were going to confront the homeowner and
remove the device that was the source

of the noise, themselves. Neighbour was advised not to as that action would be considered theft. Neighbour swore then hung up. I was then sent to the property to ensure an incident did not occur and arrived at the scene at 12.52 a.m. It was apparent there was a party underway. I requested the music to be turned down and was informed by the man who answered the door – Gerald – that I'd, 'have to speak to the homeowner, Kirsty Richardson, the lying tramp who currently goes by the name of Bethan Philips.' Bethan then descended the stairs and introduced herself as Mrs Philips. A brief argument ensued between Bethan and Gerald. Bethan then apologised for the music level, switched the music off and assured me the sound would discontinue. Satisfied the noise had abated I returned to Newport central police station and wrote up the incident report. When I typed the name Mrs Kirsty Richardson into the system it flagged her up as a warrant absconder, wanted in connection to the disappearance of her husband, Garrett, and their four-year-old twin sons, Alfie and Leo, in 2015. The photograph supplied with the report, distributed force-wide and marked as a red alert with Interpol, matched the face of the woman I spoke to, who called herself Bethan Philips.

I glance up at Jones. 'You've read the file.' It's not a question but he nods.

'Kirsty and her husband separated when the boys were three years old. She filed for divorce and moved out of the family home.'

'It's unusual for the husband to stay put. Has she reported any allegations of intimate partner violence or coercive control?'

'No. But he did begin proceedings to gain contact with the children, which suggests she was preventing him from parental access. We don't have all the details of the family court case, but the father made several reports to the police with increasing concern over the whereabouts of the twins and his wife's welfare. When Kirsty failed to attend the third consecutive court hearing Garrett's solicitor advised him that without a Child Arrangements Order in place, a DNA test to confirm his relationship to the children, or his name on their birth certificates – their births were registered while he was working away – he had no legal right to pursue a claim, and certainly not to dictate where his children resided or how much contact he had with them. Then he found Kirsty, living in Bristol.'

'Her tenancy agreement gave her landlord permission to place her on the public electoral register.' I sigh.

He nods. 'That's how he said he discovered where she was living. When he asked to see the children, she was evasive, so he admittedly forced entry into her one bedroom flat, found "no evidence the boys existed," left and called the police.'

'I take it this was when Avon and Somerset Constabulary went to speak to her and found the flat empty of possessions?'

'Yes. The police attempted to contact Garrett to update him on their investigation, but his mobile phone was switched off. They visited the house which he'd remained living in several times, but found the post piling up on the doormat. They passed the information on to CID who undertook a basic background check on the children's medical records which alerted them to the possibility of child abuse, suspected by the twins' health visitor who had already made enquiries with the local authority regarding her concerns that the boys were being neglected before Kirsty had removed them from the family home. CID then organised a multi-agency staff meeting where social services presented their opinion, after which the police decided that Kirsty should be arrested on a Part 5, Section 66, of the Serious Crime Act.'

The 2015 legislation makes it possible to charge an individual for causing or allowing a child to suffer serious physical harm.

'On what basis?'

'Medical negligence.'

'How did they manage that?'

'She missed an appointment with the boys' health visitor, failed to book them in for their MMR vaccines, didn't provide their GP with an up-to-date address or telephone number after their abrupt move, and never registered them with another. Alfie had a chest infection at the time and had been prescribed antibiotics which hadn't been collected from the pharmacy. Except when detectives attended the flat to execute the warrant, they discovered that she'd done a runner.'

'That was five years ago?'

'Just under.'

'Could you go and pour me a coffee? I'll have a read-through of everything we have and request copies of what we don't. We'll reconvene to discuss the case at midday.'

Everything I read reflects what Jones told me.

I'm writing up the search and seizure warrant when my phone shrills the Nokia theme tune. I reach for it absentmindedly, eyes glued to my computer screen. 'Hullo?'

'Emma, it's Miss Stewart, Jaxon's teacher. He's had a bad morning, I'm afraid. He's been screaming and has hit his one-on-one twice. He's struggling to regain control of his behaviour. Would it be possible for you or his dad to come and collect him?'

What she really means is she doesn't feel confident the methods she's using are as effective as the textbook on additional educational needs stated when she trained to work with kids who have neuro-developmental disorders or learning difficulties, and she can't get hold of Johnno so expects me to leave work and pick him up, which she knows I will because although I enjoy my job, I love my stepson more.

'Sure. Give me twenty minutes.'

I put the phone down, exhale a deep breath of irritation and log out of the system.

Jones appears at my side. 'Problem?'

'Jaxon's having a meltdown, his teaching assistant can't cope. Johnno's not answering his phone, so Mother Hen here must go and collect him and get a bollocking off the Chief for the privilege. I've emailed you a brief lowdown of our next steps. Read through it, conduct a risk assessment, compile an arrest team with Evans, choose the pool cars you want to use and list the expenses for me to sign off. I should be back here within the hour.'

I arrive outside the school in my own vehicle, pass the tight security of the reception desk and enter the head's office to find Jaxon on all fours, red-faced, snot dripping down his chin, head-banging a cushion that moves across the carpet with every thump.

He turns at the scent of my perfume, twists round to face me, opens one eye and groans.

'Hey, Jaxon. I understand you've been feeling upset. Do you want to talk to me about it?'

He shakes his head, grunts, wipes his eyes and lunges for me. I hold his hot little body against mine while he thrashes about on my lap until I feel his heartrate slow and his limbs relax. 'Shall we go home and see Daddy?'

He nods, uses my leg to pull himself upright then walks ahead, down the corridor, running his hand along the dado rail then rubbing his fingers together to rid them of the physical memory that the texture of the glossy wood provides.

I glance back to Miss Stewart. 'We'll see you tomorrow.'

'Actually, we'd like to discuss the possibility of reducing his school hours.'

I swallow the you've got to be shitting me and replace it with a, 'I'll get Johnno to call you before 3 p.m.'

She tries to explain the reasoning behind her decision, then apologises, but I'm already fighting back the tears and trying to grasp Jaxon's hand before he darts across the playground and into the road.

Johnno's car is in the driveway when I pull up outside and he's out of it before I've unstrapped Jaxon from his car seat. 'I got your voicemail and left work as soon as I could to come straight home. What's happened?' He bends to Jaxon's height so they're eye level. 'Are you alright?'

I explain the situation, his reaction mirroring mine when I mention the lack of adequate supervision within the infant's school to accommodate Jaxon's needs, then I'm released from parental duty, slipping almost seamlessly back into the role of investigator.

I return to HQ, sign the search and seizure warrant, hand it over to Jones and wait.

The drive to Goldcliff takes twenty-five minutes from Cwmbran CID. I'm not familiar with the territory but I know my colleagues will pass the Wetlands: two square miles of marshes and mudflats with a sea view of the Severn channel.

I wait for a text message from the arresting officer to confirm that Kirsty has voluntarily sat inside the back of the marked car, and the search to locate Alfie and Leo has begun on the property before I allow myself to exhale a long breath of relief.

The first hurdle has been crossed.

Now for the difficult part: getting Kirsty to admit to murdering her ex-husband and two young sons.

MELANIE

Then

I ran the length of the hall, the silk evening gown that accentuated my slim physique clung to my legs, slowing me down. The damask curtains in the lounge caught my eye as they blew against the wind that burst through the sash window.

I flung open the front door and it thumped against the wall.

I ran towards Brandon's retreating form, down the path to the gothic pillars, the gargoyles leering at me from their pedestals. One pointed toe of my heel caught on the hem of silk wrapped round it and I tripped and fell in front of the wrought iron table. The shock of pain as my knee hit the concrete stole the breath from my throat. I lay on the wet ground, listening to the *ding* of the rain hitting the glass, watching it bounce off the patio slabs. A tree branch creaked; the gale strong enough to set a car alarm off from somewhere nearby.

I awoke to the unwelcome shrill of my bedside alarm

clock, began my morning routine and tried to forget about the dream: my subconscious replaying the night Brandon died in a fictionalised montage each time I lay down on our bed and closed my eyes.

But it was no use. Regardless of how much alcohol I consumed, how much cocaine I snorted, nothing could replace him.

Sex helped. It provided me with a release. As did shopping.

My job paid well. It also funded my grief-fuelled binges.

It was during one such weekend I got knocked to the pavement from behind, swept off the street by the scruff of my jacket, and deposited into a strange car. I didn't feel my face hit the glass, my head lolling against the side window each time my abductor braked, until I saw the bump on my cheek the next morning, my nerves no longer numbed with booze or by the class A substance that left white dust on the shiny placemat parked on the edge of the coffee table in my home. The place I wasn't sure I'd ever see again.

I stared at Danny's reflection in the mirror above the mantle. He sat on the armrest of the sofa, legs spread, palms face-down on his large thighs – a relaxed pose that betrayed the hint of violence in his dark eyes.

'What are you staring at?' I swung round to face him. 'Why are you here?'

'Pack an overnight bag.'

'Why? I'm not going anywhere.'

'You're a mess, and as you've no one else to look after you I feel it's my duty to see you right.'

That's how I ended up on a psychiatric ward at St Cadoc's.

★

Dr Watkins put the journal down and gave me a smile that caused the creases at the edges of her eyes to reveal her age. 'I get the impression you've come to accept Brandon has died and you've begun to address the influence your past experiences have had on your present circumstances.'

'You're either psychic or very intuitive.'

'I prefer to think I'm skilled at my job.' She paused, leaving a notable gap in speech I knew preceded an insight on my behaviour. 'I've noticed you often flatter me when we discuss certain topics that I perceive you consider too intimate. I get the impression you've chosen to inject humour into our conversation to avoid an uncomfortable subject. I'm interested to know what you think about my observation?'

'I find it difficult to accept kindness more than criticism because of the way my mother was quick to indicate my faults and the way I sought my father's approval despite his parenting failures.'

'I'm going to bring this step up in your self-awareness to the attention of the manager during our next meeting.'

I left the consulting room feeling confident I'd worked through most of my problems, then walked, quite literally, into another.

Kirsty Richardson.

I'd met her during recreation after lunch one gloomy afternoon a couple of weeks into my stay. She'd switched the television over as soon as I sat in front of it, took the book I'd been eyeing from the shelf but didn't bother to read it, and had done her utmost to unsettle me until I wanted to score bloody lines down her arms with my nails.

Her gaze felt cloying on my skin. 'Mel,' she cocked her head my way.

'Kirsty.' I walked round her, raising my foot higher than necessary to avoid stumbling over hers. I lost my balance and she shot me a look of barely contained triumph.

'How did your session with the head doctor go?' she sneered.

'Good. I've a feeling I'm going to be leaving here soon.' I wanted to rub it in.

She appeared to be thinking of a comeback then unexpectantly asked the one question I was still unsure of: 'Where is home?'

With Brandon, was my initial thought. But although our love would never die, he had.

'Wherever I end up.'

I'd taken an instant dislike to her and couldn't figure out why she seemed intent on annoying me. But then we were seated beside each other during a group therapy session about managing our emotions. And when we were asked to share our coping strategies, she said that she found it helpful to imagine murdering people who made her angry. I laughed because I understood. I did it too.

After our session, she followed me to the smoking area and offered me a cigarette.

'So how would you do it then?' I said, leaning forward to allow the support worker to light it in the same flame as Kirsty's.

'Do what?'

I waited until the support worker had turned around and walked a few paces and lowered my voice. 'Kill someone?'

'Oh, well, it depends. Take my husband for instance,

he deserves a slow painful death. So I'd probably get him drunk, wait for him to pass out and set fire to the bed.'

'He must have really hurt you, huh?'

'How about you?'

'I don't know if I hate anyone *that* much.'

'No cheating boyfriend, no mother-in-law who thinks the sun shines out of her son's arse?'

'No. I've got no ties.'

'You're lucky,' she said with a sigh. 'I wish I could erase my history and walk out of here someone else.'

'I'm sure it can be done.'

'Yeah, I guess anything is possible.'

We discussed other things then, but the idea germinated. I'm sure now that was her intention.

When she brought the conversation up again, a couple of days later as we sat beside each other to eat lunch, I was already questioning why I'd never considered doing it myself, before. There were many times I'd wished I could disown my heritage and I knew it could be done. Criminals used aliases all the time. It was how they got away with committing crimes.

'I sometimes wish I could be someone else,' she said.

'Yeah, me too.'

She held my gaze for a few seconds, then she gripped my arm, forced me towards her and kissed me.

I was stunned, confused, and my skin tingled all over. I'd never kissed a woman before. Had never even thought about it. But it felt right. Before the butterflies that had begun swarming the moment our lips met had a chance to settle in my stomach she said, 'There is a way we could swap identities.'

'I suppose there are but why would you want to?'

That's when Kirsty told me how challenging it was going to be for her to rent a property once she was discharged from hospital.

'I don't have a credit history and I've been out of work for a while. I've got the money, but no landlord is going to take a tenant on with no previous fixed abode, no referee…'

I had my own reasons. Every day I spent in there was money out of Danny's pocket. Money I'd have to make back for him as soon as I was discharged. My surname belonged to my father. The man who'd walked out and left me with my mother who made me feel like a ghost. I didn't want to associate myself with the name Melanie Driscoll anymore.

It didn't seem like that big of a deal to let her use my birth certificate and bank card to obtain a citizen card in my name and use it as photographic ID to put a deposit down on a new place for her to live, using her own money. Besides, the idea of pretending to be her for a while seemed fun. Afterall, it was only acting. And it would only be temporary.

'I guess no one has to know unless we tell them.'

'Exactly,' said Kirsty, eyes sparkling with excitement. 'And it won't be forever.'

I envisioned it would be like borrowing a sander from Toolstation. When we were finished pretending to be each other, we could revert to ourselves.

'Do you think we'd get away with it?'

'There's only one way to find out,' she said.

I was discharged three weeks later, sober, wiser, stronger.

We met as planned in McDonald's. We ate cheeseburgers and fries and slurped strawberry milkshakes.

'What's your mother's maiden name?… Which doctor's

surgery are you registered with?... Which pharmacy do you collect your prescriptions from?'

We made mental notes of the answers, tested each other based on the questions someone who didn't know us might ask, and practised our new signatures using the straw to write with the dregs of our drinks on the table, watching the swirls and strikes of unfamiliar lettering evaporate in the morning sun.

Kirsty handed me the key to her car, said, 'You'll have to apply for a photocard licence from the DVLA.' She looked as excited as I felt to be testing her new name. 'My paper licence is due for renewal, so they don't yet know what I look like. You can then use it to open a bank account in my name.'

Brandon had taught me to drive but we couldn't afford to run two vehicles, so I'd never taken my test.

'We'll meet here at the same time on the same day next month.'

Kirsty was seated in the same spot as promised four weeks later.

I showed her my new ID.

'Great,' she said.

She was late the month after.

'Traffic,' she said, sitting sideways at the restaurant table, her eyes fixed on a spot across the road where a man stood, feet apart, leaning against a shop wall behind a bench, with his head down. His features were disguised by the cap he wore and the jacket that was zipped up to his nose.

'Who's that?'

She followed my gaze to where the man stood on the pavement. 'Oh.'

'Is that your husband?'

'Yes,' she said.

'You said you were separated?'

'We are.'

He cast a glance her way but his face was shadowed by the towering building behind him so I couldn't see what he looked like and he was slouched in such a way that I couldn't determine his height.

'Does he make a habit of stalking you?'

'Have you got my medication?' she said, ignoring my concern.

We swapped boxes beneath the table.

It was one of the reasons we continued to meet up. Our doctors knew what we looked like, so we'd had to sign up to new health centres, but we still had to take our own pills.

'I've got to collect the twins from nursery.'

'You didn't tell me you had kids.'

Why had she felt the need to withhold from me the fact she was a mother?

'Boys. They've just turned three years old.'

'Isn't that something we should have discussed before swapping identities?'

She avoided looking at me and stuffed the pill packets into her handbag. 'See you next month.'

'Make that twenty-eight days.'

She didn't laugh.

I left McDonald's with a band of doubt wound round my skull and returned home with a tension headache.

Kirsty told me she'd left her husband, that he was mean. She'd never mentioned they had kids together. It was her idea to swap identities. She said she had moved away to make a fresh start. But if that were true then why was her ex waiting for her outside?

Had she lied to me?

The last time she sat opposite me there was a visible tremor in her hand as she withdrew my capsules from her handbag to swap with the tablets I retrieved from mine, and her lip quivered when she said, 'Goodbye, Mel.'

'Where's Garrett today?'

She lowered her gaze.

'Kirsty?' I reached out a hand to place on hers and she flinched.

'He found me. He must have followed me from here to the flat I was renting in Bristol. He took the kids and said if I didn't come back with him that I'd never see them again.'

'Arsehole.'

'That's not all,' she said, eyes like saucers. 'He collected me from the flat, then drove me to the letting agency to return the keys.'

'Please tell me he didn't come inside, overhear a member of staff call you by my name?'

'No.' She glanced down at her lap. 'But he might have found out another way. Apparently when you sign a tenancy agreement it allows the landlord to notify your local council tax office and you're automatically registered on the public electoral roll. It's a form of fraud prevention or something. I'm sorry, Mel. I should never have dragged you into my mess.'

'You don't know for sure that he's aware you're renting the flat in my name?'

'He hasn't said he knows, but that isn't proof he doesn't.'

I found the note a few hours later, folded up inside

the box when I pulled the blister packet out to take my anti-depressant.

Forgive me.

I have no choice.

I drove to the conventional looking, semi-detached house Kirsty shared with her husband. The three-bedroom Victorian property overlooked the mud-coloured river.

I tried to imagine the things Garrett had done to Kirsty which caused her to scream out in the night, remembering her voice echoing down the corridor of the psychiatric unit.

I recalled my parents arguing about my mother's affair with Jason, the black eye my mother wore the following day. The split lip a boyfriend gave her when she dared to question his motive for bringing a homeless drunkard back to our house.

Her husband beats her.

I crawled the car away from the kerb and returned home and sat on the IKEA sofa Danny bought when he'd refurnished the house Brandon had once owned.

My stomach groaned in hungry protest.

I counted the coins in my purse.

Apart from the name on my sole form of photographic ID, nothing had changed for me.

The following month I waited for Kirsty, ordered our usual choice of food and drink, and sat in the same spot between the counter and window with a view to the door.

When she hadn't arrived an hour later, I called her, but her phone was switched off. I had no other way of contacting her except for the address typed at the top of her prescription.

A few days later, I detoured past the bowling alley in the car now registered in my name – the insurance and tax paid in full up to November – on my route home from The Neon where I'd spent three hours with a client watching a live cover band ruin the original songs, hoping Kirsty would see me cruising the street outside her home, come outside and explain her behaviour to me.

Every curtained window was lit from behind, humanoid shadows darted past them, and parked in front of Kirsty and Garrett's house was a police car, its soundless blue lights flickering in my peripheral. There was a van parked behind it with Crime Scene Investigation written across its side. And further down the road another marked: Dog Section.

I did a U-turn and sped off, fear flooding my chest.

It felt as though my legs were treading through quicksand as I entered the house.

I sat on the sofa drinking coffee, thumbing through my burner phone, using the browser's incognito tab to disguise my IP address while I searched the internet to feed my guilt with news updates, until the sun rose over the distant beacon walls.

MISSING HUSBAND AND TWIN BOYS FEARED DEAD

Last night police obtained a warrant to search the address of a Newport residence, where Garrett Richardson lived alone.

His wife and the mother of their twin boys, Kirsty, took their sons against an order of the court that was made last month. Police received intelligence suggesting Mrs Richardson had fled to Bristol but were not successful in locating her or the children.

A warrant was issued to arrest Mrs Richardson on suspicion of child neglect, and the boys – whose names will remain anonymous to protect their identities – were officially reported missing.

Mr Richardson called Blaenau Gwent Police to report a domestic disturbance yesterday afternoon at the address he'd shared with his family. During the phone call he stated that his wife had turned up carrying a knife, using threatening language and behaving aggressively. But when police arrived, they found the front door unlocked and the property unoccupied.

Due to information the police uncovered during their inquiries, they now fear that the father and children are deceased. The search for Mrs Richardson is ongoing.

The article was implicit in its assumption that Kirsty was responsible for the murder of her family.

My bank manager, doctor and the DVLA believed me to be her, and until I spoke to her she would continue living as me. Yet I had no idea how to find her.

She'd taken advantage of the fact I was dosed up on psychiatric medicine, had played with my emotions by kissing me when I was impressionable, and had manipulated me into swapping my identity with hers.

My hand shook so violently that the phone fell from my damp palm, skidded across the carpet and landed beneath the television stand.

I knelt on the floor, slid my hand underneath the unit and felt around for it. My fingertips touched the sleek black object just as someone began hammering on the front door.

I slammed the phone onto the coffee table and went to answer it.

BETHAN

Now

Footsteps pad down the corridor towards my cell. The lock turns, the door opens. 'Your solicitor's here.'

I follow the police officer into an interview room.

I've only ever seen them on TV. They're not dark, cramped, or stinky. But bright, minimalistic, and smell faintly of linen fresh Febreze.

I haven't slept all night but declined my offer of coffee and toast. I can't stomach breakfast when I'm facing a life-term in prison for a crime I didn't commit.

'Take a seat and take as little time as you need to discuss your charge with your solicitor,' says the female officer before exiting the room.

He looks up from the wedge of paperwork in front of him and gestures for me to sit.

'I'm being framed for something I didn't do.'

Derek, who offered to act as my solicitor, makes notes, occasionally asking me to 'clarify aspects of my story.'

When I've finished, he puts the pen down and tells me to plead guilty.

'Have you not listened to a fucking word I've said? I didn't do it.'

'I've done my background checks, Kirsty.'

'I don't believe this.' I stand.

'You were caught smoking cannabis on the bonnet of your headteacher's car at the age of fourteen. He gave you a detention.'

'What?'

'You and two of your friends followed him home, threw a lit firework through the letterbox set into the front door, which set alight his house.'

'No.' I shake my head, but because I haven't eaten anything it makes me dizzy.

'You were arrested for shoplifting three times at the age of fifteen and placed into foster care.'

'No!'

'You received a six-month custodial sentence in a Young Offenders' Institute for Actual Bodily Harm against another girl living at the children's home.'

'That wasn't me.' I begin pacing the room.

'Police reports suggest they were called to attend the property you shared with your husband and twin boys four times over the course of a two-week period leading up to the day you murdered your family.'

'Garrett was not my husband.' I laugh at the absurdity of the situation.

'Social Services had your sons on the at-risk register.'

'I don't have any children.'

'Where's Melanie?'

'I'm Mel.' I jab my chest so hard it hurts.

'You stabbed your husband. You were sectioned under the Mental Health Act to St Cadoc's hospital. You met Mel on the psychiatric unit. She collected you the day you were discharged, in a car that had previously been registered to you. You took advantage of her psychological vulnerability and got her to rent out a flat in Bristol under her name which you used to house your children after coercing her into assisting you in abducting them, after which she hasn't been seen.'

'This is ridiculous, Derek. You know I had nothing to do with their deaths.'

'*Suspected* deaths. You were wanted in connection to Garrett, Alfie and Leo's disappearances. The police only have circumstantial evidence to support their working theory that you murdered them.'

'So? What difference does that make?' My stomach gurgles and pinpricks of sweat dot my forehead.

I shouldn't have drunk so much last night.

He consults his notes. 'Just a moment ago you said, "Garrett *was* not my husband" and "you know I had nothing to do with their deaths," despite the fact the police cannot prove Garrett or your sons are deceased without their bodies.'

'Can't you see I'm being set up?'

'You deny having children, which supports the histrionic and fantasy proneness elements of the Borderline Personality Disorder diagnosis that your psychiatrist formulated.'

'Kirsty. Set. Me. Up.'

There's no other explanation.

He retrieves a piece of A4 from the back of his notebook, held between printed pages of damning files copied from the Disclosure and Barring Service. The small print on the lower right-hand corners of each are dated last Tuesday. He pushes the handwritten document across the narrow table and observes my reaction.

'Doesn't data protection law prevent you from accessing sensitive information about an individual without their permission, or that of the police?'

'Humphrey recently informed a dear friend of his that, "in the event of my death please consider my wife. She's trying to kill me." What do you have to say about that?'

I strongly suspect that Derek is 'the friend'.

'It's bullshit.'

'At the very least the Crown Prosecution Service can charge you with identity fraud and bigamy.'

'What?'

'You claimed to be someone else to marry another man despite the fact Garrett hasn't officially been declared dead and won't be until either you tell the police where to find his body or seven years have passed since he was officially reported to have disappeared and the police consider applying for a death certificate.'

'You have no proof.'

'Gerald told PC Malone he came across your photocard driving licence.'

'He just happened to find it, did he?'

'Where's Humphrey?'

'Away on business.'

'His passport hasn't been used to vacate the country for eleven months.'

I shrug. 'He told me that he had to go abroad to sort out the contract for a property he sold.'

'He was admitted to Ysbyty Gwynedd Hospital's A&E department a fortnight ago with a dislocated shoulder after a vehicle collision in Llanberis. The mechanic called Gerald – as he was listed as Humphrey's next-of-kin – informed him the car had been written off and that it had been released to the insurers for third-party inspection. You're driving around in Humphrey's hire car, which means you were in Snowdonia with him when he had the accident.'

This is my get-out-of-jail-free-card.

'You know I was. We spoke about it during our last dinner party. We went to his holiday cottage for a break. And yes, Humphrey had a car accident. And he did suspect someone of wanting to harm him. He told me. The garage called him while I was driving. I heard half the conversation. Humphrey told me the mechanic said he suspected someone had tampered with his car.'

He nods. 'The fuse modulating the ABS had blown and the TCS was switched off. The brakes failed and the wheels lost traction, causing him to crash. But he got medicated, had his arm bandaged up, returned to the cottage in the early hours of the morning via taxi, his hire car was delivered to the cottage at 9 a.m. – you signed for it because he's right-handed and couldn't do it himself with his dominant hand in a sling – then he vanished.' He pauses, narrows his eyes. 'What did you do to him, Kirsty?'

'I didn't d—'

'Where did you kill him?'

'I didn't k—'

'You wanted him out of the way.'

The door handle comes down. I glance over to it.

'So you could continue screwing around with my wife.'

Derek knows about me and Kim.

'Why would you want to represent me if you think that?'

'I was instructed to.'

By Kim no doubt, which means she must care for me as much as I do her.

I'm still gawping at him when a casually dressed man appears in the doorway.

'Detective Sergeant Jones,' he says, entering the room.

DS Jones tells me to sit, take a breather, and asks if I'd like a hot drink.

I point to Derek. 'Only if I can throw it at that prick!'

'No, you can't. And if you threaten him or anyone else a second time, I'll add affray to your charges.'

I snap my mouth shut so fast I bite the inside of one cheek. Though I'm too numb with anger to feel it I can taste the metallic tang of blood.

'Are you ready to answer our questions?'

'Get him out of here,' I say through gritted teeth.

'Do you wish to seek alternative legal representation?'

'Yes. Call his wife, Kim.'

'She's no longer practising,' says Derek.

I turn to DS Jones. 'It's a shame she gave up a career in law, but I suppose she must be grateful to her husband for providing her with, quote unquote, an allowance.'

'You're entitled to legal counsel from someone still registered with the Solicitors Regulation Authority,' says Derek, ignoring my sarcastic remark.

I aim my words at the detective. 'I'll represent myself.'

Derek snickers and I shoot him a venomous look.

He moves towards the door. 'Then on your head be it.'

DI LOCKE

Now

I re-read the transcript of the interview Jones conducted with Kirsty this morning. There's nothing within it that screams *guilty*, but...

We have a possible motive for her wanting rid of her first husband, Garrett. The original team proposed a case against Kirsty for the false imprisonment of her children to avoid them being removed from her care. Though that doesn't explain why she'd want to kill them after going to so much trouble to keep them away from their father. And according to Derek – the legal representative no longer acting as her solicitor who's now turned character witness for the prosecution – a motive for the murder of her missing husband, Humphrey. Because, he says, she was 'munching' his wife, Kim.

But conjecture is not strong enough to convict, and without forensic proof, we don't have enough evidence to charge her with Humphrey's murder as well as Garrett, Alfie

KISS ME, KILL ME

and Leo's, nor the disappearance of her friend, Melanie Driscoll.

The wind outside my office is howling, and leaves and the occasional bit of bracken pelt the window. Kate knocks on the glass-fronted door. I look up from my computer, smile as she enters the room and drops a coffee on my desk.

'We're out of sugar,' she says apologetically, though her eyes suggest the bag hasn't been replaced due to budget cuts.

'No problem,' I whisper.

'What's not a problem?' comes a voice from the other end of the line I have on speakerphone.

Kate turns and leaves the office.

'My apologies, I was talking to a colleague.'

'Right, well, you've called Ebury & Stott Insurance Limited. Noah speaking. How can I help you?'

Hopefully, a lot quicker than your automated voice recording service and subsequent music-free hold time of seventeen minutes.

'Detective Inspector Emma Locke. Your website doesn't appear to have an email address I could have used to request the information I need on a tight timescale.'

'I'm afraid if it's data protected then I can't help y—'

'Here's where I'm at, Noah. I need a one-syllable answer to the question I'm going to pose to you so that I can continue to hold the individual I have in custody, who without forensic evidence to prove they have committed the crime we strongly suspect they have will be released on police bail pending further enquires. And we don't want that because we believe they are a risk to public safety.'

Noah checks the legitimacy of my phone call by having

a supervisor dial through to the main number the police website publicises while we continue to talk, and three minutes later – a lot sooner than if I'd have scanned and emailed through a warrant or sent a locally based officer from outside the county to hand deliver one to the man – I have the reply I was hoping for.

'Lord Humphrey Eustace Philips' life insurance policy was renewed prior to the first working day of last month to include his wife, Mrs Bethan Philips, as his sole beneficiary. Although you haven't specifically asked, I am willing to voluntarily inform you that should Mr Philips die, she stands to inherit a one-off payment of one and a half million pounds. However, this amount is subject to inheritance tax.'

'Thank you, Noah. You've been very helpful.'

According to Gov.co.uk Bethan Philips pays a tax rate of 40% on the £1,175,000 inheritance remaining from the £325,000 allowable amount, meaning she's eligible for approximately £705,000.

Enough to kill for.

I'm typing this newfound knowledge up when Jones steps into the office looking smug. He darts a side-eye glance at my monitor. 'His will was amended last month too. Bethan inherits his estate, which is also worth approximately one point five million quid, give or take.'

'Nice one.'

It's a shame it's not enough to prosecute her with.

I scan the MG3 where Jones has collated everything that we have on Kirsty so far. 'I can't authorise a request to refer with this. We have four bodies unaccounted for.'

'What do you want me to do, find them, dig them up and

conduct autopsies on them myself in order to quicken the process?'

I struggle to disguise the fact I'm unimpressed with his attempt at gallows humour. 'I want blood. Even trace fibres or DNA isn't going to suffice in this instance because we expect—'

'Hairs, skin cells and saliva to be distributed between all the individuals who at one time lived with each other, I know,' he interrupts. 'I have done this before, Emma.'

'What about the hire car that Kirsty drove here from Llanberis in?'

'It's clean.'

'Have our North Wales policing division swabbed the E-Class yet?'

He nods. 'Her fingerprints aren't on the fuse-box of the Merc, so we can't even charge her with vehicle tampering.'

I direct him to the screen of my monitor, to the photographs taken during the search on the house she shared with Humphrey I'd snap up in a heartbeat if I ever won the lottery.

'Their property is a bombsite. Half the floorboards upstairs have been ripped up and most of the paintings that Gerald says he saw hung on the wall a fortnight ago at their second-to-last soirée are gone. I want to know what she was looking for.'

MELANIE

Then

I didn't recognise the man who stood on the front step because I hadn't seen his face before. 'Mel,' he said, as if we were old friends being reacquainted.

I took a step back, groped behind me for something to swing at his head, knock him out with.

He didn't need to barge his way into the house, kick the front door shut and trap me after introducing himself. His presence was all that sufficed to know how much danger I was in.

The fact Garrett was there meant Kirsty and the boys had escaped his clutches. Meaning she must have feared for their lives to betray me as she had. But at least she hadn't killed her family as the newspaper article had suggested.

I smelt the vodka on his breath before he gripped my waist like a belt with one of his muscular arms, forcing my spine against his stomach as he led me down the hall and into the kitchen.

I felt his cock straining against his jeans and stiffen as

he pressed his crotch against my arse. I winced and tried to wriggle out of his grasp, but he held me firm. Though thankfully he tired quickly of his clothed assault and shoved me off him and into the empty wine cabinet that was built into the wall at the far end of the kitchen, several feet away from the units and the door.

There was no way out.

'Have you got any booze?'

He didn't wait for me to reply before he opened the fridge, the cupboards, and pulled out drawers looking for a hidden bottle I'd assured him wasn't there.

'You know where Kirsty is,' he said, matter-of-factly, darting his eyes around the room with increasing desperation. 'Tell me where she's taken my kids.'

'I don't know.'

And I didn't. But if he didn't either, that meant they were safe – for now.

'A dishonest whore, how original,' he said, finding a can of lager that had been hidden behind a large jar of Nescafé parked to the side of the built-in cooker. 'Who saves one of a four-pack?' he laughed, opening the can and bringing it to his mouth.

'I really have no idea where they are.'

Garrett had his back to me a second long enough for me to withdraw a knife from the rack and plunge it into his neck.

DI LOCKE

Now

J. T. Hughes, Humphrey's accountant, is no less forthcoming than his clients and business associates who all but one refuse to entertain the idea their close and dear friend is gone. And after I've spoken to him, I've got to contend with Jones' moodiness.

'You've sent me on some wild goose chases in the past, Emma, but scouting the cliffs of Seawall for a corpse during high-tide in winter must be the finest example of an unattainable goal I've ever had the displeasure of hoping to execute.'

I give Jones a look so sharp it hurts my eyes too much to hold it.

'While we're almost certain we'll find Humphrey's decaying remains buried in the garden of his holiday cottage in Snowdonia we have to eliminate the possibility Kirsty told us the truth, and that her husband returned home with her, lied to her about having to go away on business, and instead of booking a plane ticket jumped into the ocean.'

Protocol.

Suicide among men is one of the least talked about global crises to date. Yet despite what little attention it gets, alongside heart disease and cancer, it is one of their commonest killers.

'Besides, I thought you could do with a trip to the Welsh countryside, inhale some salt air into your lungs.'

'In golf-ball-sized hail and fifty-mile-an-hour wind?'

'It's brought colour to your cheeks.'

'My face is red from windburn and numb because it's minus two degrees out there.'

'Alright, don't twist your knickers over it. I've had a rather productive morning while you've been working outbound. It's amazing how much can be done in this office when you're not gracing us with your noisy tea slurping or pen-over-desk rolling.'

He has the decency not to disagree with me about his annoying habits. Though he can't help but remark on the fact I'm usually chewing nicotine gum and like to snap it against my teeth to annoy him.

He takes a chair from an unmanned desk and brings it round to dump beside mine.

'Before Humphrey bought and sold property developments, scammed people out of their savings for timeshare investments and dubious pyramid schemes he conducted business with some corrupt individuals. Some of whom dabbled in illegal enterprises.'

Jones' eyes sparkle.

'One of them washed money through his mate's car valeting business and received a percentage of commission for the risk. But money laundering is only as lucrative as you can afford for it to be, unless of course it's procured through much more profitable means, so he also dabbled in unsecured loans. He's got a vast criminal record and has spent a considerable amount of his life residing at various properties owned by Her Majesty's Pleasure, making new friends to play pool with. One of whom has an auntie who suffers from bipolar disorder and has the tendency to purchase things on impulse, and whom, during one of her manic episodes decided to buy from one Lord Humphrey Eustace Philips some company shares which Humphrey sold knowing they would make a loss as they had already dropped to half their worth in just under a day. As you can imagine the woman's husband was not impressed when he learned his wife had lost their entire savings and the man who'd taken their twenty-thousand pounds retirement fund had scarpered to Snowdonia with his wife to holiday on their money.'

'He would have wanted payback,' says Jones.

'It's possible Humphrey had a *lot* of enemies. But this one particular individual has a nephew with a much worse criminal record.'

'Offences such as?'

'Armed robbery and GBH.'

'That could be why those floorboards got lifted and the manor was left in disarray,' says Jones.

'Kirsty was looking for something before her arrest. I want you to have a word with Patrick Daly and find out why his vehicle has been flagged up on ANPR cameras four times within four miles of the Goldcliff property in the past two days.'

Jones' eyes widen at the name. 'Paddy Daly?'

Ex-heavyweight, gangster and one of HMP Cardiff's most regular residents since he lost his boxing licence for breaking the jaw of a potential opponent before getting in the ring with him.

'That's right. It was Paddy's auntie whom Humphrey scammed, so you don't need me to tell you how unlikely it is we're going to find Humphrey's body, nor how likely it is that Paddy is responsible for Humphrey's disappearance.'

Although it's still possible Kirsty killed him, it means we now have two people with a motive to want Humphrey dead and both had the opportunity to take his life. Vincent, Paddy's uncle. And Paddy himself.

BETHAN

Now

I have two options. Neither of them good.

If I come clean about Humphrey's death, the police find his body and a post-mortem confirms it was accidental, I face a minimum custodial sentence of two years in prison: one year for obstructing a coroner and another for preventing the lawful and decent burial of a body. If they don't find him, they'll sentence me to twenty-five years in prison for his murder. I'll be eligible for parole at the age of forty-eight. Unless I plead guilty to voluntary manslaughter, using loss of control as my defence, the maximum penalty for which is ten years. An unlikely conviction because, before Humphrey fell and hit his head twice and I attempted to conceal his body, I tampered with his car, which makes his death appear premeditated.

Karmic law is working against me to ensure I cannot prove my innocence; I covered all bases to avoid getting caught when killing my husband only for him to die in an accident. An event he appears to have foreseen because he never submitted the prenup and he told Derek he thought I was trying to kill him. I suspect Humphrey did so after finding the driving licence that contains the photograph of me that I got Danny to sign to authorise, beside Kirsty's name, date of birth and address, which I threw in the refuse bin a month ago during a spring clean, intending to shed myself of the weight of my old skins, but somehow Gerald found then showed Humphrey. I believe Gerald, suspecting I was cheating on his friend and having somehow recently discovered it was with Derek's wife, then convinced Humphrey I intended to kill him to claim his life insurance policy, and insisted Humphrey name me as the sole inheritor of his possessions in case anything happened to him, as the police would then consider me a suspect in the event of his death. I'd bet my favourite pair of Louboutin's Gerald also kept hold of the driving licence for safekeeping and was only too eager to produce it to the detectives when, after he deliberately named me as Kirsty to PC Malone, they began making enquiries into her family's disappearance.

DS Jones enters the room. The tall, slim-built, dark haired, handsome detective sergeant who interviewed me, returning to pile on the pressure.

The police have no key evidence (CCTV footage, ANPR camera hits, website searches, emails, text messages, or evidence suggesting plans) which means they can't prove premeditation. But to charge me with Garrett, Alfie and Leo's murders they only need me to tell them where and how I disposed of Humphrey. To prove me capable of murder.

'What's with the sudden sale of antiques, Kirsty?'

'No comment.'

'Why did you trash the house?'

'No comment.'

'The house *appears* to have been burgled but we know otherwise.' He pauses. 'What did you need the money for? Twenty grand or thereabouts is a lot of wonga, Kirsty.'

He waits for me to reply and when I don't take the opportunity he continues.

'Do you know why Humphrey, an upstanding member of the community who associated with councillors at the local freemason's lodge, scammed Paddy Daly's auntie out of such a substantial sum of money?'

The Messenger?

I shrug.

He remarks upon my body language 'for the benefit of the tape' then answers his own question. 'According to Gerald, Humphrey's first wife betrayed him. I suspect Humphrey feared you'd do the same so he lavished you with gifts and plied you with affection to prevent you from straying, which landed him in debt, forcing him to sell property, including his yacht etc. I suspect his loss of status gave you an excuse to murder him or you planned to replace him with your lover, Kim.'

'No comment.'

'Paddy is a conman, Kirsty. He told you his auntie bought some company shares from Humphrey that immediately made a loss which he wanted recovered in full, with interest. But Vincent says his wife has never even spoken to Humphrey and he gladly showed us a building society statement dated today that proves their savings – far much more than we were told existed – remain intact.'

'No comment.'

'I suspect Paddy had some influence on your decision

to take the items he suggested you sell to a dealer he recommended.'

'No comment.'

'I suspect those paintings you sold to Paddy's mate were each worth triple the amount of money he gave you for the ten of them.'

'No comment,' I hiss, more pissed off at having been mugged off than I am for being accused of something I haven't done.

We're interrupted by a knock on the door.

'Detective Inspector Emma Locke,' says the smartly dressed woman seating herself opposite me. 'You murdered Mel too, didn't you?'

'What? No!'

'It is confirmed by a member of staff that on the day of your hospital discharge Mel collected you from St Cadoc's and drove you home.'

'This is too much.'

'I put it to you that you used Mel, a vulnerable woman, for your own financial or sexual gratification – I haven't yet decided which best applies – then you murdered and disposed of her, just like you did with your husband, Garrett.'

'Stop!'

'How much money or possessions did you pilfer from her before you took her life?'

'It's gone too far.'

She slides photographs across the table. 'Yes, it has.'

I jump off my seat.

She holds an image up to me. 'Garrett. A physically fit gent, in his prime. Murdered.'

'No.' I shake my head.

'Humphrey. Your kind, rich husband. Murdered.'

'No.' I squeeze my eyes shut.

'Alfie and Leo, four years old. Two healthy, happy, little boys. Murdered. I also suspect you murdered your easily led lover, Mel.'

She has no picture of Kirsty but when I blink, I can see an accusatory expression on her face.

'No.' I cover my ears, but I can still hear DI Locke talking.

'Murdered by you.'

'No, no, no. I didn't kill them.'

'You're going to get five life sentences, to run concurrently, if you're convicted.'

I don't want to tell her Kirsty took the twins and ran in fear of her husband, their father, because if they find her then she'll get into trouble for taking them against the order of the court and the police will want to know what happened to Garrett.

The words Kirsty wrote on the pill packet I found when I opened the bag come back to me; I have no choice. The only way I'll be able to divert the detective's focus is to confess.

'I left Humphrey at the quarry.'

DI Locke nods to DS Jones who vacates his chair and leaves the room while I fill her in on everything that happened. After a short interval he returns with a cheese sandwich, a packet of salt and vinegar crisps and a scalding tea which he hands to me without a word while DI Locke continues throwing questions at me until I feel as if I'm suffocating beneath them.

'We need a body,' she says. 'And as you claim to be the last person to have seen your husband, and admit to failing to seek medical assistance for him after he fell, odds are that you're the only one who can help us recover him.'

She gives me some Google Earth shots, asks me to pinpoint an estimated location. Then she uses a tool on an iPad to narrow it down to a grid reference by asking me specifics about the surroundings: estimated tree heights, their density, the approximate yards separating them from one another, and the types of birds that nest in them.

The unit's IT department can use the GPS signal on our phones to find the exact spot, but without the phones it will take them longer to obtain the network records than the time they have available to remand me in police custody.

I circle the area with a red biro, the pen shaking in my hand.

I hadn't put much thought into what he'd look like until now but the idea of him decomposing beneath the thin blanket of slate makes me want to hurl.

DI LOCKE

Now

It's been an excruciatingly long twenty-four hours, and I'm beginning to lose patience as we near the end.

DI Vickers of North Wales Police has been keeping me updated since the CSIs he's assigned have begun their search of Dinorwic slate quarry, paying special attention to the location Kirsty circled on the image Jones printed off from Google Earth. But so far, they've only been able to recover a dead field-mouse, a child's nappy and a chewing gum wrapper.

'We've got to find him.'

'It's been almost a week since Kirsty says the incident occurred,' quips Jones.

'He'll have begun to putrefy, and he's been exposed to the elements.'

'It's been raining. Any residual blood will have washed away,' he says.

'Vickers has requested authorisation to supply the forensic investigators with dogs.'

Cadaver scent from a single drop of blood or the plaque from a tooth can be detected through fifteen feet of snow.

'Let's hope they recover him before our time is up.'

'We've only got three hours and fifty-six minutes remaining,' he says.

'I don't need reminding.'

We can apply to hold Kirsty for a further twelve, but we'd need to provide the CPS with hard evidence to expand custody beyond the legal remand limit and I'm concerned she's not medically fit to withstand another six hours (in two-hour blocks) of interviews considering she hasn't slept since the night before her arrest – which means she's been awake now for approximately thirty-two hours.

When an offender manages a restful kip it's usually a red flag signalling a lack of conscience, low empathy, a feeling of superiority, a belief they'll get away with the crime they have committed. Innocent folk are too worried to relax.

I try not to concern myself with the fact Kirsty is displaying signs of insomnia because I can't prove it's been caused by her arrest. Besides, we have a bigger problem.

It's now looking likely Kirsty will be eligible for release.

We have no proof Kirsty was aware that police had sought to arrest her when she removed the twins from the family home, and as she didn't travel far – setting up home in Goldcliff under a pseudonym – there's no evidence that she's a flight risk. The incident of arson never accrued legal involvement, the shoplifting charges are considered minor as she was a youth at the time the offences were committed, and the ABH charge is spent so we have no reasonable grounds to suspect she would breach any bail conditions imposed.

I spend a fraction of the time we have remaining making enquiries into Mel's life, taking notes as I do. I scan the bullet-pointed list the team have developed in the hope of discovering something that might tell us what may have happened to her and if Kirsty had anything to do with her disappearance, where she may be.

Volatile relationship with her deadbeat, cheating father.

Co-dependent, insecure mother.

Temporary stepfathers with criminal records, addictions, and violent or paedophilic tendencies.

No relationship with stepmother and stepsister.

Non-existent relationship with stepfather, Paul.

Grandmother diagnosed with schizophrenia.

Hospital admission for attempted suicide after the death of her boyfriend, Brandon.

Sectioned under the Mental Health Act in 2015 and diagnosed with drug-induced psychosis and severe depression.

Mel ticks several boxes that suggest she has the potential to be a repeat offender, but with no criminal record there's nothing to indicate a typology she could be defined with. Unlike Kirsty.

Something's niggling me.

I re-read the information we've acquired on both women so far to compare Kirsty's trajectory against Mel's.

Five years after marrying Garrett, Kirsty gave birth to their twin sons, Alfie and Leo. She was admitted to St Cadoc's psychiatric unit three years later, after stabbing her husband in the arm. She was diagnosed with Borderline Personality Disorder (now termed Emotionally Unstable Personality Disorder), which is characterised by affective dysregulation – or emotional instability to the layperson – cognitive distortions, impulsivity, difficulty maintaining relationships, and a predisposition to other diagnosable mental health disorders, such as anxiety, depression, mania, eating disorders, addiction and self-harm.

That's suspect.

I think of the way Kirsty's acted since she's been in our presence. Her behaviour is evidentially inconsistent with her medical diagnosis. But BPD or EUPD is a lifelong condition. And as a disorder of an individual's personality, its symptoms are extremely difficult to disguise.

I continue skim-reading the notes, positive I'm on to something, though I'm still unsure what.

Garrett made several phone calls to report domestic disputes shortly after Kirsty was discharged from hospital. Police attended the property four times, but although no legal action was taken, the PCs notified the local authority concerning their visit. Kirsty breached the Child Arrangements Order granting Garrett custody of the children, and was served to appear for contempt of court, so she took the boys to Bristol, rented a flat there and placed the twins into a local nursery. But Garret claimed she returned to Newport with him, which is when he made the phone calls to the police, and Social Services placed the children onto the at-risk register.

According to the transcript of the telephone call Garrett made to police the day he reported his wife and children missing, Kirsty fought him and snatched the boys. The warrant was issued for Kirsty's arrest on the assumption that she abducted the children, fearing she'd lose contact with them. Police visited Garrett to update him on the investigation and found the property in disarray. Due to the nature of his allegations they conceded Garrett had come to harm. None of them have been seen since.

I eye Jones, seated across the room. He straightens in his chair and flattens his palms on his chinos.

Then there's Mel, who fell asleep in a bath after spending two consecutive nights drinking and crying over the loss of her boyfriend. Her gran found her, called an ambulance. It's recorded in her medical notes as a suicide attempt. She took the anti-depressants her doctor prescribed, but never returned for a repeat dose. She continued working but started partying hard, binging on cocaine. Strung-out and hallucinating, her boss drove her to The Priory in Cardiff so she could clean up, but she became violent while withdrawing and the staff couldn't pacify her, so the police were called to contain the situation. She was driven to A&E at the Royal Gwent to detox under medical supervision, and someone there recommended a psychiatric assessment at St Cadoc's. She was diagnosed with drug-induced psychosis, became agitated and aggressive with staff when they recommended that she stay to rest and recuperate, and refused treatment, so she received a mandatory twenty-eight-day Section 2 order of detainment. She was medicated and counselled using high-intensity psychotherapy under a Section 3 order, then discharged twelve weeks later.

A flash of lightning crackles in the gunmetal-grey sky, momentarily drawing my gaze towards the window.

If Kirsty planned to murder her husband to relocate her children to avoid prosecution, she would have been intelligent enough to know that taking on a false identity would decrease her risk of getting caught.

Thunder roars. A receipt skitters through the air and rain slaps it against the window.

Mel went missing shortly after Kirsty's hospital discharge. Her trail stops three months after she stepped out the doors of St Cadoc's.

Rain pelts the glass. It sounds like someone's thrown a handful of rice at the window.

What if Mel stole Kirsty's identity when she left the psychiatric unit?

I picture wedding guests tossing rice into the air at a bride and groom walking arm-in-arm down an aisle.

What if Kirsty is Mel?

You can't get married without a birth certificate and photographic ID. As soon as the registrar had typed Kirsty's date of birth into the computer along with the rest of her personal details they would have known that Kirsty was already married to Garrett and was attempting to commit adultery. They wouldn't have accepted her and Humphrey's notice of intention to marry without evidence she'd obtained a Final Divorce Decree, as well as Humphrey's wife's death certificate. So we know she used a false name to obtain a marriage licence – I've had two DCs investigating how Kirsty managed to commit bigamy since her arrest – but we had no reason to suspect her surname and maiden name weren't one and the same. Nor enquire as to whether her maiden name was legally procured when the CSI team I allocated to search the mansion attempted to locate Bethan Miller's birth certificate within the property. Because investigators found Kirsty's driving licence, and Kate received confirmation from the DVLA that it wasn't a forgery.

'Of course.'

I flick back through the notes and slam my palms down on the desk when I find the name: Brandon Miller.

'Boss.' I turn my attention to Jones, and he waves me over. 'You've got to see this.'

I leave my desk, cross the room, and stop and stare at the screen of Jones' laptop where there's a scanned copy of Bethan and Humphrey's marriage certificate.

It seems we've come to the same conclusion.

'DC Winters contacted Newport register office and asked for a copy of Bethan Miller's birth certificate. They told her th—'

'There isn't one.'

'How did you kn—'

'A hunch. Have you ch—'

'Yes. I'm waiting for confirmation from the deed poll service but as you can see the date of birth listed on the marriage certificate matches Melanie Driscoll's, so I think it's obvious that she changed her name to Bethan Miller.'

Though I can't say why she felt the need to alter her Christian name, I can understand Mel might have taken her deceased boyfriend's surname in the hope of keeping him alive, which, according to the medical notes we've obtained, supports Mel's psychiatrist's belief that her grieving process stopped at the denial stage.

There's nothing legally preventing Mel from changing her name. She's not suspected of a criminal offence and we've only believed her to be missing since we began investigating Humphrey's disappearance and learned of Garrett, Alfie and Leo's disappearances, and subsequently her and Kirsty's friendship.

'If that's Mel we've got banged up in that cell, it means Kirsty's still missing,' says Jones.

'Once we have definitive proof of her identity, we can direct our focus exclusively on what's important, which is to find that family.' I point to the scanned photograph of Garret and the boys that's blue-tacked to the wall.

There wasn't a photograph of Kirsty in the property when police attended the domestic disturbance reported to have occurred at the house she shared with her husband and sons, and found it a mess, the residents gone. It's not unusual, as mums are often the ones holding the camera and taking the pictures. But what detectives did think strange was that without any living family members or known friends they struggled to find anyone who might have a picture of Kirsty with her family who could corroborate her identity. And with only the small black and white profile shot on her photocard driving licence, until now we had nothing to refute the fact that the woman that we have in Interview Room Three was Garrett's wife, or the mother of his kids.

Relying on Mel's mum, Sam, who moved to Spain to be close to her brother, has also proven difficult. 'I could never afford a camera,' she said, when asked. And when I said Spanish authorities would have to visit her address to assist her in finding a photograph of her daughter as a matter of urgency when conducting initial enquiries into our arrestee's identity, she said, 'There's no point looking. I don't have any.'

I suspect their relationship isn't close considering she hadn't spoken to her daughter in years and didn't seem at all bothered about her wellbeing.

I enter the interview room alone.

If that's Mel seated in front of me, she was the last person to have seen Kirsty, Garrett and the boys, before they vanished. But it doesn't explain why she stole her friend's identity.

If she's lied to us about who she is, then what purpose will it serve her since she's admitted to leaving Humphrey to die, unless she's trying to cover something else up?

'He was right there,' she says, stabbing the map with her fingertip. 'How could he have disappeared? Unless...'

'Unless?' She, thankfully, doesn't detect the annoyance in my voice.

'I took a picture of us with Humphrey's phone before he fell. When I looked at the photograph there was a man stood further up the hill of slate, above us.'

'Someone witnessed you leave him lying injured on the ground. You didn't think to tell us this before?'

Neither did the man, it seems. We have no reports of anyone witnessing the incident.

'Does Humphrey have a OneDrive account?'

'Yes.'

Without the phone we can't access the memory card, but with his username and password we can hack into the folders of saved items on the Cloud registered to his mobile phone and any other devices he has linked to his Google account, find the picture and use it to appeal for the man to come forward and tell us what he witnessed.

Someone knocks on the door.

'Come in.'

Kate opens the door. 'A word, Inspector.'

I stand, and she steps aside to allow me past as I exit the room. I close the door behind me.

'I've just received the call logs from Vodafone, and with them confirmation that both Humphrey and...'

'Call her Bethan.'

'Humphrey and Bethan's mobiles were disabled from Google tracking and any searches made in north Wales, whatever they were, were scanned via the main London exchange.'

I can understand why Bethan would want to remotely and anonymously access a community IP address by switching on the incognito tab, and unlink the microphone app which allows vocal recognition and voice recording to avoid keyword detection if her intention was to murder her husband, but I can't explain why Humphrey did the same.

Kate continues. 'The mobile phone mast situated nearest the cottage in Llanberis hasn't picked up a signal from Humphrey's phone since the day Bethan told us he fell and injured his head.'

CSI haven't found a speck of blood in the bathroom where Bethan says she showered when she returned home that evening nor any evidence of the bloodied clothes she told us she'd burned on the fireplace.

I glance at the clock on the wall.

We're almost out of time.

★

I return to my desk and email a copy of Bethan's mugshot to Sam – something I'm allowed to do now that we have confirmation from the Royal Courts of Justice that Bethan Philips is not Kirsty Richardson, but is in fact Bethan Miller, born Melanie Driscoll – and await her reply.

She might also be able to help fill in the gaps of information we have about her daughter, who would have needed an enrolled deed poll to open a bank account yet there doesn't appear to be any record of her having applied for one using any of the names we know her by, which is odd.

How has Bethan been supporting herself for the past five years?

Bethan has admitted to swapping identities with Kirsty to enable her to escape her marriage to Garratt. So now everything's resting on the Major Investigation Team finding Humphrey's body and proving her responsible for his murder so we can charge her.

Though Bethan says Garrett was physically abusive and controlling, we only have evidence that supports his allegations that Kirsty was violent towards him and neglected her children. Both theories provide suggestions as to why it's proving difficult to locate Kirsty and the children, but had they run away from or been harmed by Garrett, it's much harder to explain why he hasn't yet been found even if his disappearance was voluntary. Which is I suppose why the detectives involved in the original investigation reasonably and appropriately considered it possible Kirsty had taken his life.

Sam responds to my email sooner than expected. I'm

surprised too that she wants to talk to me and offers to call
the mobile number – my work phone – supplied generically
to every email I send, offering to speak with her at 1 p.m.

> Yes, the woman you have in custody is my Mel. The
> photo you sent me reminds me of how much she looks
> like her father.

> I'm free to chat when I finish my shift at siesta.

I pick up the phone to call the CPS.

The designated caseworker I've been liaising with gives
me her verdict. 'All the evidence we have on Bethan is
circumstantial. You haven't yet identified and located the
male from the photograph Bethan says she took minutes
before Humphrey fell the second time. Without the discovery
of blood, an object or material belonging to Humphrey at the
site of the supposed crime there's no forensic proof of death,
and therefore no justifiable reason to extend the hold time
on Bethan's custody. Even though she's confessed to gross
negligence by failing to dial 999 or attempt resuscitation
she's stated some valid reasons for not doing so: no phone
signal, which we've been able to prove; a lack of first aid
knowledge; she froze, a scientifically proven response to
trauma; and her belief that her husband had died as she says
he'd stopped breathing by the time she'd stopped panicking.
This means we must prove her responsible for his death by
omission, which we can't do without his body, which would
need to be forensically examined via an autopsy before we
could ascertain an official cause of death, and this would
mean conducting further inquiries that are going to take far

longer than a twelve-hour extension. She was not present to confirm her verbal agreement during the phone call to the brokers when Humphrey added her name to his life insurance policy, nor was she an attendee of the drawing up of the will at Derek's law practice which dilutes the theory that her motive was financial.

'I must also add that we have no evidence at all to link her to the disappearance of Mr and Mrs Richardson or their sons. Even though she provided the DVLA with a photograph of herself to obtain a driving licence in Kirsty's name, records show she was the legal owner of the vehicle at the time staff inform us she collected Kirsty from St Cadoc's hospital, suggesting neither Kirsty's identity or car was stolen, but rather handed over to her. Whether that was consensually or coercively we cannot prove.'

She pauses to take a breath before continuing. 'As you've had her in custody for twenty-three hours and fifty-seven minutes. I'd advise you to let her go while you continue your investigation.'

As I approach a slack-shouldered Jones I glance across to Winters and notice she's rubbing the exposed skin of her forehead behind her fringe and I'm made suddenly aware of the flagging energy in the incident room.

They're both tired. We all are.

Jones darts his eyes up at me with a knowing look in them.

'Give her bail and put her under surveillance.'

Aware that we're on to her, Bethan might not return to the scene of Humphrey's so-called accident. But if she's concerned that she may have left evidence that could implicate her in his death, whether the incident occurred where she told us it did or elsewhere, it's likely she'll lead us to his body.

It'll also give me time to speak to her mum, and collect information on Bethan's movements, find out where she was between leaving St Cadoc's and marrying Humphrey five years later.

Because if she gained financially from Brandon's death and she intended for Humphrey to die it's possible there've been other victims between.

BETHAN

Now

I stand in front of the desk at the custody suite. The police have insufficient evidence to charge me for Humphrey's murder.

The officer behind the desk reads the legislature from the screen of his computer. 'You are being released from custody on pre-charge police bail pending further investigation in accordance with Subsections 37, Part 2, and Section 34, Parts 2 and 5 of the Police and Criminal Evidence Act 1984. You are restricted from residing anywhere except Wildflower Manor, Goldcliff, Gwent. You are expected to present yourself to Newport Central police station in twenty-eight days. Failure to surrender will result in a breach of bail which will lead to your immediate arrest for obstructing the course of justice.'

I exit the building and walk down the road to the bus stop for shelter, the cold hard rain slashing down from a thunderous grey sky as if god himself is pissing on me.

I have seven pounds in my pocket but no phone to call

an Uber, and no idea how much the ten-mile journey home will cost. I drop fifty pence into a payphone – probably the only one in Cwmbran still standing – that stinks of piss and has a window missing, to dial through to the only person I have any hope of answering my call so early in the morning.

Kim arrives in her black Range Rover twenty minutes later.

I open the nearside passenger door and I'm hit immediately by a waft of cedarwood, amber and patchouli perfume.

'Christian Dior. Nice.'

'You're soaked.'

I hoist myself up and land onto the seat.

'Sorry, it took me so long to get here. Traffic was murder. Sorry, that was a thoughtless word choice.'

I slam the door and put my seatbelt on. 'It's fine.'

I'm too tired to give a shit.

'I expect you're looking forward to your own bed. Memory foam mattress, soft pillows…'

Her eyes flit from the wing mirror, to me, to the rear-view mirror, to the windscreen, to the wing mirror, and back again so fast that just watching makes my head spin. Her one hand on the steering wheel grips it so tight her knuckles are white and the energy radiating off her causes the air in the cabin to thrum. 'Are you high?'

'I don't drive under the influence.'

'Then what's wrong?'

'Did you do it? Did you kill him?'

'I didn't kill Humphrey.'

She gives me a sideways glance, smiles and pats my knee.

I get the sudden urge to push her hand further up my leg, down the waistband of my trousers and into my knickers.

'What do you think happened to Kirsty and the boys?'

'I don't know.'

A lie. Because on some level, I do. I think I've always known.

'Were you and Kirsty an item?' She says it so blasé I almost believe she isn't jealous.

I give her a sideways glance. 'No.'

The rumble of the tyres on the unlit, half-mile-long road is the only sound to fill the space between us where, before my arrest, it would have contained continued chatter and laughter.

Kim parks the car directly in front of the house.

I guess this is goodbye.

'You had visitors earlier.' When she doesn't expand, I give her a quizzical look and she adds, 'The local press was outside.'

I inspect the mud-trampled lawn; the proof is evident. I scout the shadowed hollows between the trees, listen out for a shuffling footstep upon the undergrowth. 'They're not here now.'

'There was a journalist here this morning.' Her dark eyes are trained on me as if she's anticipating the killer blow that she suspects I'm capable of.

'How do you know?'

'I was here.'

'Why were you here?'

'The police needed keys to enter the property for CSI to conduct their search – the warrant to do so wasn't ready until they'd shut the door after they arrested you. Derek sent me, told me to let them in. Otherwise they would have used a battering ram and broken the door down.'

'You have a key to my house?'

'Derek does. Humphrey gave it him in case of an emergency. Do you want it back?'

'Yes.'

'I'll get Derek to bring it over later.'

'Thanks,' I say, a little bitchier than intended.

Could Derek, not Gerald, have found the driving licence? Could he have entered our home in search of evidence of my unfaithfulness – which he'd always suspected, and I'd blamed for his obvious dislike of me – while Humphrey and I were in Scotland celebrating our honeymoon, and found it then? And not as he told the police in the refuse bin where I'd dumped it last month?

I turn to Kim. 'I guess this is it then, for us?'

She doesn't even have the decency to restrain the impulse to laugh. 'You know there wasn't ever an "us", I'm married.'

'So am I.'

'It was just a bit of fun. I love Derek.'

'Keep telling yourself that if it makes you feel better for cheating on him with me, Kim.'

I exit the car and watch Kim drive away, back to her husband and her safe, comfortable life where she exists like a trapped butterfly.

I was just a fantasy to her. An escape from the monotony of her Stepford-like existence. Even if she daren't admit it, Kim's no different to me or Roberta. We're just trophies on the arms of rich men. Exchanging affection for the privileges they offer in return. There's a term for what we are: whores.

I tread around the circular lawn and head for the porch. I reach the door, shove my key in the lock, and startle at the snap of a branch near the hedgerow behind me. I ignore it and push open the door, flick on the hallway light, and enter the house. I close the door behind me, drop my handbag onto the floor below the coat stand, then unbutton my jacket, shrug it off and hang it up. I kick off my shoes, stretch my tired feet and tread upstairs for my slippers. I put them on, remove my makeup, comb my hair, then head down to the basement.

A sound above – wind probably, blowing a branch into the side of the house – leads me to select a bottle of red from the shelf closest to the concrete steps and my only exit, rather than walk further into the bowels of the cellar where my favoured brand is kept.

I carry it up to the kitchen, uncork it, fill a glass to the brim, glug it down, wipe the residue from my chin, pour another and take it with the three-quarters empty bottle along the hall and into the drawing room.

I put the bottle down and lean behind the plant stand to switch on the billiards table lamp. A set of keys jangle from the other end of the room as though someone has flicked them to get my attention.

I turn slowly to the corner to where a hulk of muscle sits, and a wave of terror floods my chest.

DI LOCKE

Now

I'm about to enter Greggs, salivating at the thought of my morning bacon roll and looking forward to a much-needed white americano when Vickers calls. 'We have blood.'

Cadaver dogs detected the scent of human remains. A blood spot was found on a piece of Snowdonian slate. It's being lab-tested. The results are expected to be available by midday. The sample will be compared to the saliva on Humphrey's toothbrush, which CSIs removed from the country manor during yesterday's search. But even if it's a conclusive match, even if it's cranial, it doesn't prove he's dead, or that he was murdered. It supports his wife's story: that he suffered a head injury at the site where she states he fell.

'Of course, you do,' I sigh.

About ninety per cent of our most useful evidence is discovered after we've released a suspect on bail.

'I'll update the team, but I'd like to see the preliminary results before arresting her again.'

I'd usually eat in but I'm in a hurry, so I pay for my food then take it to the car, hoping to finish it before I'm disturbed.

I close the car door and manage a slurp of coffee before my phone chimes.

'Hi, it's Sam, Mel's mum. So... my daughter's being accused of knocking the old codger off his perch, according to Wales Online?'

'I can't divulge investigative details that aren't public knowledge, but I can tell you that she was released on bail earlier this morning.'

'It's in the news article I read that she's calling herself Bethan and that she was arrested on suspicion of murdering Norman.'

'Norman?'

'Her husband. I was disappointed not to have been invited to the wedding and I must say I'm surprised he made it. He wasn't in the best of health when they met back in 2015. I thought he'd be dead by now.'

'Do you happen to know Norman's surname?'

'Oh, it's not him then? She found another old codger to fleece, huh?'

As soon as I end the call, I ring Jones, ask him to find out all he can about Norman Webb.

I'm still mulling over everything Sam told me as I pull up behind Johnno's Mazda.

'Mel replaced the boozy, drug-fuelled nights out that often ended in her blackout with an expensive taste that meant dining out with old men and conning them into funding her extravagant lifestyle was necessary to ensure it continued. Norman was one of those men. He was in his seventies when Mel began dating him,' Sam told me.

His wife had died ten months before they met. His daughter didn't like Mel, called her a gold-digger, said she didn't want Mel nursing her father in his final hours, predicted Mel would inherit his money when he died.

'She wanted a sugar daddy and he was happy to oblige. Though I couldn't tell you why she wanted a father figure, I guessed it was because Norman was able to provide her with financial stability. Something we lacked after her dad left us.'

Sam's relationship with her daughter was fraught with tension before they lost contact with each other shortly after Sam met a backpacker while visiting her brother in Spain.

'Mel was in her early twenties and was more than capable of taking care of herself. My third marriage to Paul was on the rocks, so I didn't feel like I had anything to hold me back. I left Wales three months later, moved in with Liam and divorced my husband. My brother helped us buy a place. Mel was living with Norman in his three-storey on the Caerphilly Road in Bassaleg when I moved to Spain. She went off the rails when Brandon died, got into drugs and started hanging out in seedy bars so I was glad she'd calmed down after Danny had got her into rehab, despite the fact she was settling with a man old enough to be her grandfather.'

Sam didn't worry when she hadn't heard from her daughter. 'I assumed she'd put the past behind her, made a new life for herself just as I had done. I hoped she'd finally stopped playing games with married men and had found someone to settle down with.'

No guesses as to where she learned that from.

I sip the final dregs of my coffee and stuff the last chunk of the breakfast roll that's stunk out the cabin into my mouth before I exit the car and walk towards Johnno. He's sat listening to the radio with the engine idling when I approach.

He smiles as I open the passenger door, the wind slamming it shut behind me. 'Are you prepared for the biggest case you've ever fought?'

He's talking about the Special Educational Needs meeting we're about to attend concerning Jaxon's schooling, for which we've been advised to seek alternative arrangements.

'Sure.'

'Hey,' he says, nudging then cupping my chin between his thumb and forefinger to plant a soggy kiss on my dry lips. 'We're crime partners.'

'You're a journalist.' I shrug him off.

'I meant, if they refuse to give our son his right to an education, I'll expose them, and you can cover my tracks.'

I give him a weak smile in appeasement.

'We've got this,' he says, putting a hand on my shoulder.

I'm feeling homicidal when we leave the building forty-five minutes later. Time I feel I've wasted trying to convince two professionals that I cannot home-school and provide my son with a roof over his head if I leave a career in policing I spent years training for and a lot of money working towards. I had to restrain the impulse to rip up the Education and Health Care Plan and stuff it into their tea when they blank-stared me after I told them I had no intention of leaving my job to educate my son.

Johnno pulls me against him, and I rub my cheek against his stubbly face.

'We're never going to stop having to fight for his right to the same education and healthcare services as his peers.'

'That's why I chose you to be his mother.'

'It's so tiring.'

'I'm proud of you,' he says.

My phone rings.

I withdraw from his embrace to answer it.

'Jones. What have you got?'

'Norman was diagnosed with bowel cancer in 2014. When he discovered it was terminal in 2016, he requested his GP write Do Not Resuscitate on his medical notes. I also managed to speak to his daughter, Karin. She told me that her father stopped speaking to her when he made Bethan his next of kin. Norman died in 2017, leaving his entire estate to Karin, who relished kicking Bethan out onto the street.'

We know she vacated the two-bedroom townhouse that Brandon bequeathed to his parents and that Danny purchased after her brief return from St Cadoc's. Because when Kirsty disappeared, she changed her name by deed poll and skipped town.

'Okay, thanks. Can you find out where Bethan was for the next two years?'

It's possible Bethan killed before she left Humphrey to die. She had a large enough window of opportunity to do so and people rarely go from being law-abiding citizens to committing murder. There has to be some evidence of a prior attempt at someone's life.

I'm back in my office, seated at my desk, drinking percolated coffee – my second hit of caffeine in less than three hours – from the staffroom cafetière and scrolling through my emails when Jones enters the room to dump an incident report relating to another case on my desk, and our mobile phones *beep* simultaneously. He reads his Instant Message Alert first. We release a synchronised gasp and brush arms as we slip through the door to head upstairs.

We follow the tapping of fingertips on a keyboard to the desk at the far end of the forensic technician's room.

Kate swivels her chair round at the sound of our entrance. 'Lavender oil. It's great for insomnia.'

Do I look *that* bad?

'Your text message said you had a face.'

She nods. 'The image is grainy. The zoom's distorted the pixels. But the night Bethan claims Humphrey took his tumble a man driving a black Jaguar displaying a number plate containing the letters GTY drove to a petrol station in Rhayader.'

'Where's that?'

'A historic market town in Radnorshire, Powys. Do you want the population total?'

I glare at her.

'Who's the Jag registered to?' says Jones.

'Mr Cecil Montfort. He lives in one of those static homes on the Lighthouse Park Estate in St Brides.'

A retirement village eleven miles away, replete with coastal path walks, and a sandbank beach.

'His car was stolen last month. Cecil suspects it was

taken on a Wednesday, but it wasn't reported missing until the Sunday afternoon because he keeps it locked up in a rented garage. According to the crime report, he drives to the supermarket once a week or to his daughter's once a fortnight. But she's been away and before she left stocked his cupboards. There's a small shop on-site he uses for bread and butter, his ham, eggs and milk get delivered to his door weekly from a local farm, and he's recently recovered from a cold, so he's had no need to leave the house or felt well enough to drive anywhere. His grandson offered to collect the car for him so he could go to St Bridget's church to leave flowers on his wife's grave. When he got there the car was gone.'

'Why hasn't the car been flagged up on ANPR cameras?' Why wasn't the man caught driving the stolen vehicle arrested? Why wasn't the car returned to Cecil?

'Cecil mistakenly gave his grandson – when he was on the phone to the police – the vehicle registration to an old car he owned, which he traded in for this newer model. It was the same colour as well as make. He found the logbook in a drawer yesterday.'

I restrain the impulse to raise an eyebrow.

'Let's see what this bloke looks like.'

'I printed you off a copy of the CCTV image.'

She hands it to me.

Recognition sparks.

Sleep deprivation and excitement cause me to stutter. 'It's Garrett.'

He's alive.

BETHAN

Now

My body turns to ice. I drop the glass of wine in my hand and it smashes in half, shatters at my feet, the plum coloured liquid sloshing over my shimmering nude tights.

Garrett is slouched at one end of the chaise longue, a large whiskey in his hand. He swirls the liquid inside, pours it down his throat, then slams the glass onto the arched unit above his seat and glues his eyes to mine.

My heart feels like it's convulsing.

He stands, walks towards me, crushing the glass beneath the thick rubber soles of his loafers.

'You have Humphrey's key.'

The one he had on him when he died.

He sneers, comes to stand in front of me, tilts my chin up to meet his cold, hard gaze, and my stomach does a backflip. 'Ga—'

'Shush.' He presses a thumb against my mouth.

I gag from the strength of his aftershave.

'Listen.' His voice bounces off the bare walls.

I grab his wrist, try to jerk his hand away from my face, but his shoulder tenses with barely contained aggression.

'Your husband was worth a lot of money.'

'He made some bad decisions and lost most of it.'

'I'm not talking about the house,' he says. 'I've checked the land registry. It belongs to his ex-sister-in-law. Who's married to Rupert, who owns the croft next door to the cottage in Llanberis you and Humphrey stayed in. It was the first timeshare property he invested in.'

'You've done your research.'

'That I have.'

'What do you want?'

'Enough to make my silence worthwhile.' He laughs and squeezes my jaw, digging his fingers into my cheeks until I'm sure they'll bruise.

I cross my arms to hide the fact they're trembling.

His eyebrow twitches. 'That's right, my little murderess. I saw him knock himself out, when he fell. I saw you check his pulse, attempt to bury him in a shallow grave then leave him to die.'

'You're the man in my photo?'

He nods, strokes my jaw with his thumb. 'I waited until you'd gone before I dragged him up off the bed of slate you left him on.'

'What?'

'His pulse was faint, but he was talking. He coughed and spluttered, choking on dirt, said he'd tried to get up when he heard you walking away but that he couldn't using only one arm.'

'He's alive?' My breath snags.

'I got him walking but he was delirious, wheezy and staggering, and his arm was broken. He kept moaning about the pain.'

'What did you do?'

'I told him what I'd witnessed at the quarry, how long I'd been following you, that you stole my wife's ID, and that you'd killed Kirsty and the boys.'

'No.' My hand reaches for my mouth and I shake my head.

'He told me you'd plotted to kill him, that Gerald suspected something was amiss from the beginning of your relationship. He said it was Gerald's idea to implicate you for Humphrey's murder in case you somehow went through with it.'

By advising Humphrey to change his life insurance policy and his last will and testament to include me as his sole beneficiary, and writing a note claiming I would be responsible if he died in suspicious circumstances.

'Why would he tell you all this?'

He shrugs. 'Because he knew he was about to die? He also told me that he sent someone to your house, Rick? Patrick? To offer to buy some paintings from you to clear a debt or something. He said he used the money from their sale to hire Derek to provide you with legal protection, for some reason. Which you snubbed, apparently.'

I assumed Derek had come to my rescue as fast as he could because he cared about me, because I was his friend's wife, until I learned he knew she was cheating on him with me. But that doesn't explain why Humphrey would ask Derek to represent me should I be charged with his murder.

Unless it was a ploy to increase a jury's sympathy with

KISS ME, KILL ME

the man whose adored wife was responsible for his murder, to cover the fact it was really intended that Derek lose the case to ensure I was convicted.

'Where's Humphrey?'

'He passed out shortly after our conversation.'

'Did you check his pulse?'

'He stopped breathing.'

Like he had when I thought he'd died?

He studies my reaction, but I'm too incensed to express the emotions that are swarming inside me like enraged wasps.

'What have you done with him?'

'I left him where he lay, just as you did.'

So why haven't the police been able to find him?

'When your fellow inmates learn you killed two kids, you'll wish you could join him.'

I should have killed Garrett when I had the chance. I should have pulled that vegetable knife from the rack and ploughed it through his neck just as I imagined. But I couldn't. Not until I could prove what I was convinced he'd done to his wife and the twins.

DI LOCKE

Now

Jones straightens, while I continue staring at the image of Garrett Richardson.

'Fancy a trip to Goldcliff before our shift ends?'

'We don't need Bethan to identify him,' he says. 'Kate did that from the photograph printed in the newspaper.'

The article that was published five years ago when Garrett was suspected of having been killed along with his children.

'I don't think Bethan's aware that Garrett's been stalking her, or for how long.'

'What reason would he have for doing so though?' he says.

I shrug. 'I don't know for certain that *he* has but Cecil's Jag has been caught on ANPR cameras in Tesco's car park on Spytty Road and it was flagged up at the petrol station in Rhayader.'

Garrett was travelling alone.

'Did he follow them there and back or was he invited by Bethan to help dispose of Humphrey?' he says.

I tap the top of my computer. 'He travelled up to north Wales before them.'

'Where are the boys?' he says.

'He could have harmed his children.'

And his wife.

'Stalkers don't stop until they get whatever it is that they want from their victim,' he says.

The stalking process occurs in five stages: enjoyment watching someone who's unaware they're being followed; the victim's acknowledgement that they're being followed; pleasure intimidating their victim; confrontation; elimination.

'If Garrett is responsible for his family's disappearance, he might be intending to hurt Bethan.'

I drive while Jones directs me along the three merging A-roads onto Nash Road. The countryside route takes us past rows of dead corn, acres of rain trampled wheat fields, a farmhouse, a couple of cottages, and some bungalows dotted between scrubland.

'Take the next right onto Goldcliff Road.'

We pass a stream that runs alongside a small hamlet where a lone duck floats on the surface of the water, scanning for fish.

'Take the next left,' says Jones, almost too late.

The road narrows into a lane that branches off onto two dirt tracks, both extending upwards. The smell of wet seaweed filters through the vents blowing hot air into the car.

He directs me left again. The private road curves gently at a bend then dips suddenly.

I brake with a squeal to avoid two deep potholes and tut.

'Sorry, I should've warned you,' says Jones. 'But in my defence, I wasn't behind the wheel when directing the search team after Bethan's arrest.'

I reverse then drive cautiously around the potholes but the concrete gives way beneath the tyre causing me to swerve to avoid a sudden drop in the verge and a damaged ball joint from a kerbed wheel.

Most of the frost has thawed, leaving the meadow that's visible behind the property through a wrought iron gate, boggy.

The hire car's parked sidelong, directly in front of the porch. And about fifty yards behind it, fronting the gables, is another vehicle.

One I wasn't expecting to see here.

'Call for back-up.'

BETHAN

Now

Garrett pushes his nose into mine, his breath hot on my mouth, then retracts, circles the room and stops in the doorway.

He's blocking my only exit from the drawing room. The house phone is in the morning room. I'm at his mercy and I can't call for help.

'You killed your wife. You murdered your own children. Kirsty was a good person. She was my friend. She only wanted to get away from you.' A sob erupts from my throat.

'The police can't prove anything without Kirsty's body. And they'll never find it.'

'It. Are you so completely emotionless you view the woman who gave you children no different to an object?'

'She was a fucking bitch. She took those kids off me. No one fucking does that to me.'

'They weren't possessions. They didn't belong to you.'

He takes a step towards me. I take two steps back.

'You're no better than her. You think you know

295

everything. You think you can get what you want from us men, then fucking leave us to pick up the pieces.'

'She didn't steal anything from you. She gave you two beautiful little boys and you punished her for wanting to protect them.'

'I would never have hurt them,' he says, closing in on me.

'But you did.'

I don't consider the consequences.

I barge past him, surprised he doesn't try to stop me, and run down the hall into the morning room.

I tug out the key to the gun cabinet from the box inside the mahogany desk drawer.

'Excellent,' says Garrett, from the doorway.

I open the framed glass door, withdraw the middle rifle, which I know is the only air gun that's loaded, and aim it to fire like Humphrey did when he was about to press the trigger. Except this isn't clay pigeon shooting. I zone in on Garrett, point the barrel at him, and prepare to strike.

Then comes the sound of wheels on gravel, a car door slamming, footsteps crunching across the stones, voices: one male, one female, drawing my attention to the bay window.

I keep the gun trained on Garrett to investigate who is talking through a slat between the curtains.

The blood in my veins cools instantly. DI Locke and DS Jones are walking towards the front door. Behind their parked unmarked car is the glossy Jag I saw in Snowdonia I now know was being driven by Garrett. And a little further back Derek's black Range Rover.

I forgot Kim said Derek was going to return the spare key.

The knocking on the front door is so hard I can hear the

rattle of the old oak vibrating the wooden waggon wheel rested against the side of the porch.

'Go on,' says Garrett, edging closer. 'Do it. Shoot me.'

That's what he wants.

Whoever it is that's responsible knocks again, louder this time.

'Hit me in the stomach, the chest, anywhere. Prove yourself the psycho they think you are.'

Impatient, and having obtained the key from Derek, one of the detectives presses it into the lock and pushes the front door open.

Garrett smirks. 'Drop the gun, I'll pick it up and shoot you in the eye, hold the detectives hostage. Death by cop.'

Great. Not only is he impulsive, but he's also suicidal.

It'll take ages for the Welsh police to call through for the firing squad's attendance.

'Shut up,' I snarl.

I have seconds to decide what to do.

I point the rifle at the ceiling that's survived two world wars and press the trigger, ducking to avoid a spray of plaster.

'Drop the gun,' yells DI Locke from somewhere down the hall.

'It's Garrett,' I scream. 'He's holding me hostage. He's going to shoot me,' I manage before he clamps his hand round my mouth.

'Not another word,' he warns.

He wasn't prepared for my sleight of hand. He wanted them to think I was holding him hostage.

'Put the weapon down,' shouts DS Jones. 'Unload it, drop

it and kick it out here,' he orders. 'If you're holding it when armed response get here...'

Garrett smiles at me. 'Your prints are on the gun. You fired it.' He removes his hand from my mouth, holds his palms up mockingly.

I take the opportunity to speak. They might be the last words that leave my lips before I'm arrested. 'He killed them. Kirsty, Alfie and Leo. His own wife and children. He's a murderer.'

DI Locke's silence unnerves me.

Does she believe me?

Until Garrett had shown up at my house all those years ago, I'd assumed Kirsty was the abuser in their marriage. At least that's how the media had portrayed her. The articles described the domestic disturbances reported by her husband to police in the weeks leading up to her and the boys' disappearances. I'd met her in the psychiatric hospital after he'd accused her of stabbing him. And she'd gone missing using my identity. But then he barged his way into my home, and I turned everything onto its head. I began to suspect he'd tormented Kirsty until she'd stabbed him, either in retaliation or self-defence, having been pushed beyond her limit of reason. Her actions leading to some form of breakdown which resulted in her being sectioned. I think she wanted to swap IDs in the hospital because he threatened to remove the children, stop her from having access to them. But then when she took the boys and he found them in Bristol he told her he forgave her, coaxed her into returning to him. She accepted his apology, as most women do to violent partners, and came back to the house where, I assume, he killed her and the children. Then he called the police, made a series of false reports concerning domestic abuse before faking his own disappearance. What I don't know is where he's spent the past five years, his resentment multiplying for my part in his wife's initial escape. And I don't know when he began stalking me. It can't have been until recently otherwise he'd have shown his face before now. I suspect he always intended to frame me for their murders but witnessing me burying Humphrey gave him the perfect excuse to execute his plan now.

'I know nothing I say or do can reverse time, alter what I did, and I deserve to be punished for it, but Humphrey was alive when I left him and would have survived had Garrett not been there, seen me leave and chosen to end his life. But Garrett murdered his family because he couldn't stand the thought of them being happy without him.'

And that's so much worse.

Garrett shrugs. 'You've given them motive.'

'Back off,' I hiss.

'Let's play dangerously,' he whispers, grabbing the nozzle, jerking the gun up, and squeezing my trigger finger, forcing me to fire a second shot.

Half a plaster cast bunch of grapes hits my shoulder before Garrett's fist connects to my face.

I'm still holding the rifle as I land on my spine with a crack.

There's shuffling down the hall.

Blue lights flicker in the gaps between the waving silver birches.

'The police are here,' says Garrett, turning and strolling to the doorway.

'Where the fuck are you going?'

He laughs, leaves the room.

'What are you doing?'

They'll kill him.

Or they'll think he managed to evade a bullet to the head from me.

'Shit.'

I remove the cartridge from the chamber, throw the rifle across the room, stand, lock the gun cabinet, drop the key into the box and slide the drawer closed all with my sleeve-covered hand, and walk cautiously down the hall.

Headlights pierce through the darkness. The police vehicle squeals to a stop in front of the porch. Someone jumps out of the car. Two sets of footsteps land on the ground. 'Stand back,' orders a male voice.

'Get down on the ground,' a woman demands.

Though I can't see him, I know it's Garrett they're commanding.

The male officer rounds in on him as I reach the porch. 'Now,' he yells.

Their voices fade to the *thwomp* of their target falling to the ground.

Garrett lands on his side, clutching the collar of his shirt. The female police officer lunges forward, her knees hit the ground beside him as his foot begins to jerk uncontrollably.

Blood seeps through the fabric of his shirt and onto the gravel.

'Don't move,' says a man's voice as my arm is forced behind my back, the other joining it, my wrists cuffed. Then I'm bent forward, marched towards the marked car and lowered into it with a firm hand pressed down against the crown of my head to prevent resistance.

I watch the reflected image of the manor shrink in the wing mirror as the vehicle traverses off the drive and onto the dirt lane. When we hit the narrow, private road another set of blue lights split the dark green fields and the ebony sky in half.

DI LOCKE

Now

I'm waiting for the call from – ironically – PC Malone, the police constable who kicked this entire investigation off after she'd attended the Goldcliff property in response to a report made by a neighbour concerning a complaint about loud music disrupting her sleep, to confirm Garrett's hospital discharge from Gwent Royal.

Jones isn't interviewing him or Bethan due to the Firearm Related Incident we were both involved in. After our Critical Incident Debriefs, I declined the offer of an intensive two-hour long counselling session and insisted I conclude the investigation into Humphrey, Kirsty and the boys' whereabouts from behind my desk.

Jones enters the room, rubs his eyes and blinks several times.

I push my untouched coffee across the desk towards him. 'You look like you need it more than me.'

'How much kip did you manage last night?'

'Probably not much more than you.'

Three and a half hours.

Johnno begged me to stay in bed until 6 a.m., but I'd already slammed my second two slices of bread into the toaster by 5 a.m. Once I'm awake I have no hope of going back to sleep. Especially with a kid who's up at the crack of dawn or as soon as his Melatonin has worn off- whichever comes sooner.

'In light of her confession the CPS have agreed to charge Bethan with Humphrey's attempted murder.'

Which is what a live burial comes under.

If PC Dowd hadn't tasered Garrett, he might have used the screwdriver discovered in his pocket – the one we believe enabled him to enter the garage he stole the Jag from – to injure PC Malone. His resulting trip to A&E was a necessary precaution, a box ticking exercise due to the fact he'd hit his elbow on the gravel hard on his way down.

The key for the Jag was hung on a hook above a fully stocked toolbox in the garage Cecil rented, which explains how Garrett was able to steal his car without heating and damaging the wiring.

That's what we arrested him for.

Securing him in custody for a crime he can't deny was our only way of ensuring he couldn't evade the law a second time.

The footage from the bodycams the PCs were wearing when they entered the house provided us with no evidence to contradict Garrett's claim that *he'd* been held hostage by Bethan. If CSI find her prints on the gun that he says she threatened to shoot him with, the CPS will agree to charge her for the possession of a firearm with intent to cause fear of violence on top of everything else we can pin on her.

The rifle Humphrey owned was designed to shoot over twelve feet in range, and though it couldn't kill you, injure or maim you it could. I've been advised it's not worth pursuing a charge for possession of an illegal weapon because handling a gun without a licence is a lesser crime.

After filing an incident report and getting formal approval to designate Winters to prep the interview room, I give her the go-ahead to conduct Bethan's interrogation.

An hour before lunch, after a short nap in a hospital bed under the supervision of PC Dowd and PC Malone, Garrett is driven to the custody suite.

Unlike crime fiction in books and film there's no two-way mirror. But I can watch Chapman questioning Garrett via live link to the audio-visual recording if I sit in the tech room upstairs using Kate's monitor, and don't talk or blink in case I miss something vital.

I'm eating a toasted cheese sub roll with pulled beef and mustard dressing, chomping on it so vigorously I'm almost swallowing each mouthful whole, and practically starving myself of oxygen to eat it as fast as possible while Jones watches me with amusement, sipping his vending machine coffee. By the time I'm done Garrett's videoed interview has just passed the introductions.

He looks directly at Chapman. 'You said you can place me at the scene of Humphrey's murder.'

'I said we have you on CCTV filling the tank of a stolen vehicle – a Jaguar with the registration GTY – at a petrol station in a town midway between Newport and Snowdonia. We can also place the car on ANPR cameras during the time that it was missing in various locations. Including near to Bethan's home and Llanberis.'

'Yeah, I nicked it.'

'Are you admitting to being present in the vicinity of Humphrey's fall?'

'Yeah. I saw the whole thing.'

'The GPS signal on your phone does place you at the scene.'

'I was following Bethan.'

'Why?'

'I left the holiday park to buy some fags in the local shop and I saw Mel's ugly mug on the front cover of a *Home and Garden* magazine. She convinced my wife to leave me, stole her identity, then disappeared off the face of the fucking earth. I must have wasted hundreds of hours in the past five years trying to track her down online, only to hit a dead end every time.'

He's been staying at a holiday park.

'What was in the magazine that led you to her?'

'It was an article about their wildflower garden winning an award. Mel was stood beside this old, rich dude, Lord Humphrey Philips. I scanned the article and realised she was calling herself Bethan and I thought, I bet he doesn't know who she really is, so I went down there to confront her but that place is like a fortress. They live down a lane just off a private road so there's nowhere to park without being seen. It was too risky to hang around so I pulled over up on the main road hoping one of them would get in the car and drive past. No one did so I came back the next day and just kept circling the area until this car crept right up to my rear bumper, beeped at me, then overtook me. It was her. She drives like a fucking maniac.'

'How long ago was this?'

'At the start of summer.'

'This year?'

'Yeah.'

He's been following her for at least three months.

Chapman tilts his head, inviting him to continue.

'I was concerned for her husband. I thought he might end up missing too.'

'You thought Bethan had something to do with Kirsty's disappearance and feared something similar might happen to Humphrey?'

'I needed proof.'

'Right,' says Chapman.

He hasn't once mentioned the boys.

'I crept close enough to the manor to overhear them discussing plans for a holiday in Llanberis. I had the date and the time they planned to leave. The address was online. A holiday let turned timeshare. I was already there when they arrived.'

He's confirmed the timeframe the vehicle was flagged up on camera.

'Just over twenty-four hours into their holiday a taxi pulled up to the cottage and I saw Humphrey exit it wearing a sling. I guessed he'd had a fall. The next day she's driving a different car. They stopped off at this hotel-restaurant. I watched them through the window from the comfort of my car as they stuffed their faces. When they left, I drove a few vehicles behind them all the way to the quarry. I thought, what's Lord Fool doing panting up there at his age? I followed them to the summit of the quarry. They had an argument. I couldn't hear what was being said. She pushed him. He fell and hit his head.'

'You didn't report what you'd witnessed to the police.'

'I was scared of her. If she was capable of making my wife disappear, lying about who she was and killing her husband, what would she do to me when I told her I knew?'

'All the more reason to tell us so we could put measures in place to protect you.'

He leans his elbows on the table and extends his hands to emphasise his supposed openness. 'Okay, I wanted her to suffer.'

'You were intending to enact your own brand of revenge?'

'I was going to withhold the information as leverage.'

'You were planning to blackmail her.'

'My parents are hard up. They've been bailing me out for years. I thought the money would come in handy. She owed me anyway. It's her fault Kirsty left me.'

His parents know he's alive. Have been in contact with him all these years?

'A moment ago, you accused Bethan of *making your wife disappear*, now you claim she helped Kirsty to leave you. Why would your wife need help to leave you?' says Chapman. Dismissing Garrett's remark or waiting for the opportune moment to question him about his slip-up?

'You're twisting my words.'

Chapman needs to pull Garrett back onside. And he does, swiftly.

'What happened after Bethan pushed Humphrey?'

'I left, like I told you.'

'So he fell, hit his head…'

'And I thought I'd better get out of here in case she sees me.'

'You were close enough for her to spot you, so you didn't come to his aid. Instead you... what?'

'I walked back down to the car park and drove back to Newport.'

'You witnessed a murder and you walked back down to the car.'

'That's what I said.'

'And you didn't report the incident to police because you intended to blackmail her.'

'Look, I know how it sounds.'

'That's accessory to murder for the purpose of financial gain,' says Chapman.

'If you have a body, which you don't.'

You cocky, arrogant prick.

'We're having trouble locating Kirsty and your sons too. Any idea where they might be?'

He turns to his legal aid who nods his assent for Garrett to continue. 'No,' he says, glancing round the room, flicking his nails like counters, *click, click.*

Nerves or boredom?

'What happened, Garrett? We have the domestic violence reports you made to police in the weeks preceding Kirsty's disappearance. We know you claim she stabbed you, which resulted in her being admitted to St Cadoc's. Did something similar happen this time?'

'I don't know.'

'She didn't work here, when she returned to Newport to move back in with you, after renting a flat in Bristol using Bethan's ID. And even if she squirrelled money away it would have run out by now. She hasn't used her old bank account or tried to open another since the day you – the last person to have seen her – reported her missing. No one's seen or heard from her for five years, Garrett. Instinct tells me she's dead. I just want to find her, so she can be laid to rest. Preferably buried beside the twins.'

My muscles tighten in anticipation.

'Do you know how many people enter this room and lie, but can't take the heat when faced with a prosecutor in the Crown?'

My skin prickles with nerves.

'If it was self-defence, there are protocols we can take. Advocates we can assign you who specialise in Intimate Partner Abuse who'll support you during the trial.'

Garrett's breathing hard and fast.

'I thought I was here for nicking a car?'

'You've been charged with taking a vehicle without the owner's consent.'

'Then why am I still here?' He stands abruptly but Chapman's used to challenging behaviour and doesn't even flinch.

'I have a few more questions I'd like to ask you, Mr Richardson. Could you please remain seated?'

He does, reluctantly.

'We took a swab from you when you entered the custody suite.'

'Yeah?'

'When we logged your profile on the system it flagged up a match to a crime one of my colleagues was assigned to investigate two years ago.'

He narrows his eyes. 'Two years ago, I hadn't ventured further than the holiday park.'

'That's when the body was discovered.'

'Body?'

He seems rattled.

'Her head and hands were missing so we had no way of identifying her through dental records or fingerprints. There were no identifiable features except she'd obviously suffered quite a beating.'

'Beating?'

He's parroting Chapman. A common defence tactic when an interviewee knows he's about to be confronted with hard evidence to prove him culpable of something he thought he'd be able to evade the blame for.

'There were bone fractures the forensic pathologist was able to prove were older than the estimated date of her death.'

He presses his lips together.

'Could you explain to me how your DNA got onto the female's body?'

He folds his arms.

Shit. He's losing him.

'Is she your wife, Kirsty?'

He looks affronted, straightens his spine.

'You told my colleagues shortly after your arrest that Bethan, who was known as Mel at the time we are discussing, stole your wife's identity.'

'She did.'

'We have evidence that they voluntarily swapped ID.'

He shrugs.

'We know that you attended the flat your wife rented in Bristol using Bethan's ID.'

He glances down and around the room in boredom. Not the reaction I'd expect from a loving husband whose wife and children mysteriously vanished. No matter how many years have passed since the event I'd expect him to want closure. That is of course, unless he knows how they disappeared.

'What reason did Kirsty give for leaving you to move to Bristol with Alfie and Leo?'

'She didn't.'

'Could you explain to me why your wife might have wanted to alter her name to move out of the home you shared?'

'No idea.'

I look at Jones. 'At least he's not no commenting.'

The interview continues this way for over half an hour then cuts to a short break when Garrett insists he needs the toilet almost immediately after Chapman produces the printouts of the ANPR camera shots and a copy of the CCTV image from the petrol station, placing Garrett in Rhayader.

What story is he going to cook up while spraying the urinal to defend visiting a town one hundred miles from where Bethan and Humphrey were staying?

'Do you want another coffee?'

'Please.'

Jones re-enters my office carrying two steaming cups. 'I bumped into Chapman in the corridor. What he said to Garrett before recess must have worked. He thinks he's going to break. Said he's blinking loads and keeps tapping his foot.'

He's agitated.

The first part of an interview is aimed specifically at fact-finding, asking questions, paraphrasing and then summarizing the arrestee's responses for clarification.

The second part is fault-finding, to present evidence to contradict their version of events to discredit the reliability of their story. The third part is to assign blame. After the re-introductions, the second instalment hits a grand start.

The interview recommences.

'Okay. I'm going to tell you something. But I don't want it used against me.'

'I must remind you, Mr Richardson, that anything you say may be given in evidence.'

'I know that. It's just…' He bites his lip and leans forward. 'Look, Kirsty pushed me too far. She knew exactly which buttons to press and she kept on hitting them, over and again.' He emphasises this by slamming his fist onto the table with each word. 'Kirsty took my kids away from me. She would have done it again if I hadn't stopped her.'

'You needed to prevent her from removing the children from your care again.'

'I found her address easy this time because she was using that dumb bitch's name, but I might not have been so lucky if I had to find her again.'

'You were afraid that discovering her might be more difficult the next time she left you.'

'I told her that if she came back to live with me, I wouldn't keep her away from the kids. I wouldn't punish her for leaving. I wouldn't hurt them.'

'You promised not to harm her or the children if she returned.'

'I said I was sorry for fighting for custody, for causing her to think the only way out was to run away.'

'You apologised for using the children as weapons and assured her it wouldn't happen again.'

His eyes glint as he wipes a bead of sweat from his upper lip.

He's not about to cry, he's hoping that Chapman's eating the bullshit that he's feeding him.

The change of Chapman's tact is notable only to me.

'I can see this is upsetting for you, but you're doing very well, Garrett. I really appreciate you being so open and honest with me, it's incredibly helpful.'

He laps up the praise like a thirsty dog. His shoulders relax and his hands still. He's forgotten or no longer cares his every word, every movement, is being recorded and may be used as evidence against him in court.

'I loved Kirsty the second I saw her. But she changed the moment she moved in with me. We used to have fun together, but she wanted to go out with her friends all the time, dressing up like a slag and getting wasted, flaunting herself in front of the lads, making herself look whorish. But as soon as the... when they were born... she stopped going out, focused everything on them. It felt like she didn't want to know me anymore. When she took them to Bristol, we hadn't had sex in months.'

'Priorities shift when you have children.'

He shakes his head. 'It was like I wasn't there anymore.'

They, *them*, he's refusing to identify the boys or acknowledge that they're his.

'She'd got what she wanted from me.'

'He was jealous of the twins,' says Jones from his seat beside me, eyes pinned to the screen.

Chapman goes to speak but Garrett dismisses him. 'I wanted her to suffer, like she made me.'

Garrett wants to dominate the interview. Chapman lets

him take charge. Now his defences have dropped he'll incriminate himself.

'She always put them first.'

Bile climbs up my throat.

'I didn't know who Bethan was when Kirsty visited her in McDonald's that day or that they'd swapped ID. I only learned that later. I followed Kirsty, watched her from the opposite side of the street. I wanted to make sure she was going to pick the k— them up from nursery. Kirsty knew I was there, she was glancing round, looking for me. I let Kirsty go on ahead of me and followed Bethan back to a house. I Googled the address. It was listed to a Melanie Driscoll as she was on the public voting register at the time of the last general election. Kirsty was in the bedroom when I got home, stuffing clothes into a suitcase. She was planning to leave me again with the kids. I couldn't have that.'

'You weren't going to let her take the children this time.'

Chapman homes in on what Garrett is about to reveal, disinterested at this stage in reconfirming Bethan's earlier statement.

'She said, "I'm going. There's nothing you can do about it."'

'She was leaving you, suggesting you couldn't stop her.'

'That fucking bitch put it into Kirsty's head that I was no good for her.'

'Bethan convinced Kirsty you were a bad influence.'

'I was angry. I saw red and I lost it. But I didn't kill her. I swear on my mother's grave.'

Jones groans beside me.

His half-baked confession doesn't wash with me, and

neither thankfully, does the traumatic amnesia defence wash with Chapman.

'So what are you saying?'

'There might have been a confrontation. I might have hit her. I can't remember. But that's all. Just a slap.' His eyes widen, begging Chapman to sympathise with him.

'For the record you're admitting to having hit Kirsty during an argument the day she disappeared?'

'I can't remember who threw the first punch. It was a fight. She gave as good as she got. She's not the victim in all this.'

I feel my body stiffen with the impulse to wipe the smug smile off his face.

'A moment ago, you said you might have slapped her. Now you're admitting to having punched her.'

'She hit me first.'

'You admit you're responsible for hitting Kirsty during a fight shortly before she went missing?'

'Yeah. But that's all it was, a fight. I didn't kill her.'

'She was alive when you what?'

'I left her there.'

'Where?'

'In the house. I left her in the bedroom.'

'And the boys?'

'I don't know anything about them.'

The chair flips over beneath me and I'm across the office, the door is flung open towards me, and my feet are moving along the carpeted incident room under a red mist of my own. Though I'm fully conscious of my actions and completely in control.

Once I'm outside I lean over the bonnet of my car and whack it hard with my palms flat, straighten, and unlock it with my key fob intending to reach inside the glovebox to light a cigarette I know isn't there because I haven't smoked in months.

Evans is standing at the smoky glass window overlooking the car park. He sees me, taps the glass and signals to the phone in his hand. I head inside and call out for Jones to follow me on the way to his office.

I knock three times out of politeness and enter ahead of Jones when Evans invites us in.

'Sir?'

He hands me the phone, mouths the name of the caller.

'Vickers?'

'Interpol have informed me that they've received a call from a French airport where security have detained a gentleman for using a stolen passport to fly a private plane into the country.'

'Okay.'

'He claims he's intending to stay at 13117 Route de Ponteau, Plage des Laurons, Martigues. That's Ponteau Road, Laurons Beach for us English speakers who chose to study Spanish instead of French in school.'

'Right.'

'He has a Welsh accent.'

'Humphrey was on his way to Derek's vineyard?'

'They've sent me a snap of his mugshot and a scanned copy of his passport photo. It's him alright.'

BETHAN

Now

HMP Eastwood Park is my new abode. The external paintwork on the two-storey building looks clean and fresh, and the communal area and canteen are, but my cell is the size of the broom cupboard at Wildflower Manor and it smells of sweaty metal.

As I'm on remand I can't access any of the education programmes yet, and the waiting list for access to the prison library is restricted to inmates already sentenced, so I spend most of my time reading worn books, yellowed with age, the covers missing, chewed, or the edges ripped off for roaches that I've been handed down by my cell-mate Charmaine.

After Garrett was charged with Kirsty's murder, he took a vow of mutism and refused to answer any more questions.

Charmaine updated me on the investigation when she arrived last Tuesday, for her second shoplifting stint. She was released on Monday, picked up and relapsed hours later, stealing a multi-pack of razors from Boots to sell in a pub she got into a fight in to fund her heroin habit. The police were called, she was arrested and charged and driven back here on remand Tuesday afternoon.

Most of the women here are drug addicts. Charmaine seems to have calmed down since they put her back on a Methadone prescription. But she'll be back out on the Gloucestershire streets again in a few months. Will she reoffend? Will she yo-yo back and forth into the system like most of the repeat offenders in here?

She flushes the toilet. The stink fills the room. 'It's blocked again,' she says, wiping without shame while I pretend not to watch her expression.

She pulls the curtain back, a wave of shit floods my nostrils and I gag.

I turn away from the stink and back to the chapter of the book I've been trying and failing to read for the past ten minutes.

'The police have confirmed the human remains found inside that suitcase belong to Kirsty.'

I close the book, throw it on the bed. It doesn't bounce, the mattress is too hard.

'How?'

'The boys' mitochondrial DNA matched the hard tissue DNA that was extracted from her bones.'

'Who told you?'

'Russ.'

Her boyfriend who's still using street heroin and who visits her every week.

She knows who I am. My face has been plastered across every front-page copy of *The Argus* since Humphrey reappeared. Discussions are underway between a production team and ITV to create a true crime documentary about the case starting from when the investigation into Garrett and the twins' disappearance was first opened.

'Johnno Locke covered the story.'

A relation to DI Locke perhaps?

'Said death seems to follow you.'

I guess it does.

First, Maddison, then Brandon, then Norman, then Kirsty.

After Norman's death his daughter Karin inherited his house, kicked me out, and homeless but determined to seek financial independence, I was forced to live in a cramped bedsit, buying groceries with the money I scammed off men online.

I used the same lines every time: 'I've just lost my job and I can't pay my bills; my mum's sick but I don't have the money to visit her; I'd love to meet you but I don't have the finances to travel; my sister's been diagnosed with a rare form of cancer and the only available treatment is experimental and therefore expensive so I can't afford it; I'd love to accept your marriage proposal, just wire me the money to pay for my flight over so we can start planning the wedding.'

I never got caught because the moment the final payment reached me, I'd close the fake account I'd set up for the purpose and reappear on another online platform using a different name I'd found in an obscure chatroom and the profile image of another attractive female model. But the money didn't last long, and it never felt like enough. I suppose I got greedy. That's why I began hanging out in bars. I didn't want to go back to providing escorting services, but I knew I couldn't survive long off handouts. The fees were high so the men who used the agency were wealthy enough to afford them and my pay was so good I didn't notice the commission the company took from my wages. But what I really wanted was a permanent income, a long-term partnership with a man who wanted female companionship from a woman who could run his household and attend social engagements with him, but who did not mind the lack of sexual intimacy.

A trophy wife.

Humphrey fit the bill perfectly.

If it wasn't for Garrett nicking that Jag, following us to the quarry and witnessing Humphrey's fall, the police wouldn't have had any reason to suspect he was still alive, was responsible for Kirsty's murder.'

I swallow a lump of fury.

He still discusses Alfie and Leo as if they were inanimate objects, just possessions that he discarded when they were no longer of use to him.

I couldn't make it to Kirsty's funeral for obvious reasons, so I visited the chapel to light a candle in her memory and the prison chaplain said a prayer for her instead. I'm not religious, but it's so quiet in there I almost imagined she was at peace.

Humphrey returned from his convalescence at Gerald and Roberta's château last week. I can't call him. All numbers must be approved by the governor. My mother has disowned me. Gran won't speak to me. But my father agreed to talk to me. He's accepted my Visiting Order too, so I'm hoping to see him on Saturday. We have a lot of catching up to do.

DI LOCKE

Now

I tuck Jaxon into bed, kiss his soft little forehead, wondering how monstrous a man must be to murder his own family.

Johnno's standing in the doorway when I turn to switch off the light and place the battery-operated nightlight at the end of Jaxon's bed. It leaves a muted colour-changing glow to melt into the stark white duvet.

For a kid that dislikes sleeping, he has an entire Argos catalogue of soothing objects to make his bedroom as comfortable as I find lounging on the sofa, eating Aldi's own-brand chocolates and sipping tea while Johnno threads his fingers through my hair.

I have Johnno's face in my hands, his five-day-old beard as rough as sandpaper against my palms, his lips smashing against mine, his soft tongue darting into my mouth and violating my senses, when my mobile phone forces us apart.

'Winters?'

'I'm just back to the unit from Duffryn. I wanted to call you before I write up the report.'

'You've finished interviewing the grandparents?'

'And the twins. The child protection order will stay in place until they're settled, and the guardianship order has been made by the family court, but for now social services and CAFCAS have agreed for Alfie and Leo to remain in their care.'

It was Garrett's comment about the holiday park, his parents subsidising his living costs for the past few years, and his refusal to discuss the boys during his interview with Chapman that made me suspect the parents might know where the boys were and wonder if they were living in a static caravan like Cecil.

As soon as Garrett's face had been flagged up on CCTV – due to the facial recognition software we'd applied to it, using every individual we had images of who had some kind of relationship to Bethan after her arrest – Kate had been tasked with finding out where Garrett's parents lived. We couldn't risk sending anyone to their address until we had Garrett in custody to lessen the risk of him panicking and taking the boys deeper into hiding. But after Mr and Mrs Richardson Senior had sold their house in 2010, they'd stopped voting and paying council tax so Kate hadn't been able to find them. As soon as I finished my call with Vickers, having just learned Humphrey was alive and kicking and living in the lodge on the farm at Gerald's vineyard I called the Lighthouse Park Estate manager's office. The man who answered confirmed that a Mr and Mrs Richardson lived there. I kept him on the phone while I texted Winters their address, to ensure he didn't inform his longest tenants that a detective was about to visit their home to question them about harbouring their fugitive son.

'How did you know which holiday park they'd be living on?' she'd asked, afterwards.

'I guessed Garrett stole Cecil's car because he knew the old man's routine. That he lived on the same estate.'

I can hear seagulls squawking down the line. 'How are the boys?'

'Happy and healthy,' says Winters. 'They were as oblivious as Garrett's parents were as to their mother's murder.'

Garrett told his parents that Kirsty was depressed, couldn't cope, had left the boys in his care. They'd gladly taken them in when he told them he'd secured a job overseas. A ruse so they wouldn't expect he'd killed their mother and was struggling to parent two energetic boys on his own.

'Have you organised for a Victim Support volunteer to visit the family?'

'Yeah, all set up for tomorrow.'

By the time I've put the phone down I'm too agitated to fuck but the need to press myself against Johnno, to feel his skin on mine, is overwhelming. The urgent sexual desire a reminder that I'm still alive.

Afterwards, too restless to sleep, I wait until Johnno begins to snore, prise his arms off my waist, and climb out of bed. I dress, leave the bedroom, creep downstairs, and enter the kitchen. I sit at the pinewood table decorated with scorch marks and dents Jaxon has made by cutlery we probably no longer own. I boil the kettle, pour coffee, but I'm buzzing enough without it. I flip open my Kindle but can't get into the story of a lovelorn couple and their sexual escapades that border on criminal.

I send Johnno a text message, knowing that before he gets out of bed, he'll check the notifications on his phone, won't panic to find my side of the king-size empty. Then I grab my keys and leave the house.

I drive the four miles to Carleon, park on the street and walk down to the bridge. I rub my arms to keep warm while I navigate myself through the sludgy bracken and nettle infested gorse using the Ordnance Survey Map I revised.

I stand just beyond the hollowed space where Kirsty had been left discarded like rubbish inside a suitcase at the edge of the railway line.

In this secluded spot in the dark of night I let the tears fall, feel my body convulse, and thank the universe my child is still breathing.

I may not have conceived Jaxon, his behaviour might be challenging most of the time, some days are tougher than others, but he has two mums: the one who birthed him and the one who stepped into his life to prove herself worth his love. I am blessed where others are not so fortunate.

Although Bethan's allegations cannot be proven, they also cannot be disputed; according to Bethan, Kirsty's motherly instinct to run from her abusive husband to protect her children is what led to her ultimate demise. And if her death serves only to remind me of what I have and inspires me to ensure I don't become complacent no other person has had such a profound effect on humbling me.

I wipe my eyes with the sleeve of my jacket, place my hand on the bark of a nearby tree, its branches lit only by the dim orange glow of a streetlight overhead, and whisper goodbye.

Author's Note

The idea for this novel, as with most of my crime fiction, stems from everything I learned while working within the sphere of forensic mental health.

Murder is not always violent, but it is classified as the most serious of crimes. The motive often relies on one or more of the following: status (power and control), financial gain, passion (sex, love, jealousy), or revenge.

Bethan's motive is likely a mixture of the first three. She wants to live a life of luxury and in order to achieve that is willing to marry someone rich. She chooses men who are older because they are statistically more likely to suffer health problems and die sooner than their younger counterparts. Her attraction is also in part a result of her upbringing. Her father's perceived abandonment of her means she is continually searching for a father figure, a man to take care of her. Although Brandon was much closer to her own age, it's possible that his death paved the way for Bethan to choose partnerships with older men because she associated true love with him, and she feared being hurt again. With her experiences of grief, beginning with the death of her friend Maddison, it's possible she views life as temporary and disposable.

LOUISE MULLINS

While her intimate relationships are all short-term, possibly because she's witnessed her mother Sam's constant struggle to maintain one, she is bisexual, and does appear to be prepared to commit to Kim. And this might also be perceived as a reaction to her mother's continued swing between over-protective or uncaring behaviour.

Bethan's relationship with her grandmother appears to be her only consistent and stable one, yet Elin struggles with her own demons: schizophrenia, characterised by auditory and visual hallucinations, and delusions. This disorder predisposes close family members to anxiety and depression.

Together these genetic and environmental factors create the perfect balance of damaged identity, warped desires and a lack of emotional support that might motivate someone considering murder to commit the act.

Acknowledgements

I'd like to say a huge thank you, firstly, to my long-suffering husband Michael, whose encouragement and advice are unconditional.

My three kids, for driving me insane enough to want to live in my own alternate universe for the duration it takes me to write each book.

Ieuan Lewis, for his friendship, patience, advice, but most importantly his mechanical expertise. Any mistakes concerning this aspect of the plot are entirely my own.

Kerry Watts, for always spurring me on when this writing lark feels like I'm treading through quicksand in a storm and cheering for me when I hit the mudbank looking like I have.

Sarah Voisey, for your friendship, laughs, and tea.

Rhea Kurien, Dushi Horti, Claire Rushbrook, Holly Domney, and the rest of team Aria, for giving my writing the opportunity to shine.

Daimler, despite your heavy workload and two hundred plus assembly stations you were able to find an English speaker to explain the production process of German engineering, including the manufacturing of galvanised panels, and the fascinating use of emu feathers for precision paintwork, so thank you.

A special mention must go to the men and women who work for or with the United Kingdom Police Service, putting their lives on the line each day to protect the public in their fight against crime.

I received invaluable advice from several professionals whose areas of expertise included: forensic anthropology, pathology, forensic science, and odontology to ensure the procedural aspects of this title were written as realistically as possible. I would not have been able to do this without the selfless detectives working for Blaenau Gwent Police.

Although Detective Inspector Locke and her colleague Detective Sergeant Jones are fictional characters, I hope I have given the real Major Investigation Teams working for the Serious Crimes Department of the Central Intelligence Unit justice.

For the support they offer hybrid authors like myself, I must thank the entire blogging community who review and promote our titles. I am extremely grateful. I couldn't do it without you.

I must thank my early beta readers for their objective honest literary criticism which continues to inspire my writing.

And, lastly, I offer a huge thank you to my readers all over the world who have purchased my titles and for believing in me. Reviews are important to us, it helps other readers to find our work, so once you've turned the final page of this book please share your thoughts and recommend this title to a friend.

Please help other readers to find my work by leaving a review on Amazon.co.uk/Amazon.com and Goodreads.

https://www.amazon.co.uk/Louise-Mullins/e/
BooJoLYBKU

https://www.amazon.com/Louise-Mullins/e/
BooJoLYBKU

https://www.goodreads.com/author/show/7484872.
Louise_Mullins

Purchase Kindle and paperback copies of all my titles
here:

https://www.louisemullinsauthor.com/

Be the first to hear about new releases by 'liking' my
Facebook author page:

https://www.facebook.com/LouiseMullinsAuthor/

where you can sign up to review titles before they are
published and enter competitions to win signed copies
of my books.

You can also follow me on Twitter where I regularly post
book reviews:

https://twitter.com/MullinsAuthor

And Instagram:

https://instagram.com/MullinsAuthor